BLOOD CONSPIRACY

BROOKLYN SHADOWS BOOK 2

BY BROCK E. DESKINS

"First, we rearm while Marvin figures out a way to remove these bombs. I'll have to contact the enclave and let them know what's going on. I may have an inflated opinion of myself, but I'm smart enough to know when I need help."

"I'm surprised to hear you admit it."

"This is about more than me. This is a threat to all... mother—!" I brake to a stop and watch the figure in a hoodie walking across a section of Prospect Park. "How do you turn the headlights off?"

Lesile taps on the control screen and the car goes dark. I turn the wheel, mash the accelerator, and speed through the grass. I spot the glow of a phone or music player and understand why he doesn't notice me until I'm right on his ass. Francis looks over his shoulder and jumps straight into the air, but he's a fraction of a second too late. He gains just enough height to make the impact truly spectacular. The bumper catches his ankle at almost eighty miles an hour, bumps his head off the top of the windshield where it meets the roof, and catapults him at least twenty feet in the air.

I slam on the brakes, spin the car sideways, and leap out of the door before it comes to a stop. I'm sprinting toward him almost before he hits the ground. Francis staggers to his feet just in time to give me a clean shot at his neck. My blade seeks home at a dead run and launches his decapitated head back into the air.

"Gotcha, bitch!"

Marvin and Lesile jump out of the car and run toward me. "Leonard, look what you did to my car!"

ISBN 978-1-951510-57-2

For information address Crossroad Press at 141 Brayden Dr., Hertford, NC 27944
A Macabre Ink Production -Macabre Ink is an imprint of Crossroad Press.
www.crossroadpress.com

Crossroad Press Trade Edition

CHAPTER 1

There are times I think some people's entire purpose in life is to piss me off. Why am I pissed? Other than being my default mood, it's because I'm running. If man were meant to run, he wouldn't have invented the cab.

When I was turned into a vampire the night they recalled prohibition, no one ran unless they were chasing someone or someone was chasing them. So why am I running? Because I've been dogging this asshole across rooftops and through parks for the last half an hour, a Groundhog Day-type reoccurring event that has taken place four times in the past two weeks with the same guy.

Why am I chasing him? Victim of circumstance. Way back, one of the few real friends I ever had tried to create a cure for our *condition* and it worked. The only problem was that it worked by turning our insides into something resembling Coney Island mustard.

Last year, someone figured out how to change it from a vampire poison into a vampire fertility drug. Creating vampires is not as easy as the movies make it look. Even when you are trying, there's something like a ninety percent mortality rate. My buddy Percy managed to alter the Cure and knocked the odds down to something closer to fifty-fifty.

Not only was he able to create a little personal army, but those created using the Cure are total assholes. They tend to be aggressive and driven to feed more than necessary. We vampires have tight rules governing our feeding habits. Paramount amongst those is discretion. These guys and gals Percy turned were never brought into the enclave and explained the rules, so

I have been chasing these dickheads and others like them all over the Brooklyn skyline and beyond for the past year. They get one chance to join the fold and act right. So far, I've reined in three and put down eleven. Like I said, they're assholes.

Normally, this work would go to the Sheriff's—the law enforcement branch of the enclave. That became a problem when Percy managed to subvert or replace most of New York's Sheriffs and made them part of his schemes. Now we have a bunch of temps and loaners who are about as useful as a rowboat in the Sahara Desert. It's not that they're incapable, and they are out there bringing some of these guys in, but there's a political goat-screw still going on, and they're a big part of it. Percy's failed coup resulted in what could best be described as UN intervention, and we all know how smoothly those operations go.

As a warder, I have to deal with violations occurring within my ward, but I'm paid to take down anyone outside of my territory as an independent contractor, so I don't bitch too much—unless they make me chase them.

My target leaps and vanishes over the side of the building. I hear him hit the roof of another edifice just as I gain the ledge and make the jump after him. It's a fifty-foot span and a ten-foot drop, but it's an easy hop until the guy rips the top off a roof vent and launches it at me like a Nolan Ryan fastball.

With no way to avoid the impromptu projectile, I point Shalonda, my .500 magnum revolver aptly named after an irate DMV employee, and squeeze off a round. The sound of the slug striking the roof vent is lost amidst the thunderous discharge, but I know my reactive shot strikes true. I manage to alter the projectile's course, but not enough to keep it from hitting me in the shoulder and throwing off my trajectory. Thanks a lot, Newton.

I strike the far roof and go into a tumble. It almost looks planned as I use my heightened reflexes to roll to my feet. I barely get my sword in line to intercept the pipe aimed for my head. The two lengths of steel clash with a resounding clink, and I say a silent word of thanks to the guy who made my blade when it accepts the impact without complaint. I have less appreciation for the boot to my chest. I roll with the impact; there isn't a whole lot of choice in the matter, and take a hasty shot when I come to a kneeling stop near the edge of the building. I curse at Francis' back when he bolts, and my round takes off the corner of the roof access instead of his head.

"Come on, Francis, sack up so we can end this!"

Francis ignores my challenge, and the pursuit resumes. The fire escape shakes so hard when I land I'm sure it's going to tear away from the wall. I drop over the side and hit the filth-strewn alley thirty feet below at a run. Francis kicks a dumpster into my path, which I easily high jump.

For a minute, I think he's going to run out into the streets. We're in a decrepit part of the borough with little to no traffic, but all it takes is a bum with a cellphone to shoot a video of two guys racing down the street at thirty miles an hour on foot with yours truly wielding a sword, pistol, and a murderous look to create all kinds of unwanted attention.

I almost breathe a sigh of relief, ironically of course, when Francis makes a fifteen-foot vertical leap and bounds up another fire escape. The steel framework shakes under our pounding footsteps until we reach the top and resume our rooftop chase scene. I snap off a shot at a dead run and curse again when the round catches the flapping tail of his jacket instead of his spine.

Francis leaps over the side of the building, arms and legs windmilling for balance. I mimic his form and make the long jump after him. Francis strikes the next building hard and rolls. He must have hit the central support beam, because I land right after him and break through the fucking roof of the abandoned loft. There's a resounding crash of wood and metal, and I feel myself falling once again until I hit the upper-level floor. I crash through and barely manage to stop my plummet with an outstretched arm. My sword flies from my grasp and skitters across the floor. My legs kick at empty air, and my left arm is pinned to my side.

"Fuck me." I slap at my blade lying well beyond my reach.

Francis walks out of the darkness with an enormous grin plastered on his face, casually bends down, and picks up my sword. "Gladly."

"Well this is just perfect," I mutter.

"It certainly is for me." Francis kneels in front of me and gloats. "Well, well, well, if it isn't the famous Leo Malone."

"I like to think I'm more notorious than famous."

"The difference being…?"

"Chicks. The ladies love a bad boy."

Francis stands and raises my blade to take off my head. "I'll be sure they get it right on your tombstone."

"Hey, Francis, what has three strikes and no balls?"

"What?" he asks without losing his self-satisfied smirk.

"You."

The 440-grain slug tears through the half-rotted floorboards without slowing. The crotch of Francis' pants explodes in a spray of cotton and gory bits of his junk. He releases the most horrible, ear-piercing shriek I've ever heard come from a human being, and let me tell you, I've been witness to some really fucked up shit.

Francis drops my sword and rolls around on the floor holding his ruined groin and screeching. Still unleashing his hellish caterwaul, he sprints across the large, open room and jumps out the window. Vampires have an amazing healing ability and even possess some limited regeneration, but there has to be something left to grow back. I don't know how much damage I did, but I'm pretty sure that even if it does grow back, it won't ever look right.

I hear multiple footsteps pounding up the stairs, and the powerful beam of a Maglite plays over me just before a woman shouts, "Freeze, NYPD!"

Just when my night was starting to look up.

"I got you now, Malone!" Castillo shouts.

Anna Castillo is a homicide detective with a real hard-on for yours truly. She's Captain Ahab to my Moby Dick, pun intended, and a huge pain in my ass. She's at my back, and the hood of my jacket is pulled over my head, so I know she doesn't have a positive ID on me. I grab my sword, lift my arm straight above my head, and fall the rest of the way through the floor amidst the sharp cracks of several gunshots.

It's a good twenty feet to the ground floor. Normally, I

would have been able to take the fall with the agility of a cat. Unfortunately, my trench coat catches a nail or something and spins me off balance enough that I hit with all the grace of a two-hundred-pound bag of shit.

Despite my less than Olympic-quality landing, I quickly gain my feet and run like a scolded dog out of the building and into the night. Other than blowing a guy's genitals out through his ass, this night really sucked.

CHAPTER 2

"Look for the vic," Castillo ordered the uniformed officers backing her up. "Angel, follow me before the prick can crawl away!"

"Aw crap, we just ran up the stairs," Angel complained as he tried to catch his breath.

"Move your fat ass, Lopez!"

"Hey, I have feelings you know!" Angel snapped back as he hastened to keep up with his partner.

"You and your feelings both need to go on a diet."

Angel reached the ground floor seconds after Castillo. They played their flashlights all around the empty, cavernous chamber. Locating nothing other than scattered bits of trash, a filthy mattress, and a burn barrel, Angel shined his light onto the ceiling and through the hole.

"Where the hell did he go? No way he didn't break a leg from that height."

"Fuck, fuck, fuck!" Castillo railed and stomped around in a circle in what Angel liked to call a micro tantrum and destroyed the darkened corners of the room with her flashlight. "Come on; let's get back upstairs before those uniforms fuck up my crime scene."

"You're just making friends everywhere tonight," Angel replied as he tramped up the stairs behind her.

He was breathing so hard Castillo thought she could feel his breath on the back of her neck despite him being several steps behind her.

"I don't need friends. All I need is Malone's balls hanging from my rear view mirror."

"Have you ever thought about just getting a cat?"

"I have a fucking cat!"

"Maybe you need two cats."

That was Angel's nice way of telling her she was being a bitch. Castillo knew she was, and she didn't need anyone else to tell her so. Angel was like a brother, real family and not just her partner, and he knew when she got like this she was railing against Malone and not him or their fellow officers.

Castillo paused at the top of the stairs and sighed loudly. "I'm sorry, Angel. It's just that I was this close to having his ass this time. Anyone find our vic?"

"No one here, but there's some blood," one of the uniforms answered.

"Keep away from it. I don't want anyone contaminating the scene. I can still get this sonofabitch if any of it is his. Someone get on the horn and get forensics down here ASAP."

Castillo crept toward the hole in the floor, taking great care to avoid touching any of the blood spatters. She trained her light around the jagged edge of the void and studied the darkened, glistening point of a protruding nail.

"I got you now, you bastard." She crouched next to the cavity Malone had made in his fall, examined the smaller hole in the floor, and shined her light along the far wall and up at the ceiling. "I'm thinking this is the shot we heard. See if you can find the bullet, and watch your damn feet."

The uniforms began searching the area for the bullet, carefully avoiding the blood spatters while Castillo hovered near the bloodstained nail like a mother eagle watching over her egg. She refused to move, let anyone else near it, or took her eyes off it for the entire half hour it took the CSI unit to arrive on scene. Even then, she only backed away far enough to let the forensic team capture the sample, which they did only under her close supervision.

"I'll transport those to the lab myself," Castillo insisted and took the two different samples in hand. "Let's go, Angel."

They left the scene for the uniforms to secure and CSI to continue processing. Castillo preferred to drive, so she took the wheel of the unmarked car and raced across town to the New

York medical examiner's office as if she were delivering a new heart to a dying transplant patient.

"Sergeant, just because we're cops doesn't mean we're allowed to do eighty down the BQE."

Castillo curled her lip in a silent snarl of determination and turned on the car's flashers. "I need you to start an arrest warrant for Malone the instant we get back to the station. I want him in a cell when we get the DNA match back. There is no way I'm letting the little prick slip through my fingers this time."

"Two things: first, phrasing. Second, on what grounds am I supposed to get this warrant issued?"

"We saw him!"

"We saw the back of a hooded head in a black jacket in the dark."

"I know it was him, Angel, and so do you. He had a fucking sword! What other lunatic do you know carries a goddam sword?"

Angel shrugged. "I don't know; a yakuza ninja?"

She loved Angel, but sometimes he could be a bit thick, and she wasn't just talking about his waistline. "I swear to God, I am going to reach across the seat and dick punch you."

"You know what? Forget about the cat. You need to get laid. I don't care if it's by man-flesh, woman-flesh, or robotic, but you need it bad." Angel took several blows to his thigh and forearm as he tried to protect himself from her wrath. "You feel better now, beating on your partner?"

"A little."

"Seriously though, when's the last time you went out?"

That was a touchy subject for Castillo. She used to go out all the time and had a social life. She used to have friends and even an occasional lover. Working homicide exposed her to some gruesome stuff, and the hours could be brutal, but it wasn't until her job dropped her into Leonard Malone's shadow that her world went truly dark. It eclipsed any source of light or joy from her life.

It began nearly ten years ago. At the time, she thought he was just a thug or maybe a mob hit man. Death and mayhem seemed to orbit him like a celestial body collecting meteors, pulling them into his gravitational field. On the occasion that she could place Malone in the area, often only peripherally, people vanished with barely a trace. Most of them were homeless and had criminal records, so the department didn't put a lot of effort into pursuing them.

Suspected crime scenes appeared to be scrubbed free, the only proof of something happening coming from an occasional witness who saw or heard something. Then last year, he was right in the middle of several gruesome murders, and Castillo tried to get something, anything, she could pin on him, but nothing ever stuck. She could never get anything more than circumstantial evidence, but tonight was going to be different. She could feel it.

"I don't know. I haven't had the time or the patience to put up with that kind of bullshit."

"I'm just saying maybe you should take some time to chase a dick other than Malone."

"Not gonna happen. I'm going to chase it, cut it off, and feed it to my cat."

"At least leave mine alone, I still use it."

Castillo quirked an eyebrow and teased Angel to break her pissy mood. "Really? I thought that ended after fifteen years or so of marriage?"

"Nope, every Thursday like clockwork. Ladies' night, baby!"

Castillo braked hard in front of the main doors to the medical examiner's office and stormed inside. It was late, and the cavernous halls were nearly deserted. A thin white man in his early thirties waited in the foyer.

"Parker, thanks for coming in," Castillo said.

"No problem, I love being woken up at two o'clock in the morning to do blood work that can't possibly wait five more hours until my regular shift."

"Quit your bitching, and let's get to your lab."

"I don't need an escort."

"I'm not letting these out of my sight."

"It takes a few days to do a complete run-up, you know that, right? Are you going to lurk around my lab for an entire week?" Parker asked.

"I'll leave when I see them put in the cooker. No one touches these other than you, and I want every test and every movement logged. If it moves so much as a millimeter, I want it logged."

"We have a term for anal-retentive quality control. It's called SOP."

"Look, I've been chasing this guy for half my career, and I don't want to lose him again because of a lab mistake. I need this to be your sole focus in life until you can get me enough information to at least hold my perp until you get a full analysis."

"All right, I'll call you the minute I have anything."

Castillo left Parker once he began the process of extracting the sample. She found Angel in the lobby talking to someone on the phone.

"Angel, you get my warrant?"

"I have Judge Reinholt on the phone now. He's less happy about being woken up than Parker. He wants you to tell him that you personally ID'd Malone at the scene."

"Give it to me." Castillo put the phone to her ear. "I saw Malone at the scene before he fled."

"Do you have any physical proof?" the judge asked. "I've issued you three warrants for this guy in the past, and he's walked every time."

"I have blood evidence, one of which I am certain will link him to the scene."

"Why can't you just pick him up and bring him in for questioning?"

"Because his scumbag lawyer will have him out in minutes without something stronger to detain him. He also lives in a goddam fortress and practically never leaves it, so it will be all but impossible to pick him up on the street."

"All right, Castillo, but this is the last one you're getting from me unless you have him on video committing a murder and performing a running commentary as he's doing it, so you best make it stick."

With any luck, it would be the last one she ever needed. The phone chirped the moment she hung up and handed it back to Angel.

"Lab guys found the bullet," Angel said.

The smile that spread across her face was a true Kodak moment. One unlikely to be seen again until Malone was strapped to a table as they pushed a lethal cocktail of chemicals into his veins. "I got you now, Malone."

CHAPTER 3

Avoiding the influx of cruisers is easy enough as I make my way back to where I stashed my old Yamaha. Seeing as how my loft isn't far from the scene, it doesn't take long for me to get home even when I drive a circuitous route to get there. I wouldn't put it past Castillo to have my place staked out already, so I stash my bike a block away and sneak in like a thief. I use the steel stairs running up the side of the building to my office to get inside despite failing to find anyone watching my house.

I follow the inner stairs down to the ground floor and pull the hidden lever to open my secret workshop. A section of concrete lifts up and rolls back to reveal another set of steps leading into an old water, gas, and electrical conduit I use as a workspace and armory. Putting my phone on speaker, I call my lawyer as I replace Shalonda's barrel.

"Christ, Malone, what now?" Will Stepanek grouses.

"I'm probably going to need you first thing in the morning if not sooner."

"What does she have this time?"

"Nothing."

"Nothing?"

"Far less than she thinks."

"Like what?"

"She saw the back of a guy's head wearing a hood."

"No, she saw the back of a *person's* head unless you opened your mouth and spoke."

"Of course not."

"Good, what else?"

"She may have seen a sword, oh, and possibly a recovered slug."

"May have?"

"It was dark."

"So she saw a shiny piece of metal. What do you think ballistics will say about the slug?"

"It won't match anything I own."

"All right, this won't be a problem."

"I never doubted you. I'll give you a call when she picks me up."

I disconnect Will and finish replacing Shalonda's barrel. I won't have it on me when they take me in, but minimizing the number of ballistic matches I leave around the city is just good practice. Even Will would have a hard time getting me sprung if I got picked up carrying a gun that's a ballistics match to any crime scene on record.

After locking up my armory, I pull a bag of blood from my refrigerator in the area I loosely refer to as my kitchen. This isn't the first time I've tangled with Francis, and it's been a while since I had a warm meal. It would probably be a good idea for me to get something proper to eat before I do it again. Francis is on my list because he was staying well-fed and leaving bodies around the area for the cops to find. He might be an amateur but, if I don't top off my tank, I could find myself on the wrong end of the betting odds.

Kicking back in my ratty recliner, I think about how he almost got me as I looked like a square peg jammed into a round hole. That was sloppy, and I should have been able to avoid it. It was another sure sign I was past due for a proper feeding. It's not as if I deny my nature or have some moral objection to feeding on humans.

As far as I'm concerned, people rank right along with cows, and the ones I choose are less than cow shit. So why do I go so long between feedings? I used to be a junky, the only difference being that I needed my drug to survive. Any time I feed, I'm afraid the dragon is going to get me. I can't lose it again, and not just because the enclave will hunt me down and kill me if I do.

I close my eyes and let consciousness slip away. I find myself in the dark, but not the darkness inside my loft or down some alleyway. The smell of wet soil and green vegetation fills my nose. It's hot and humid beyond belief, but it doesn't bother me. I shed such mortal concerns long ago. I'm naked and covered in grime. I lope down the narrow path like an animal on the hunt, wet fronds slapping at me like the brushes of an automated car wash.

I can hear the chattering of voices ahead and smell their fear carried by invisible air currents. They know this is a dangerous place to be. They've all heard about the quỷ rừng, or jungle demon, but life has to go on. After years of war, danger has become part of the norm; life is a privilege that could be taken in an instant. I'm about to show them the truth of that.

I slow to the deliberate crawl of a stalking leopard and peer through the thick vegetation. The men are gathered around a small fire. There's six of them, and although a couple of them are armed with type 56 assault rifles, I know they're not Vietcong or soldiers. They're just farmers and scavengers who likely wandered too far from their village to return before nightfall.

It was their bad luck to run across my path, because none of them will ever make it home. I tense my muscles and lunge. I'm only halfway across the clearing when the ground gives way beneath my feet, a rope cinches tight around my ankles, and I'm hoisted off the ground. The men weren't here by mistake, they were hunting demons, and I fell right into their trap.

Two of the men raise their rifles, and gunfire destroys the jungle's tranquility. I feel the thirty-caliber rounds slam into my body like the stinging of a swarm of hellish bees. I've been feral for over a year, and my fingernails are more like the claws of an animal than a man. I curl up and slash the rope suspending me upside down with a single swipe. I land on my feet with an impossibly fast flip and hunker into a predator's crouch. Two of the squints are rushing at me with machetes in hopes of liberating my head from my shoulders.

I kill one with a punch to his scrawny neck. The other one takes a swing at me, but I grab his wrist in one hand and his throat with the other, but I don't kill him. I lift him from the ground and take off at a dead sprint. His buddies decide that shooting me is worth the risk of hitting their friend and resume firing. Bullets whizz past and snap leaves and branches all around me, but I'm lost within the jungle in an instant.

Fifteen minutes of running puts a few miles between the hunters and me and my midnight snack. No less than a dozen holes riddle my body, but those are mostly healed before I stop running. They hurt like hell, and now I'm starving. Forcing my body to heal takes an enormous amount of reserves, but I brought a refill. I toss the drained body into the foliage when I'm done with him. Rage courses through me, the anger directed at the men who tried to kill me and at my own stupidity. There's only one village within walking distance, and that's where I'm headed.

I find the two gunmen in the village amongst the crowd gathered around a large bonfire set in the center of a clearing created by a few bamboo and grass huts. Everyone is armed with something. A few have guns, but most grip machetes and farming tools in nervous hands. The stench of fear is almost overpowering, and it only heightens my bloodlust.

Armed with my dinner's machete and my inhuman speed and strength, I rush into the mass of human cattle with a bestial snarl. What they had hoped was safety in numbers becomes a hindrance with my brutal tactic. The gunmen can't shoot without hitting their own, and people knock each other over and trample their friends and family beneath panicked feet.

I try to pick out the gunmen first, but I'm like a shark in a pod of seals. I lash out with blade and claw, cutting through flesh and shattering bone with contemptible ease. In less than a minute, there's not a living soul within the orange ring of firelight. A few fled into the jungle, leaving the bodies of dozens of their friends and family lying in a twisted heap on ground.

But there's still life within the village. I can smell the sweat and fear and hear the furious beating of hearts coming from a large hut. I tear the bamboo door off the wall and hurl it twenty feet to land in the bonfire. The wail of infants and the screams of children assault my ears.

A girl probably only twelve or thirteen-years-old rushes at me with a knife gripped tightly in her fist and held high. I lift her from the ground by her throat and hold her at arm's length, laughing as she stabs me in the forearm and shoulder. I grab her wrist with my free hand and squeeze until she drops the knife. She curses me and spits in my face. I look her in the eyes and see only a shadow of fear hidden behind her fiery rage.

The dull thud of incoming mortars or distant artillery breaks my focus. I startle awake and realize it's not explosions but someone pounding on my door.

I don't have any physical need for sleep, but old habits die hard, and I'm pissed for letting myself doze off. The flashback wasn't unexpected, and I don't have to be a shrink to know what triggered it. I've been through enough therapy I'm probably entitled to at least a Masters in Psychology by now.

Shalonda is safely hidden in my armory, and I've already tossed last night's clothes in the furnace. I can hear Castillo screaming about a warrant through my half-inch thick steel door. Mentally prepping myself for a verbal prostate exam, and possibly a physical one as well, I swing the portal open and give her my best Lurch impression.

"You rang?"

"Stow it, Malone. I have a warrant for your arrest and to search your shithole loft and office."

Visits from Castillo are a lot like an IRS audit. No matter how much you prepare for it, it's still an unwelcome and deeply unpleasant event. I send Will a quick text.

I open the door with a dramatic flourish. "Mi casa es su escena del crimen."

Castillo pushes her way inside with Angel following closely behind. "Don't get cute with me, asshole."

"Aw, you think I'm cute? I thought I felt some sexual tension between us, but I thought it was just a hemorrhoid. So what bit of flimsy evidence that my lawyer will tear apart and make you look like a complete psycho bitch brings you here this time?"

"You know damn good and well why I'm here. Now face the wall, and put your hands behind your back."

"Make sure you read me my rights," I remind her as a squad of cops storm into my home. "You wouldn't want me to get away on some sort of technicality."

"You have the right to shut the fuck up. If you choose to waive that right, you might fall out of the back of a moving squad car. You have the right to your shitbag lawyer. If you can't afford your shitbag lawyer, you will be provided one who is not paid enough to scam the system and get you off."

"You sound even more bitchy than usual, Castillo. Are you getting enough sleep…or dick?"

"Don't go there, Leo," Angel warns me. "She gets real crotch-punchy when you say things like that."

"Keep talking and I'll throw you both out of the car."

"Perfect, you know how we suspects like to be roughed up by heavy-handed cops. I know my lawyer is looking to buy a bigger boat."

Castillo growls, properly reads me my rights, marches me to her unmarked car, and shoves me into the back seat. Angel climbs into the passenger seat as Castillo takes the wheel, and we're soon cutting our way through morning traffic on the way to the station. I half expect Castillo to taunt me the entire way in hopes of provoking me into saying something incriminating, but it's a silent ride with neither of us letting our egos take control of our mouths.

Will is standing in front of the precinct doors when we arrive, a briefcase clutched in one hand and several loose papers in the other. Castillo literally growls like a dog when she sees him and pushes me past.

"Detective Castillo, why don't you save us both some time and yourself a great deal of embarrassment and let Mr. Malone go now?"

Castillo stops and spins to face him, a fierce scowl carved onto her face. "Because I have him this time, and not even your slimy tactics or his girlfriend are going to get him off."

"You don't have anything to hold him on, Castillo, and you know it."

"I pursued him halfway across the burg and saw him at the scene."

"I got reports from four uniforms who all say they only saw someone in a black coat, and none of them saw a face or could give any kind of physical description at all."

"They don't know him like I do."

"Did you see his face?"

"I don't have time to debate procedure with you, Stepanek. If you want to try and get him out, you know the system."

"You're going to lose your badge one of these days, and a damn shame it will be."

"Yeah, I'm sure you and Malone will be heartbroken."

Will never leaves my side while I'm booked in and processed. It wouldn't be the first time Castillo rolled up my personal liberties and beat me with them. Most people would be offended by it, but I can respect a person who will break the rules to get the job done.

I'm processed quickly since ninety percent of the pertinent information is just copy and paste. I'm such a regular I should have a punch card. She sits me down in the interrogation room and begins the typical back and forth of questions and answers. It's an imbalanced system with far more questions than answers, and all the answers come from my lawyer, which are "my client does not need to answer that."

I'm impressed that Castillo is able to keep it up for an hour with nothing more than an angry twitch in the corner of her eye. It's a good thing Will is here, or she would probably have hit me with her chair by now. An officer steps into the room and drops a Manila folder on the table in front of Castillo. She opens it up and reads the contents.

"Why is your refrigerator full of bagged blood?" the detective asks.

Will answers for me. "He has a medical condition that requires frequent transfusions which he prefers to be done at his home instead of a hospital."

"What kind of condition?"

"The kind protected by privacy laws. You have nothing on my client, Castillo, so let's end this and stop wasting each other's time before I have to talk to your captain or the DA directly. We both know they aren't going to prosecute on this flimsy evidence. Hell, it's not even shaky, it's outright mythical."

"I just need to hold him until I get my DNA results back."

"Which can take a week, and no one is going to let you hold him that long with what you have."

"Call your lab guy," I tell Castillo.

"He won't have a complete markup yet."

"Call him anyway. I bet he has enough to end this interview."

Castillo glares at me with a mix of anger and suspicion. "What do you know, Malone?"

I return her vitriolic stare with a smile. DNA tests are useless on vampires. Our bodies absorb the blood cells of our victims into our veins, capillaries, and tissue. We have more divergent DNA in us than a porn star.

She pulls out her phone and taps in a number. "Parker, what's the status on my samples?"

"I was hoping to finish running them again before I called you, but they're a bust."

"What the hell are you talking about? I watched them taken myself."

"I don't know who took them or how, but I've gotten cleaner samples from a peepshow jizz mop. There's gotta be markers pointing to at least half a dozen different people."

"In which sample?"

"Both."

"I don't know what the hell is going on, Parker, but if I find you have been compromised, I swear you will never see the light of day!"

"Hey, don't threaten me because your people screwed up! You want to come look at the security footage? Be my guest. I have every second of my day recorded, a day that started way too damn early on account of you."

"You can bet I'm going to look at that footage."

Castillo ends the call and looks as though she is about to hurl her phone against the wall.

I quirk an eyebrow and ask, "Is there a problem?"

"You knew that sample was crap!"

"Did I?"

"I don't know what you did or how you did it, but I'm going to bury you, Malone."

"Well, while you are out buying a new shovel, I'll be taking my client home now," Will says.

Castillo gives us an imperceptible nod, and Will escorts me

out. She doesn't bother to issue any more threats and just sits staring at the wall, likely trying to decide whether or not to just shoot me next time.

"So, what is with the blood in your fridge?" Will asks once we're outside.

"Like you said, I have a medical condition."

"Just for my own curiosity, are you a serial killer?"

"Would it be a problem if I was?"

"Are you kidding, defending you if you got caught would make my career. I would be the white Johnnie Cochran."

"I don't think you have the rhyming skills or endearing personality."

"I can be endearing!"

"You are the only person I know who is less likeable than I am."

"That's very hurtful. I'm glad I have your money to wipe away my tears."

CHAPTER 4

"I had him!" Castillo railed.

"You did, but you shouldn't have," Captain Starks insisted. "I just spent the last half hour getting my ass chewed off by Judge Reinholt because you tricked him into issuing a warrant under false pretenses!"

She knew this was coming the moment Parker told her of the lab results, but that foreknowledge did nothing to calm her fury or ease her humiliation.

"They weren't false! I saw him!"

"According to every other cop on scene, you saw the back of a hooded head poking out of a hole in the floor."

"They don't know him like I do. I know it was him."

"I don't give a damn what you know or what your gut tells you. The next time you arrest Malone, you had better catch him in the act, standing over a body, with a weapon in his hand, and a videotaped confession. Do you know who judges talk to? Judges talk to mayors, mayors talk to governors, and governors talk to senators who talk to the president. When shit rolls that far downhill it's a building-sized pile by the time it lands on my desk! You're a good cop, but your obsession with Malone is going to cost you your badge and maybe even get you put in jail instead of him."

"Malone is maybe one of the biggest problems plaguing this city, and no one else seems to realize it. He has a refrigerator full of blood for fuck's sake!"

"In jars or something?"

"In bags, like from a hospital. He says he has a medical condition."

Captain Starks grinned. "You think he's a vampire or something?"

"I think he's Dexter fucking Morgan! Maybe he does have a medical condition, or maybe those are his trophies."

"I don't care if he's the next Osama Bin Laden. You need to back off unless your evidence is concrete enough to build the foundation for his prison."

"I won't arrest him until it's a sure thing, but I'll never back off. He's a killer, and I'm going to prove it."

"Just make sure you can prove it to the point even his own mother thinks he's guilty."

CHAPTER 5

Katherine is parked in front of my loft and waiting for me when Will and I arrive. Not only is she a striking blonde bombshell and the assistant DA, she's a half werewolf who could do a lot better than me. Even after a year, I still wonder how I got so lucky in finding someone like her who is willing to tolerate my bullshit.

"Hey, Kat," Will calls through the open window of his car.

"Hi, Will. I guess you didn't need me."

"Naw, Castillo had jack shit like usual."

I lean into the open passenger door after I get out. "Thanks again, Will."

Will sticks his arm out the window and waves as he drives off. Katherine wraps me in her arms the instant I turn around.

"Shouldn't you be at work?" I ask.

"Shouldn't you be in jail?"

"Of course not, why do you think I pay Will so much and bang the DA?"

Kat pushes me away and punches me in the chest. "Ass."

She hooks her arm in mine, and we walk into my loft. I growl when I see my place looks as though someone burglarized it. My armory door is still closed, so I assume they didn't find it.

"Goddammit," I curse when I see the open door of my refrigerator.

Castillo's people obviously got word to leave it alone and "accidentally" forgot to close the door.

I toss the ruined blood bags into my furnace. Most of the ashy contents are strewn onto the floor where they were obviously raked through quite thoroughly. I need to call in for a resupply. Our blood people belong to the same section that does our emergency body cleanup, so I get the typical amount of shit from the guy before he places my order. Other than keeping them busy, I don't know why they give me so much grief.

"Are you going to go out again tonight?" Katherine asks.

"I have to. This guy is a real problem, and he's smarter than most of the others I've brought in lately."

"Are you going to have to feed?"

Kat accepts the requirements of my nature, but it doesn't come easy. I'd probably like her a whole lot less if it did. It's a nasty business but unavoidable if I don't want to die a horrible, lingering death while being driven into madness. Vampires can live on bagged blood for a time or take enough fresh stuff from victims without killing them, but only for so long. At my age, I only have to do a full feeding, meaning to the death, three or four times a year depending on my activities. Fights like ones I've been in the last year bumps that number up a bit. The need also increases as I get older. I don't want to think about how many times elders like Vincent have to take a life in order to maintain a healthy existence. It's a good thing there's not many of us, and it's not that hard to go unnoticed when there's seven billion cattle to feed on.

"Yeah, I can't let him get the jump on me again. I know he'll have done a full feeding after I shot him, and I'll have to do the same to be on top of my game."

She smiles at me coyly. "Speaking of being on top, I still have half an hour left on my lunch break."

It takes less than a minute before we're naked and gripped in the throes of passion. Until I met Katherine almost a year ago, I had done a good job of keeping everyone away from me. Kat was the kind of woman who would not let anyone or anything deter her when she set her sights on something. For some reason I have yet to understand, those sights got set on me, and she broke through my emotional walls despite my best efforts.

Our liaisons are often these short visits on account of my tendency to try and kill her, or anyone near me, in my sleep. I'm sure we both wonder if I'm ever going to shake my flashbacks, but we don't talk about it much. She accepts it as part of my nature, which is just one of the many things I love about her.

Our lovemaking is short and fierce, driven by the animal within each of us, an animal we both fight to suppress but let run free when we are together. It is a rare time when Kat can embrace her werewolf nature and I feel truly alive. I can go an eternity without taking a breath except to speak, but during sex, I completely forget my vampiric nature and find myself gasping in ecstasy. We lie in other's arms for only a few minutes before Katherine jumps up and puts her clothes back on.

"I better get back to work. Try not to get arrested again today."

"I'll try."

"I doubt it."

She's right. Even if I try to avoid trouble, trouble has no problem finding me.

A knock at my door just as I'm getting ready to head out for the night illustrates my earlier point perfectly. My blood order arrived a couple of hours ago, so I'm pretty sure it is someone I have no interest in seeing. A client would have gone upstairs to my office, and Kat isn't likely to be coming back tonight since she knows I am going out.

Given the fact I pretty much have no other friends, it isn't hard to deduce the likelihood of it being an unwanted visitor. It's also unlikely to be a threat since few assailants bother to knock, but I slip my blade into the sheath sewn into my trench coat and make sure Shalonda is resting comfortably in my pocket holster.

I lift the hundred-pound steel bar from the cradle and open the door. As I suspected, it's unwanted visitors. Three Sheriffs stand outside with their hands crossed in front of them. Two more Sheriffs stand next to a black van parked a few yards away with the side door open.

"Is it prom night already? Damn, I'm not even dressed yet." Sven doesn't seem to have a problem not smiling at my joke.

"Vincent requests your presence," Sven says with his Swedish accent.

"Why doesn't he ever just call? It would save money on gas."

"You have once again forgotten to update your contact

number."

"Yeah, I didn't forget."

"You will come."

It's hard to tell if Sven is asking me or telling me given his lilting accent. I assume it's not a request despite what he said earlier, so I lock up and climb into the vehicle. The van lurches into motion with a spray of gravel before the sliding door slams shut, and we're soon speeding across the Brooklyn Bridge on our way to Lower Manhattan. We stop before a black skyscraper on Madison Avenue which looms over Central Park.

Alicia, a young black woman, who is attractive despite her shaved head, slides the door open, and we all pile out. Alicia is one of the few vampires from team Percy who managed to comply with the enclave's rules and became a Sheriff. She and another former accomplice, Bryan, are still on probation and likely will be for at least a couple of more years. I was surprised at the council's leniency given the severity of their crimes, but they felt it would be easier to bring in the others if they knew they wouldn't be summarily executed. It's a damn sight more forgiveness than I would have shown.

We enter the three-story atrium designed to intimidate or awe visitors. The twenty-foot, white marble angel cradling an infant stands in stark contrast to the black marble walls. It looks down at the babe in its arms with a smile that is both serene and predatory.

I smile at one of the two security guards manning the desk inside the foyer. "How's the leg?"

He answers my inquiry by shooting me the finger. Apparently, he is still sore, at least emotionally, after I nearly blew it off with Shalonda last year during one of my epic temper tantrums. I guess I can respect a grudge holder. I'm a lot of things, but a hypocrite ain't one of them.

Sven uses a key to call the private elevator, and we're soon rocketing up to the top floor. No smooth jazz or other obnoxious music plays to entertain our brief trip up, and I do mean brief. We ascend nearly eight hundred feet in less than half a minute. The doors slide open and deposit us in another gorgeous foyer although not nearly as grand as the atrium. My escorts and I reach Vincent's office where his secretary tells us to wait outside.

I stare impatiently at a pair of tall, highly polished doors and begin pacing around the room. It's odd how I can stare through the scope of a sniper rifle for hours without twitching a single muscle, yet it takes all my reserve just to keep from kicking in Vincent's doors and storming into the room. I "accidentally" knock a crystal clown off a shelf just to break the boredom... and the clown.

"Mr. Van Graff will see you now," his secretary says.

I set the crystal piano, which was next to have an accident, back on the shelf. Sven and his posse do not follow me in when one of the doors swings open and I walk into Vincent's office. I still can't help but be impressed by his office. It's nearly as big as my loft and much grander, which is good because it reminds me to dislike him.

"Six minutes," Vincent says as he leans back in his high-backed, leather swivel chair. "It took you six minutes of waiting before you started breaking things."

"Yeah, I got laid today, so I was pretty relaxed. Was the clown important to you?"

"Not at all."

I walk over to a lighted cabinet prominently displaying several ancient bowls, tools, and stone weapons. I pick up a clay vase with Egyptian hieroglyphs painted across its surface.

"How about this one?"

"Must you always be such an insufferable little prick?"

"I'm not sure. I've never tried not to be, but I suppose it's possible." I put the vase back on the shelf but out of place, knowing its misalignment will drive Vincent insane for the rest of our meeting. "What did you want with me?"

Vincent's eyes flick between the vase and me a few times before locking onto my face. "I hear you had a run-in with another of Percy's rogues but failed to apprehend him."

"That almost sounds like a rebuke."

"Forgive me; I shall change my tone so it sounds precisely like a rebuke."

"I've brought in or put down fourteen of these assholes in the last year, and that's post-Percy and gang. How many have your Sheriffs taken care of, seven, eight? I think I'm doing pretty damn good working on my own."

"Having the police chase you halfway across New York while you are doing it defeats the primary purpose for which I hired you. Perhaps you have forgotten that the reason I contracted your expert help was to avoid precisely this kind of attention. It was not to shoot your way across Brooklyn and beyond to carry out executions."

"Even when I get the job done you still bitch. I swear it's like we're married. You can do that now you know? You don't have to drive to Massachusetts anymore. You can do it right here. Not with me obviously, but some other poor schmo who doesn't mind you nagging him all the damn time."

"The only thing worse than your discretion is your failed attempt at humor. While I appreciate your diligence, we cannot have you arrested in the process. If this latest character is proving beyond your abilities, I can assign you one or more of the Sheriffs to assist you."

"Great, can I pick the Swedish chef, or is it a grab bag for one of the other Muppets?"

"Involve the police again and they might all be coming for you. Good day, Mr. Malone."

I know a dismissal when I hear one and leave. I pause outside the door, perform a left face, and pace off five steps. Executing a perfect right face, I mule kick the wall. The barrier quivers beneath my assault, and I'm rewarded with the muted sound of breaking pottery and toppling artifacts.

"Oops, muscle spasm."

I stride briskly for the elevator with Scooby and the gang chasing after me. I spy a figure out of the corner of my eye, make an abrupt halt, and backpedal. Wyatt was the former head of the Sheriffs, but he backed the wrong horse. Due partly to his last-minute change of heart, his execution was commuted to spending the rest of his life riding the pine in The Tower.

"Wyatt, how's the desk job treating you?"

"Well, it's better than having my head cut off for treason. I find the dullness of my duties surprisingly relaxing."

"You look better."

"I suppose that was you making that racket?"

"Yeah, just a little parting gift for Vincent."

Wyatt shakes his head and grins. "You're going to go too far one of these days, Leo, and you have stepped on far too many toes to expect any kind of leniency."

"It's all part of the plan. I'd rather lose my head than have my balls cut off and put in a desk drawer."

"At least I know where to find them."

"You have fun. I'm off to chase down some baddies. Try not to get a paper cut."

Wyatt shoots me the finger as I leave. Team Edward shows me to the door but of course does not offer me a ride home. It's Friday night in Manhattan, and I don't have the patience to wait for a cab. I also don't have my wallet as I tend to leave it at home when I know I'm going to be hunting. Pro tip: if you plan to kill someone, empty all your pockets before you leave. You would not believe all the shit people leave behind at crime scenes. Damn amateurs.

That leaves the subway, which I despise beyond few other things in this life. Of course, it too takes money, but that problem is far easier to get around. I descend the steps and shut down my olfactory senses as I join the CHUDS migrating to and from the platforms.

Luckily, this platform doesn't have the floor to ceiling turnstiles. I don't even have to flex my knees to hop over. Just a quick twitch of my ankles catapults me to the other side without breaking stride. Unfortunately, I'm stopped dead in my tracks when my face pushes against the broad chest of a subway cop. I look up into the black face displaying not a hint of amusement.

"Buddy, you're lucky I'm about to go off shift. Go back and pay your fare before I slap you with a five hundred dollar fine."

"Can you cut me some slack? I forgot my wallet. I'll pay twice next time."

"You can pay once this time or you can walk."

I glare but fail to intimidate the man. With little recourse other than causing a scene that will surely get me another invitation to the principal's office, I do an about-face and hop back over the way I came.

"Hey, buddy, can you spare a fare?" I ask a guy.

"Fuck off."

"Hey!" the cop shouts before I can launch a retort. "Leave the paying folks alone."

"I pay your check with my taxes!" I shout back despite knowing how stupid that argument sounds. "That should be enough!"

"From the looks of you, I doubt your taxes are enough to pay for my doughnuts."

It's a valid point, but it still pisses me off. I storm away and stop in front of a vending machine. Looking around to make sure there are no more cops, I place a few solid kicks to the coin box and finish it off by tearing it open with my hands. I grab a fistful of change before it all clatters to the ground and feed them into the turnstile a minute later.

"Where'd you find the money so fast?" the cop asks me as I pass.

"Your mother's G-string."

This is New York, and my insult barely fazes him. No one is raising a ruckus, so he lets me pass without further challenge. I take the next car headed to Brooklyn and grab the hand bar. I never sit on a subway seat, and no self-respecting person should. The car is crowded but thankfully far from packed. Had that been the case, I probably would have gotten out and clung to the roof. I store that thought away as a future option.

I search for the tiny spark of inner peace within me so I can make the trip without cracking someone's head open. A Hispanic voice cuts through my tissue paper-like Zen, and I look to find a kid badgering the girl sitting next to him. I can tell she is not a native as she desperately tries to ignore the kid's aggressive requests to "hook up". He looks up at me and wrongly assumes I have developed some sort of interest in his activities.

"What the fuck are you looking at, *puto*?"

The girl looks at me with pleading eyes, obviously hoping I am going to come to her rescue. I could not give a shit about her problem, but I'm far less prone to letting the kid's insult slide. It takes about one-tenth of a second for the back of my fist to flick from the hand bar to his forehead and back.

The girl looks a bit frightened at my heavy-handedness but squeaks out a thank you. I just grunt in reply, thankful that everyone has cut the volume of their inane prattling in half and is now giving me just a bit more space.

I take a deep breath when I finally climb back to the surface. Vampires don't need to breathe to survive, but not doing so makes it impossible to speak and, more importantly, smell the things around you. I held my breath the entire way here to keep from gagging on the concentrated stench of humanity. Even now, the myriad smells are strong and unpleasant, but they're tolerable.

The subway doesn't run anywhere near where I need to go, so I start hoofing it across town. I don't get tired, but the waste of time pisses me off. This is definitely the last time I forget to slip some bills into my pocket before I leave. I retrace my steps from last night, taking to the rooftops and alleys so I can run full tilt without attracting attention. I wisely choose to use the front entrance of the building where I shot Francis instead of making a potentially painful and embarrassing leap to the roof again.

Yellow police tape crisscrosses the doorway and surrounds the spot where I landed after my ignominious drop through the floor. I navigate my way past more tape as I take the stairs to the upper floor. More police tape cordons off much of the upstairs, sectioning off the hole I fell through and Francis' blood spatters.

I have no clue as to where Francis hides out during the day, so my best bet is to try to track him down. It's a bit of a long shot. Vampires have heightened senses, including smell, but we're nowhere near being bloodhounds. My only hope is that, being a relatively new vampire, he hasn't learned how to consciously heal his wounds efficiently.

I take a good sniff and start following his hasty exodus across the roof and down into the streets. He might have been running in a panic, but he's kept his wits enough to avoid the populated streets and stuck to the alleyways. His retreat took him through the most run-down sections of Brooklyn, and I manage to follow the trail into Greenpoint. It's not the worst the city has to offer, but it's definitely a weak stone's throw from it.

The blood droplets have slowed, and it's getting harder to find them. I've lost the trail twice now only to pick it up a block or more away, and it's growing fainter by the step. I finally lose it altogether, but I'm sure I'm in the right neighborhood.

The block I'm on has plenty of places in which to hide out during the nighttime hours as well as some prime hunting grounds. Only an idiot hunts anywhere near his lair, but being an idiot is a prime factor in why Francis is on my shit list. I follow the sound of metal crashing to the ground not far away. A chain-link fence bars the entrance to a metal recycling company. Unless there's a pit bull wandering around the yard, no one should be inside at this hour.

Gripping my sword in my right hand, I jump up, grab the top of the fence, and fling myself over to the other side. I crouch next to the fence and survey the area. This is as good a place as any to lie low during the night. The yard is a maze of cubed scrap metal stacked ten feet high like oversized children's blocks.

I take a good, long sniff and detect a whiff of fresh blood. I had hoped Francis would take a night to lick his wounds and I'd catch him before his next feeding, but I don't think I'm that lucky. I creep around a wall of stacked steel and peer between the rows. At the far end near the fence, I spot what looks like a body. In a perfect world, I'd find Francis taking a nap and dreaming about the days when he had functioning genitals.

However, this isn't a perfect world, in fact it tends to kinda suck. The body appears to be that of a homeless woman Francis probably nabbed as she made her way to one of the nearby shelters. If he had stuck to these kinds of kills, properly disposed of the body, and wasn't such a gluttonous little pig, I wouldn't be trying to kill him. Nevertheless, he chose to do the opposite, so here I am.

I look up at the sound of shifting metal and see one wall of iron and steel lean inward just before it topples in an effort to crush me. I execute a long jump toward the end of the row that would make Carl Lewis envious. The wall of metal crashes down just behind me, entombing the corpse Francis left behind.

I roll several times and hear the impact of something striking the ground inches from my head. Tumbling to a kneeling position, I bring my blade over my head and block the length of steel Francis uses to try to split my head like an insane Gallagher. I knock him to the ground with a leg sweep and buy myself enough time to get to my feet.

Francis, the little chicken shit, won't face me in a stand up fight, rolls to his feet, and runs. He jumps up onto another row of compacted metal, but I chuck a muffler at him and knock him off the other side. My victory is short-lived. I take a few running steps before he vaults back onto the wall and hops over the fence.

I leap over the enclosure and into the street just in time to see him hurdle the fence surrounding the water treatment plant across the street. Francis lands inside the facility at the same time I reach the street. I snap off a round, and he yelps and slaps at his left upper arm where the bullet grazes him. The treatment plant is a big place, and I don't want to lose him again.

He darts between the massive, silver tanks, and I lose sight of him for a moment, but my excellent hearing picks up the sound of his feet striking the pavement. His footsteps stop, so I slow to a walk and try to pick up his scent, but the wind isn't with me. I can smell the fact he came through here, but not where he is currently standing.

Francis lunges at me from the dark cleft between two of the huge water tanks. I duck the swing, and the steel cistern rings like a bell when his bar smashes into it. He kicks out to the side, catches my thigh, and knocks me back several paces. I bring Shalonda up, but he vanishes past one of the water tanks and takes off running again.

I would rather not punch a hole in something holding a few hundred thousand gallons of water, so I check my shot and give chase. For a guy whose balance should be a little off due to some missing bits, Francis can still run.

He sprints across an open area and runs toward the man-made ponds. The grated metal catwalk shakes and rattles beneath our pounding feet. Francis hunkers behind a steel pipe sticking up out of the water at the end of the walkway set in the center of the pond.

I stop about twenty feet away. "Come out so we can end this,

Francis. I'm tired of chasing you."

"I'm tired of running. You shot my dick off, you bastard!"

"Come out and I'll end your suffering."

"Give me a chance. Fight me. No guns." He waves his steel bar over the water pipe.

I slide my pistol into its holster. "All right, we'll end this Star Wars style."

"Technically, it's Empire Strikes Back."

"Technically, I don't give a shit. Either way, it ends with you losing a lot more than a hand."

Francis peeks around the pipe and stands. He hefts his bar as if he's standing at home plate waiting for the pitch. I take two steps toward him. He raises his length of iron higher.

"Dumb fuck," he says with a sneer.

Francis brings his bar down on the water pipe's outlet valve and knocks the cap off. Water gushes out like a fireman's hose at several hundred PSI, blasts me in the chest like a civil rights protester, and knocks me off the catwalk and into the water. I kick for the surface and look for Francis, but he's gone. He probably jumped into the waterway feeding the treatment plant. Since he'll never have to come up for air, it'll be all but impossible for me to find him again tonight. He could swim the canal all the way to the East River without breaking the surface one time.

I'm hungry, wet, and crabby as hell, and the thought of getting back on the subway does nothing to improve my mood. I'll have to walk a ways before I can reach an area where the cabs run. With any luck, I'll find dinner somewhere between here and there. There's certainly an ample supply of people who won't be missed much, but like with any good restaurant, it's all about location.

I travel the darkest, scariest streets and alleys in hopes of finding a straggler to pick off from the herd. My favorite is catching some guy in the midst of a violent crime. I like my meal to be rich in irony. I say a quick thanks to Lady Luck when I hear a muffled cry coming from a narrow gap between a pair of five-story buildings.

The alley reeks of trash, piss, and shit, and I'm forced to

clamp down my olfactory senses as I step into the dark divide. Somewhere near the midway point, I pick out a pair of bodies. One is pressing the other against the wall with a hand over her mouth. Despite the overwhelming odors, I can still pick out the smell of perfume and a woman's scent amidst the heavy city stench when I take a quick sniff.

I grab the hoodied assailant by the upper arm and fling him against the far wall. I take two steps toward him and freeze in my tracks when the thug drops his hood. In a purely instinctive response, my heart pounds in my chest and an overwhelming sense of fear and pure, unadulterated hatred infuse my body.

"Hello, Leonard," Lesile greets me in a soft, French accent.

Lesile's the bitch who turned me into a monster and tortured me for weeks in a twisted crash course to teach me how to be a proper vampire. For the past eighty years, my greatest desire in this world has been to cut this bitch's head off and mount it in my loft, but now I can't do anything but stare with my mouth agape like an idiot.

I turn my head when I hear her "victim" moving behind me. She is holding what looks like a 40mm grenade launcher and is pointing it at my back. I barely have time to mutter "what the fuck?" before it discharges like a giant party favor. Instead of paper streamers, half a dozen electrodes pierce the thick fabric of my trench coat before unleashing what must be half a million volts of electricity throughout my body.

The result is instantaneous. I lose all control over my nervous system and flop to the ground like a marionette with the strings cut. A black SUV comes to a screeching halt at the end of the alley and disgorges four men in full assault gear. A dozen more figures repel down the side of the building with masterful expertise. I summon all my focus, tear the electrodes from my body, and lurch to my feet. Lesile moves faster than my eyes can track. I feel her foot strike my chest before I realize she even moved. I slam against the wall with the force of a senior citizen's car smashing through the front of a convenience store.

Before I can even think about countering, half a dozen more super Tasers fire and pump me with enough juice to fry an elephant. I'm back on the ground in an instant as every muscle in my body locks up with a steel grip. Fuck me. Just before I black out, I tell Lady Luck to eat my ass.

CHAPTER 6

It's nearly impossible to knock out a vampire, but you can run enough juice through one to sever their link with reality. By the time I regain my faculties, I'm trussed up and stuffed in the back of what I assume is one of the SUVs. I can tell we're moving, but I have no clue as to the direction. A hood covers my head, and what feels like some kind of old-school manacles binds my hands behind my back.

The cuffs must be about two inches wide and are attached by chains to my feet. I have no clue who these people are, where we're going, or what they want with me. My biggest question is what is Lesile doing with them? Were these people working for her? Are they part of some goon squad?

Lesile has always been on the fringe, pledging no allegiance to any enclave I know of. They could have killed me if they wanted to, so they obviously want me for something.

Most people would be scared shitless in a situation like this, but not me. I don't think it's courage. I think I'm just too damn stupid to be scared. I do know two things. These people are not vampires, and I am well and truly screwed.

I can't smell Lesile, so I assume she's in another car. These guys are probably just minions, so I don't bother to engage them. It's unlikely I'll get anything other than another jolt of electricity from them anyway. I'll play docile until they slip up. Then I'm going to free the beast and put the fear of heaven and hell into them just before they die.

I mark the seconds in my head but lose count after a while, so I give up. That trick only works for short distances, and we exceeded it long ago. My break comes when we stop for gas.

I can smell the fumes emanating from the pumps, but more importantly, I hear the DJ declaring 94.5 FM WPST as being the home of the best Top 40. That puts us traveling southwest and somewhere near Trenton.

Having a direction and distance isn't much, but it's something. Less than an hour later, I feel us leave the interstate when the G-force pushes me to one side of the vehicle as we speed down the long curve of an off- ramp. Our periodic changes in speed hints at the presence of toll stations, so I make the assumption we are on the New Jersey Turnpike.

Even if I'm right, it's still not much to go on. But, like a puzzle, every piece counts, and the more pieces you get the clearer the picture becomes. An interminable amount of time later, at least two hours by my count, our road trip finally ends. My handlers pull me out of the back and drop me on the ground.

"I'm going to switch your chains around so you can walk. Make a move and you're going to think you just got the chair. Got it?" one of my captors says.

"Just make sure you secure them properly, because if I get loose I'm going to kill every one of you fuckers. Got it?"

Something jabs me in the back and thigh and shocks the shit out of me once again. My body is locked into place by my own muscle contractions as the guy I'll call Sparky unhooks the chain running from my cuffs to my ankles. He removes one shackle, cuffs my hands in front of me, and reattaches the chain to my leg irons.

My handlers push me forward, warning me of the steps when we reach them, and guide me into a building. I detect the constant hum of what is probably an industrial generator or two, and the interior smells of fresh paint and drywall, but they fail to mask the musty odor of decay and years of disuse completely. I store each of these new puzzle pieces away for later use.

I hear the clacking of people typing on keyboards and the sounds of our footsteps echoing down the hallway. My hearing is keen enough I can get a guess at the length of the hall and the change in sound when we pass an open doorway or come to an intersection. We stop, I hear a door open, and I'm shoved into a room. I get a whiff of Lesile just before someone yanks the hood off my head. It's all I can do to keep from throwing myself at her when I see her standing near the far wall with a self-satisfied smile on her face. I refuse to humiliate myself no matter how pissed off I am.

There are four armed men and Lesile in the room with me, but none of them speaks. I assume we are waiting for someone else to show up. My theory proves correct when a man in an off the rack grey suit strides in. He is in his forties and of average build. His black hair is neatly cut, obviously the finest work of a poorly paid barber. Everything about him reeks of fed.

"Mr. Malone, I have heard much about you."

"You didn't hear enough; otherwise you would have killed me already."

"Why would I do that?"

"Because every minute I'm alive is a minute closer I come to killing you and your boy band."

The man smiles and gives me a disappointed shake of his head. "Are you a spiritual man, Mr. Malone? The pride of your heart has deceived you, you who live in the clefts of the rocks and make your home on the heights, you who say to yourself, 'Who can bring me down to the ground?' Obadiah said that in The Good Book."

"And Jesus said unto the Pharoses 'You'll die slow but calm. Recognize my face, so there won't be no mistake.'"

"I don't believe Jesus said that."

I shrug. "It may have been Notorious B.I.G. I get them confused sometimes."

"Your singular wit is certainly proving true, but the ease with which we brought you in is unsettling. I heard you were a supremely dangerous creature, and that is what I need. If I have been misled, I'm afraid I have little use for you."

"Oh, I'm supposed to be dangerous? As the director of this show, it's up to you to provide the actors with the proper motivation. Let's try this."

I spin around and head-butt the man behind me with the force of a major-league slugger swinging for the upper deck. Without taking a step, I flex my legs, launch myself at the guy to my front, and catch him in the chest with both feet. The impact sends him crashing into the wall ten feet away. He hits it with a meaty slap and slides to the ground. Neither men are moving, nor are they ever likely to again.

Electrodes sprout from my body before I even reach the ground. The two remaining guards pump enough electricity in me to light up Times Square, and I start flopping around like a landed fish. Little wisps of smoke curl up from my body as I try to reboot my brain.

"I had hoped for a less lethal demonstration, but I suppose that will do." The suit turns to his men. "Get some additional guards, take him below for his implant, and have someone clean this up. Lesile, I will hold you responsible for any more trouble he might cause."

Lesile's smile vanishes. She snatches the hood from the floor and bags my head before grabbing my ankle chains and dragging me down the hall. I don't even try to fight back. None of my muscles are responding, so I let her take me where we're going like a bag of cotton. I'm bounced down a single flight of stairs. The sound of running generators gets louder, and I soon reach them. The room sounds enormous and the hum echoes like an underground garage. She drags me out of the stairwell and through another door. The smell of antiseptic reaches my nose before Lesile tosses me onto a surgical table and pulls the hood off. I'm in a makeshift operating room, and she straps me down with bands made of what looks like Kevlar.

It is a far too familiar scene, and it's all I can do to keep from letting the flashback of Lesile's tortures from making me lose my shit. It's only through sheer stubbornness that I'm able to fight back my rising panic. There will be a reckoning. When I get out of this, there's going to be a Black Friday of ass whoopings unleashed up in here.

A woman with brown hair tied in a tight bun and wearing hospital scrubs walks in. She checks the straps holding me down and rolls a tray of instruments closer to the table. She holds up a small circuit board a little bigger than a postage stamp with a small glass vial set in its center.

"Are you familiar with a toxin called the Cure?" She

obviously knows the answer and keeps talking. "This is a satellite transponder. I am going to implant it in your brain. If you fail to do as you are told or attempt to tamper with it, a signal will be sent to release its contents."

"Oh good, for a minute I thought it was a suppository."

"Joke with me all you like, but you had better take this seriously. I have seen what this does to your kind, and it looks very unpleasant."

A dozen smart-assed comments spring to mind, but I keep them to myself. I'm too busy wondering what the fuck she and the Mod Squad know about my kind and how far that knowledge goes. The primary purpose of the enclave and the rules we all—mostly—abide by is to keep our existence secret. The government knowing about us is the absolute worst possible thing that could happen. My only relief is being fairly sure it's not my fault.

"It's nice operating on your kind," the doctor says as she picks up an unpleasant-looking power tool. "I don't have to worry about anesthesia or heart failure."

I wince when I feel the scalpel cut a neat line around my head. I block out the pain receptors and try not to think about what is going on. It's a bit hard to do when she pulls my scalp back to reveal my skull. The oscillating saw starts up with a high-pitched whine. There is surprisingly little pain even when she pries the top of my skull off and sets it on the table like a soup bowl.

"Perfect. Now I'll just slip this deep between the two lobes and close you up."

Knowing she is digging around inside my brain without me feeling it is certainly disconcerting. The doc sticks my skull back on as if she were closing up a jar of mayo and starts stapling my scalp back in place.

"Make sure you get it on straight. If I have a sideburn running between my eyes you're going to answer to my barber."

"I am glad you are keeping a sense of humor through all this, Mr. Malone."

"Yeah, I always keep them laughing—right up until I kill them."

The doc looks to one of the guards. "Take him away. Mr. Malone, I suggest you behave. Cameras throughout the building monitor your every movement. If you try to escape or threaten anyone, an agent can press a button and kill you instantly."

"Super. Does anyone plan on telling me just what the fuck is going on and what you want with me?"

"That information is not available to me, but I'm sure you will find out soon enough."

Someone drops the hood back over my head, and my entourage nudges me down the hall. Paint covered the only window I saw, and most of the interior smells of renovation, so there is little to give me clues as to my location. Less now that the bag is over my head again. Even with the fresh paint and drywall, I can't help but sense a familiarity with the place. I'm sure I've never been here, but perhaps I've been in something similar. It has a creepy hospital or boarding school vibe to it. I spent years off and on in schools for troubled youths. Maybe the ghosts of this place are calling out to me.

My guards escort me up a stairwell. Either this place doesn't have elevators or they don't trust me in such close confines. Lesile is walking ahead of the pack, and I can't help but be curious as to her role in all this. She's the last person I want to talk to, but my curiosity is stronger than my disgust.

"So why don't they have you in shackles?"

"Because I already have one of those things in my head, and I know how to behave myself."

"The hell you do."

"I am smart enough to know when I am beat, and I like my life too much to let my ego do something that will only result in my death. You should learn something from that if you want to live beyond the next few hours."

I count off three flights of stairs before reaching the top. One of the guards opens a steel door and pushes me inside, pulling off the hood as he does so. The door closes with a resounding clank, and I hear heavy deadbolts locking into place. I shuffle around the room, tapping the walls and stomping the floor with my boot in search of weaknesses. I don't find any. The room is perfectly square and bereft of any furnishings. Once again, I get the feeling of a classroom or hospital room.

"You should relax," Lesile tells me. "They obviously want you for something specific, otherwise you would be below."

"What happens down there, other than brain raping?"

"You don't want to know."

"You're a psychotic bitch, but you're a wily psychotic bitch. How did they catch you?"

Lesile smiles coyly and nibbles the tip of her finger. "I made a boo-boo."

With her stunning beauty and soft accent, it's damn hard to remember how much I despise her. She exudes sexuality like heat from the sun. Thankfully, she ruins the effect by talking.

"Leonard, you look like shit. I'm three times your age, and I look better than you. What have you done to yourself?"

"I've had a hard life."

"Bullshit. You do not eat properly. You should feed more, and from actual people, not from a bag given to you like some sort of refugee or zoo animal."

"You don't know anything about my life. You didn't know anything when you took it, and you sure as hell don't know shit now."

"Then tell me. We have nothing but time."

"The only thing you need to know about me is that I'm going to kill you the first chance I get."

"You were always such a shit, Leonard." She winds a lock of ebony hair around her finger. "If you don't want to talk, I can think of some other things we can do to occupy our time."

I look up at the camera prominently displayed behind what I assume is some thick Plexiglas. "I'm sure the boys on the other end would love a show."

"Let them watch."

"How about you just keep on your side of the room and tell me what they want with me?"

"I don't know, but they obviously have a use for you just as they do me."

"What's your use?"

"I help them identify and capture other vampires."

"You know, a lot of people think I'm a real cocksucker…"

"Everyone thinks that."

"...but I've never betrayed my own kind."

"Leonard, I am my own kind and no one else. The only way I could betray my kind would be to sacrifice myself out of some idiotic sense of loyalty. You should learn that if you want to survive."

"I need more than just survival. In fact, survival barely cracks my top ten."

"Then you are a fool. I gave you a wonderful gift. If you choose to throw it away, then I won't stop you."

The hours roll by in silence. Lesile may as well be a statue, which suits me just fine. I shuffle around the room, still wearing my shackles and chains, until it becomes boring. I take a seat against the wall and close my eyes. I focus on the blackness inside my mind, but I don't let myself slip beneath the surface of consciousness. My break could come at any moment, and I need to be ready to act in an instant.

I'm saved from my tedium when the door opens and the suit saunters in with a retinue of phaser-wielding henchmen. I'm not sure how long they had me sit here and stew, but I estimate it to be about a day to a day and a half.

The suit flips open a dossier and pretends to read it even though I'm sure he has it memorized. "Mr. Malone, you have quite a history—World War Two, Korea, Vietnam. KIA or MIA in every one, always near the end."

"Yeah, those Asians are a troublesome bunch."

"You must be wondering who I am."

"Not really. I never feel the need to know the people I kill."

"You certainly like to sing your favorite song, don't you?"

"If you like the chorus, wait until I drop the beat."

The suit closes the folder and smiles. "My name is Agent Snow. I am in charge of this operation."

"Fed?"

"Homeland Security. Over the last few years, the NSA picked up some pieces of electronic chatter mentioning a highly toxic substance called the Cure. Their first thoughts were of a terrorist organization finding a cure for western existence, and they handed the case over to Homeland Security. When I saw a glimmer of what was really happening I created a black op more need to know than the mission to kill Osama."

"I've never known the government to be able to keep secrets for long. This seems like too big an operation to keep quiet."

"This is the most covert black op in history. Everyone who knows anything about this is in this building. They have little to no family and cannot leave the facility. There are two phones in the entire complex, and they are more tightly controlled than the vaults in the Federal Reserve. Our funding is completely under the table. Not even the President has a whiff of what's going on here. We are completely self-sustained."

"Okay, let's assume I don't think you're full of shit. Why?"

"Necessity for one. It is rather difficult to identify your kind, but we're getting better. Can you imagine the uproar if the populace found out there were vampires amongst them and that you consider them food? There would be a panic. People would be shooting every Goth kid and *Twilight* wannabe on sight. On top of that, there would invariably be some pinko liberal movement declaring your rights as human beings and citizens. If I thought we could just feed them to your kind I'd go along with it, but liberals rarely support their causes when they find out the real cost."

"I can see why there's not armed squads scouring the countryside, but that doesn't explain why I'm here, or her."

"Now we get to the crux of our predicament. About a year ago, we zeroed in on one of the cells, captured our first vampire, a sample of the toxic Cure, and a reformatted substance that seemed to make vampires instead of killing them."

Goddam Percy and his fuck-up. What was once a goat screw just turned into a colossal disaster of epic proportions. The only saving grace I can see is the fact it is not widely known and is still contained. That won't last for long, and I begin to get a chill down my spine in anticipation of where this little speech is going.

"As you probably know, Homeland Security's primary mission is to protect our nation and people from terrorism. Many agree this is an impossible task if we are limited to defensive measures only. We had to take the fight to the terrorists but in a way that would not draw international condemnation.

Too many people are already bitching about the drone strikes and, let's face it, the drones are a Band-Aid not a cure. We needed to create small, highly proficient, and lethal strike teams to eradicate terrorist cells abroad, capable of operating for long periods of time without any support and who could not be traced back to the U.S."

I start laughing. "You dumb sonsabitches. Let me guess, you made some super soldiers, and now they're running amok."

Agent Snow takes a deep breath and nods. "We needed to develop a way to hit these terrorist vermin's nests while maintaining plausible deniability. Last year, we lost a helicopter carrying a group of Navy SEALs in Afghanistan."

"And you thought a great way to reward their service was to turn them into monstrous killing machines?"

The agent's face flushes and he shoots me a contemptuous glare. "These men would do anything for their country. Even if they woke from their comas, their injuries were too severe ever to allow a semblance of a normal life. You were a soldier once. You knew men like these, and you know living as a cripple would be worse than death. We thought we found a way to not just save their lives, but return them to duty."

"But they went rogue because you don't know a goddam thing about vampires. You didn't know the altered version of the Cure made vampires with extra bad attitudes. You didn't know unleashing a top tier predator, one whose entire adult life has been focused on killing, would spark a bloodlust and cause them to go rogue. Where's their leash? Why can't you push the button and take them out?"

Agent Snow's face is a deep shade of red, and he looks at me like a willful child who just got scolded.

I grin and shake my head. "You didn't implant it in the brain, and they cut your little bomb right out."

"Believe me when I say your model's anti-tampering mechanism is vastly superior."

"You still haven't told me what you want from me."

"I thought that would be obvious, particularly for a private detective such as yourself. You are going to clean up this little mess before it becomes an international incident and possibly a global catastrophe."

"Two words spring immediately to mind. 'Fuck' and 'you.'"

"You are hardly in a position to refuse, Mr. Malone."

"What are you going to do, waterboard me?"

"You have a bomb in your brain. I think that should be enough to convince you of your only option."

"I guess that would work on someone with a high regard for their life, so my answer is still 'fuck you.'"

"I was told you were an obstinate bastard. Your kind in general seems reluctant to cooperate. Of the four vampires we have captured alive, none would speak of their organization or society. The only exception to their reticence was when we asked them to give us the name of just one vampire. Can you guess the name they gave, every single one without exception?"

"That's kind of hurtful, yet I feel a sense of pride having made such an impact on them."

"Perhaps you value the life of another more than your own."

The suit nods to one of his flunkies and the hood drops back over my head. They prod me out of the room and force me down the hall before stopping. I hear a door open, and they shove me into another room. Someone pulls the hood off my head, and I fall into a fit of laughter when I see Vincent chained to the wall.

"And I thought I was going to have a bad day. If you think this is leverage, you really have to work on your intel. It's this quality of information-gathering that had us looking for Saudi terrorists trained by Afghani Al-Qaeda in Iraq."

"Forgive me if I doubt the sincerity of your enmity. I understand Mr. Van Graff is something of a figurehead in your society."

"More like a dickhead. You would have had better luck convincing me to do what you want by promising to kill him. But I hate being told what to do more than I dislike Vincent, so go fuck yourself."

"Perhaps Mr. Van Graff appreciates his life more than you do and will convince you it is best to cooperate."

Agent Snow and his goons leave me in the room with Vincent, but I'm sure they're hearing and seeing everything.

Despite my bravado, seeing Vincent here is deeply disturbing. Not because I give a shit about him, but because it means the government has gotten its hands on the highest ranking vampire in the entire northeastern United States. Vincent is a treasure trove of information, and if they can pry his secrets out of his head, it could bring down not just our enclave but our entire society.

I decide it's a good idea to make Vincent's importance look as poor as possible. "How on earth did they manage to get you?"

Vincent does a great job of maintaining his stick-up-the-ass composure. "It is not important."

"Please tell me it was a honeypot. It was wasn't it? What was his name? I bet he was a Filipino boy, wasn't he? I always took you for a flip sticker."

Vincent rolls his eyes and gives me an exasperated sigh. "Since you enjoy making japes as to the inference of my sexuality, let me put your assumptions to rest."

"Don't you dare!"

"I have been an avowed homosexual since 1853 and a practicing one a good deal longer than that. What's the matter? Is it no longer fun now that you know the truth?"

"No, now it just sounds like a hate crime. Who wants to be that guy? You're a real dick."

"Perhaps. This is an unmitigated disaster, Leonard, and we must figure out a way to resolve it. If that means doing as they ask, so be it."

"Do you really think they're just going to let us go if I play the part of their dog?"

"Of course not, but it will at least give us time. As much as I despise you, I know you are the most likely person to succeed in carrying out their executions and creating an opportunity to resolve this dilemma. These people do not fully appreciate what an unpredictable pain in the ass you can be."

"I do like to put on a good show."

"Make it your greatest performance."

"Hey, Vincent, did you at least get a tug and tickle before they dragged you in?"

"How did that feel?"

I frown. "Empty, hollow, and kind of dickish. I hate you."

"Nothing pleases me more."

"Not even…oh, never mind. It's not even worth it anymore. God I hate you."

Vincent has robbed me of one of my few pleasures in life. This day just continues to top out the suck-o-meter. When the time comes to pay the piper, these assclowns are going to need an unlimited line of credit. When Snow returns, I can tell he has been listening in by the shit-eating grin on his face.

"Will you do as we tell you?"

"Only under a formal statement of duress."

"Noted. I understand your desire to thwart our plans, but just because you are our best option does not mean you are our only option. Nor is Mr. Van Graff the only leverage we have on you. We are also quite aware of your involvement with Ms. Goldstein. We know she is not a vampire and, as she is a high-profile person, we would prefer not taking any actions against her to force your cooperation. Do we understand each other, Mr. Malone?"

"Do you know the fable about the king, the mice and the cheese?"

"I'm afraid I am not familiar."

"This king had a problem with mice eating his cheese, so he brought in a bunch of cats to get rid of them. Now he had a problem with cats all over his castle, so he brought in dogs. To get rid of the dogs, he brought in lions and the story continues to escalate and eventually becomes an unending loop. You've brought lions into your home, Agent Snow."

"I will keep that in mind."

"Where are these rogue vampires and how many are there?"

"We were able to successfully infect three and inserted them in Yemen to hunt out and destroy Al-Qaeda cells that are beyond our conventional reach."

"Yemen, the birthplace of the suck-o-meter."

"Their last known location was near Shuqrah in Abyan. Our sources indicate a number of deaths in the region point to our rogue operatives."

"Who are they killing?"

"They appear to still be hunting down suspected terrorist cells, but they have been getting progressively less covert."

"It sounds to me like you should just let them continue what they're doing."

The agent shakes his head. "You don't understand how sensitive and classified this operation is. If they were just killing terrorists, we might just let them go on uninterrupted. But they ceased being surgical and are creating a state of terror in the region."

"Terrorists being terrorized. Breaks my fucking heart."

"We need to control this. If any of the outside nations, hell even our own, gets wind of what those soldiers are and where they came from, there is going to be a global political shitstorm, and your people are going to be in the middle of it. This has the potential to be far more devastating for your kind than for our government. Imagine if other nations discover they have creatures feeding on their population. They won't act with our restraint."

"And you think I can fix this all by myself?"

"Lesile will go with you. She speaks Arabic and is familiar with the culture."

"It's not enough. I'll need a special tool."

"I will get whatever you need."

"This tool is a who, not a what."

CHAPTER 7

I'm assigned four handlers, but only two escort me into the prison. I sit in front of the glass and wait while my two guards loom over my shoulder a few feet behind me. I'm still wearing my cuffs, but at least I'm not shackled. That will change when I get back in the car and make the return flight.

I smile at the man in the orange jumpsuit when he sits down opposite me and presses the handset to his shaggy head. "Hey, Meat, how's life in the dog pound?"

"Not so bad when you're top dog."

"Top or bottom you're still banging dudes."

"What do you want? Conjugals are on Saturday."

"I need your help."

Meat flicks his eyes to the two suits behind me. "Who are they?"

"That's Heckle and Jeckle. They're part of the problem."

"Why would I want to help you and get mixed up in your problems?"

"For one, it would get you out of here. Secondly, if you haven't figured it out yet, these guys are feds, and they know about my kind."

Meat's expression grows dark. "What else?"

"Nothing yet, but it's only a matter of time."

"I knew you leeches would fuck up eventually. How bad is it?"

"It appears to be contained, but I need your help to keep it that way."

"Give me a sitrep."

"That thing with Percy drew unwanted attention. They got

ahold of the original Cure and the new version and created what they thought were going to be some super soldiers. They lost control, and they want me to clean up the mess."

"And I should help you because...?"

"Because you know as well as I how fucked up this can get if word spreads, which it invariably will. How long has the government been able to keep anything secret? All it takes is one dipshit with a grudge and a thumb drive to tell the entire planet."

"Your friends can get me out of here?"

"Within the hour."

"What's the job?"

"Jump into Yemen and kill three highly trained Navy SEALs made extra murderous."

"Yemen? Fuck me."

"Three lethal, special ops, extra mean killers, and Yemen is the problem in this scenario?"

"Yeah, they'll probably kill us, but Yemen is worse. It's like hell's slums."

"Then you'll help?"

Meat sighs and looks over his shoulder at the guards and the steel door leading into the visitation room. "Yeah, I'm not built for incarceration."

"You're not built for dancing either, but I bet you have some sweet moves."

"I know I'm going to regret this."

"Come on, sweltering, terroristic hell, trained killers, it's going to be a hoot."

I'm true to my word, or at least the feds are, and Meat and I are both shackled, hooded, and flown back to Neverland Ranch. We don't talk much on the flight or the drive from whatever secret airstrip our private jet uses. I can tell Meat is using his senses to try to get an idea of where we are, so I don't bother him.

We're guided through the building, taking so many turns and flights of stairs I'm certain they are using a circuitous route to confuse our bearings before sitting us down and removing our hoods. Agent Snow sits behind a desk, and the brain bomb bitch, Dr. Mengele I guess, is standing next to him. Six feds keep their super Tasers trained on us.

"Margaret, please inspect Mr. Poole."

Margaret, Mengele, I was close. The doctor sticks a small, round puck on Meat's forehead and uses one of those eyeball-examining scopes to look into his eyes. She pulls out a small computer tablet, looks at the display, and pulls off the puck.

"Temperature, pulse, and blood pressure are within normal limits. He's not a vampire, but he does display some unusual characteristics I would like to examine in closer detail."

"Interesting," Agent Snow says and flips open a folder on his desk. "Lawrence Poole, age thirty-nine, former marine sergeant, highly decorated for services performed in both gulf wars."

I snort. "Lawrence?"

"Fuck off, *Leonard*."

"Touché."

"Mr. Poole, I understand you are aware of what Mr. Malone is?"

"You mean an asshole? Yeah, it's not a secret. Everyone who has ever met him knows it. Even people who just pass idly by are instantly aware of his assholishness."

"I am referring to his vampiric nature."

"Oh, you mean that. Yeah, that too."

"He says you are something of an expert in hunting his kind. Would you care to elaborate and fill me in on the physical peculiarities Dr. Birch found?"

I interrupt before Meat can fuck up the story I spent the last few hours concocting. "Lawrence comes from a long line of vampire hunters. Have you heard of Abraham Van Helsing?"

"Like the movie vampire hunter?"

"Not like, exactly, only less glorified. Meat's great-something-or-other grandfather was Saary Tarcal until Prince Dimitrie Cantemir, the Prince of Moldavia in what is now Romania, decreed his name be changed to Saary Goatfucker after having been convicted of fucking goats. Normally, this would be grounds for execution, but the region had a vampire problem, and his was one of the few families practiced in hunting and destroying them. The prince put him on probation with the order to kill the vampires and to stop fucking goats. When the family immigrated to the United States, the kind folks at Ellis Island changed their name to Poole, likely in an ironic joke referring to the shallowness of their gene pool." I look at Meat. "If you ever have a son, promise me you'll name him Gene."

"Eat shit."

"Anyway, one night, Lawrence's father climbed through his sister's bedroom window, drunkenly mistaking it for the barn, and there they conceived him, the last of the incestuous, goat-fucking, vampire hunters. Obviously, their centuries of close contact with vampires and lack of genetic diversity has created a few minor mutations, which Dr. Birch has noted."

Agent Snow smiles in obvious amusement. "You are a funny man, Mr. Malone."

"Stick around; my eight o'clock show is different from my four o'clock."

"Mr. Poole, is what Mr. Malone said factual in any way?"

Meat twitches his broad shoulders. "More or less. He left out the part where we like to brutally sodomize the vampire before cutting off its head."

"How many vampires have you killed, Mr. Poole?"

"Three."

I turn and give Meat a surprised look. I certainly know he is capable, but I never thought he had actually done it.

"You hunted them?"

"Chance encounters. I never got into the family business."

"Do you think you could hunt them if you wanted to?"

"Oh yeah, no problem." Meat touches his nose with his index finger. "I know right off when I get close to one. They have a peculiar stink, at least to my nose. Some more than others."

Agent Snow leans back in his chair. "If you are successful in this mission, I might have a job for you. Good pay, benefits, retirement."

"I'll think about it. We ex-cons can't be too choosy when it comes to taking jobs."

Agent Snow smiles in a way that says agreement isn't necessarily required. I know Meat is just playing along. There are a dozen factors in play that would ensure Meat would never work for Snow or any government agency. Besides, such an act would cause a war between weres and vampires and would reveal his people to the world. He knows the stakes, and he knows the only two possible ways for this to end.

"Mr. Malone, I hope I can at least trust in your sense of self-preservation to work with your team whether you like them or not. I will not hesitate to set off the capsule in your head if you become a detriment to this mission."

"I'm as interested in putting these guys down as you are. We'll get it done or die trying."

"You most certainly will. Your insertion team and equipment are already prepared for departure."

There is no rest for the wicked. Meat and I are hooded and shoved back into a vehicle. My best guess is we drive for about an hour before stopping. Our handlers pull us from the vehicle and guide us to wherever we're going. I can tell from the echoing noises that we're in some kind of enormous building, likely an aircraft hangar, and I'm right. Someone pulls my hood off and I look at what appears to be the ass end of a jet similar in size and function to a C-130 and painted flat black. My gut tells me the paint is anti-reflective to give the aircraft some crude stealth capabilities.

I find Lesile already seated and handcuffed on the craft's bench seat. They sit Meat beside her and chain me to a seat across from them. It seems my sparkling personality has been rewarded with special treatment.

Lesile flashes Meat a broad smile. "Leonard, who is our burly friend?"

Meat grins back. "My name's Lawrence. Folks call me Lars, but my friends call me Meat. My good friends get to see why."

Lesile smiles even wider and leans into him. "I'm Lesile. I hope we become very good friends."

"Are you fucking kidding me?" I growl from across the aisle.

"Are you jealous, Leonard? I knew you still cared for me. No one can pretend to hate another so vocally without being in love."

"Call me old-fashioned, but I'm just a bit turned off by inter-species relationships."

Meat says, "I'll be sure to tell Kat that next time I see her."

"Who is Kat?"

"Leo's bed buddy."

"She's one of you?"

"She's half, but she's a good woman. I don't know what she sees in this prick."

"Go to hell, Goatfucker."

Lesile turns her smile toward me. "Leonard, you did not tell me you had found love. I was not sure you were even capable of it. Kat and I must have a girls' night out and share stories."

Fuck me with a stick. This is going to be one hell of a long flight. The whine of hydraulics kicking on fills the compartment as the loading ramp rises into position and seals us in. The portholes are blacked out for light discipline, and the interior is thrown into pitch darkness for a moment until the interior lights kick on. I feel a slight jolt when a tow vehicle couples onto the front landing gear and pulls us out onto the runway.

A much deeper whine fills the cabin when the engines spin up and it becomes a roar. The jet rockets down the tarmac, and my stomach sinks a bit in the split second the wheels leave the ground. I've never been a big fan of flying. In fact, the only time I have been on an aircraft was when one was carrying me to one war or another.

When we level out, one of the black-fatigued agents shouts over the drone of the engines. "It's a fifteen hour flight, so go ahead and get as comfortable as you can. With our additional fuel capacity, we'll only have to perform a single midair refueling. Agent Snow wanted me to remind you all of our capability to set off your implants from any location in the world. My team can also trigger them if you show us any resistance. This is your only warning."

I spend most of the flight studying the men holding their weapons at the ready. They try to maintain perfect vigilance, but it's a long flight, and they eventually relax. I watch for telltale body language to pick out weaknesses and, more importantly, who has the button. I'm more than a little annoyed at the fact that I seem to be the only one doing it. Lesile and Meat are too busy cozying up to one another, and I say a word of thanks for the restraints preventing them from humping on the floor.

The hours crawl by, and I have to fall back on my sniper training to find the patience to keep from going bat shit crazy out of sheer boredom. I find myself looking forward to the life and death fight with our targets and realize I may have something of an emotional problem. I should have a talk with my shrink about this. I'm sure it can't be healthy.

"All right, people, we're nearing the drop zone," the lead agent announces. "One of my guys is going to remove your restraints. If you so much as flinch before he clears the area, we're going to fry your brain. Got it?"

All but one of the agents move to the front of the cargo hold and train their weapons on us while their remaining team member unlocks our shackles. Once freed, he hastens to join his group near the front of the plane.

"In the small box near the rear of the aircraft are some electronic devices. The item looking like a wristwatch emits a GPS signal. The sat phones will allow you to track each of them in case you get separated. They will also allow you to send encrypted texts to apprise us of your mission status. Once we receive confirmation of your success, we will send you the location for the extraction point. Remember, we can set off your implant anytime and anywhere if you deviate from the mission."

"What about equipment, or are we supposed to talk them into shooting themselves in the head?" I ask.

"We'll drop your gear once all three of you are clear of the aircraft. This is a low altitude jump, so don't fuck it up."

Low altitude means under five hundred feet to avoid radar. He's right, there's no second chances if there's chute failure. I walk to the rear of the plane and retrieve the electronics package. I toss a phone and a GPS to my two teammates as the large cargo door at the rear slowly drops open. I motion to Lesile to come to me.

I have to shout over the sound of the engines and the noise of the wind as the aircraft cuts through the air at a hundred and fifty miles per hour. "Have you ever jumped before?"

Lesile shakes her head. "I never had a reason or desire to

jump from a perfectly functioning airplane."

I grab a harness and guide her in putting it on. "It's easy. The static line will deploy your chute for you, and all you have to do is glide to the ground. You can steer by pulling on the two handles just above your head. When you jump, cross your arms in front of your chest and leap straight out as if you're jumping into the pool. It's that easy."

"I still don't like it."

I clip the static line to a metal ring on her harness. "Trust me, you'll love it. I know I will."

I take a step back and kick her in the chest as hard as I can. Lesile's eyes widen as she flies from the back of the aircraft. Her enraged shout turns into a series of expletives when the static line snaps taut, pulls her harness' quick release, and she freefalls the entire way to the ground. Meat leaps from his seat and stares at the packed chute flapping behind the cargo ramp at the end of its static line.

"What the fuck did you do? She was the only one who speaks Arabic! How the fuck are we supposed to complete our mission now?"

"I don't know. I don't really think much beyond getting what I want, and what I wanted more than anything in the world right now was to kick that bitch out of the back of this airplane."

"Is she dead?"

"I sure hope so; otherwise I'm in some real shit when I get down there."

"We're moving past the drop zone. Go now!" the fed orders.

I flip Meat and the agents a one-fingered salute and jump. My chute snaps open, and I bounce a few times as the canopy arrests my fall. I see Meat jump a few seconds after me followed by a plastic crate containing what I assume is our weapons. Dropping into a desert at night is like jumping into the ocean. Thankfully, my heightened eyesight is able to pick out the details of the ground without a problem, and I make a good landing despite not having had any practice for over forty years.

I pull my harness release and let the light wind carry it and my chute away. Meat performs a decent PLF and does likewise. I pull out my sat phone and tap the "find" button. I get four blips on the screen. The two next to each other in the center I logically guess are me and Meat. Two others blink to the north and south. Since we came in from the south, I assume the one to the north is our gear and the southern one is whatever is left of Lesile.

Meat glances at my display and starts hoofing it south. With little recourse, I follow him. The terrain is rocky with a covering of sand. Low dunes lie in mounds where the wind piled up the sand like snowdrifts. Our blips almost converge on the screen after half an hour of walking. I turn in a slow circle and look for some sign of Lesile. I'm beginning to think she lost her GPS in the fall and her body is somewhere else, when the small dune behind me explodes in a spray of grit.

Lesile moves so fast I only turn halfway around before she punches me in the side of the head. I reel under the assault then find myself flying through the air when she kicks me in the ribs. I land flat on my back and look up at the sky. I barely manage to roll aside when her body blocks out the stars and she falls to the earth like a meteor. She craters the ground where my head was a fraction of a second before.

I reverse the direction of my roll and land a punch to her right ear. "Ha, bitch, take that!"

My victory is short-lived. We both roll to our feet, and I'm soon on the receiving end of a severe ass whooping. I dodge or duck two out of three kicks and punches coming for my face, but when there's twenty of them in the span of two or three seconds it's still a substantial beating.

A kick to my chest sends me flying and crashing to the ground again. I roll and push myself into the air when she tries to do a flying axe handle. I twist around, drop onto her back, and put her in a chokehold.

"Meat, how about a little help?"

"Naw, she looks like she's doing fine on her own."

"You son of a—!"

Lesile launches into the air with me clinging onto her back. She arches back and crushes me to the ground. Her head whips forward then back and brutally smashes into my face. I try to get to my feet when she rolls off me, but her legs wrap around my neck and right arm in a figure four. She punches me in the head and face several times, and there's not a damn thing I can do about it.

"You tried to kill me, you bastard! I'm going to make you regret your failure."

"My only regret is not yelling 'this is Sparta' before I kicked your psycho bitch ass out of the plane!" My defiance earns me a few more hammer blows to the face.

I don't know if Meat comes to my rescue out of pragmatism or pity. "Lesile, we'll probably need him, so you might want to wait until we're done before you kill him."

Lesile releases the vice-like leg lock from around my neck and delivers one last kick to my side. I lie on the ground looking and feeling like I was run over by a car on the expressway.

"Our gear is a few miles north of here," Meat tells Lesile.

"I'll need to feed at the next opportunity. Malone's childish little stunt has sapped all of my reserves and then some. He too needs to eat. I can tell by his feeble punches he has been denying himself."

Meat isn't thrilled with the thought of our requirements and doesn't respond. He walks over to where I'm still lying on the ground and offers me a hand up.

"Come on, killer, we need to get moving."

I grip his hand and let him pull me to my feet. "You could have said something sooner."

"Naw, it was way too much fun watching you get your ass beat by a pretty little girl."

I scowl. "She's no girl. She's a psychotic bitch and an elder. The odds weren't exactly in my favor."

"That means you're weak and stupid. Don't pick fights you can't win."

"Better to be dead than bored."

"Damn, you really are stupid."

"This from a guy with a neck tattoo."

"What's wrong with my neck tat?"

"Nothing if you want to advertise your intentional failure at life. Neck tattoos are a sign to the world that you have chosen to aim for the bottom of the social and economic barrel."

"Yeah, you're a real Warren Buffett of success. I bet bums stop and give you money."

"You are both losers," Lesile snaps. "I'm starving, so you two girls stop your catfight and let's go."

I bare my teeth and hiss at her, but I lose what little cool points I have left when she takes a step toward me and I flinch away. See, I'm not that stupid. Meat quickens his pace and falls in step beside her.

"You think I'm a loser?"

Lesile threads her arm through his and smiles. "Don't worry; I am not above slumming it when given enough incentive."

Meat grins lasciviously. "Baby, I got enough incentive to wreck a camel."

I groan in disgust. I can't wait for people to start shooting at me. I walk in a small circle and find my tracker thingy with its screen smashed.

"Way to go, bitch, you broke my phone!"

She and Meat ignore my complaint, and I have to jog to catch up with them. I feel like a little kid chasing after his older siblings, and it doesn't help my mood. Being even less techno-savvy than me, Meat gives me his tracker, and I hone in on our stash. It takes nearly an hour to find the box wedged between a stand of rocks, but the flapping parachute makes it easy to spot.

Meat tears away the chute, drags the plastic crate into the open, and pops the top. Inside are three black, flowing robe-like garments with shemaghs. I put one on and feel like a ninja in a prom dress. My mood improves when I spot the ordinance. Not only am I reunited with Shalonda and my blade, but an H&K MP-7 rounds out my ensemble quite nicely. Going up against three rogue vamps with elite military training makes me wish for an RPG, but it's hard to conceal those.

Lesile dons similar garb but of a finer, more feminine make, along with a dangling gold necklace. She conceals her H&K and rapier, with its shortened blade and simple hilt, beneath her robes. She tells us to hide our guns but display our swords.

"I am a wealthy Bedouin woman, and you two idiots are my bodyguards. You don't talk—ever. If anyone asks, I'll tell them you are mute eunuchs."

"I'm sure Malone will have no problem convincing anyone he's a eunuch, but I seriously doubt he can shut the fuck up long enough to convince anyone he's a mute," Meat says.

"Go to hell."

"We're already here, dumbass."

"Right? Who makes black clothing in a country that's hotter than Satan's nut sack anyway?"

Lesile looks like she's ready to jack slap the crap out of both of us. "Shut up and let's go. I smell food in that direction."

She leads us with eagerness in her step. It doesn't require a great deal of empathy for me to understand why. Her little fall caused significant damage, which probably took most, if not all, of her blood reserves to mend. Throw in kicking my ass and she is literally starving, and I'm not far from it myself.

I'm not nearly as eager as she is, despite my hunger. I know it is unlikely we're going to stumble upon a small Taliban camp. The poor bastards we find aren't going to be terrorists, murderers, or thugs. Just some people in the wrong place at the wrong time, but I'm not squeamish or sentimental enough for it to stop me from doing what I have to do. It's nature, and nature can be a cold, unforgiving bitch.

We hasten across several miles of sandy, rocky terrain. Just three shadows rolling across the moonlit desert. In the distance, a single, large tent is silhouetted against the star-filled sky. Only the occasional clanging of a bell from the large herd of goats breaks the silence.

Lesile sticks out her tongue as if tasting the air and motions for us to move to the downwind side of the tent. We pad clockwise around the tent and hunker behind an outcropping of rock about a hundred yards away. Despite our stealthy movements, the goats begin to shuffle as a sort of sixth sense alerts them to the presence of a predator.

"If it's all the same to you, I'll wait here," Meat whispers.

Lesile nods, understanding that while he may tolerate our requirement to kill in order to survive, he will not be a part of it. While I might take a gloomy acceptance of it, I'm not thrilled with it either. In New York, it's easy to find people I can judge as being kill-worthy, or at least someone who won't be missed and who likely places little value on their life anyway. But here, I don't know who these people are or what crimes they may have committed against humanity to warrant their deaths.

From what I can tell, they are just a couple of guys moving some goats. My conscience is assuaged only by the fact that they are men; no women or children. Kids would have been an instant no-go for me and likely would have resulted in another fight between Lesile and me.

Moving with the speed and silence only our kind can achieve, Lesile and I stand next to the eastern side of the tent seconds later. I can hear three distinctive heartbeats thrumming beneath the heavy breathing of deep sleep. I use my blade to cut a slit in the side of the tent. I nod and we both rush in. The men stir the moment we lunge, but their eyes cannot penetrate the total darkness of the interior.

Forget what you see in the movies about vampire attacks. We don't grab someone by the arm and head and chomp down on their necks. That would be way too messy, and we don't like a struggle. I leap to the far side of the tent and clock the man farthest away with the hilt of my blade. He crumples back down before he can get beyond a sitting position. I spin and punch the man behind me in the forehead. He also falls stunned to the ground. Lesile, having only one person to deal with, wraps the man in a chokehold and gently guides him to the ground as he loses consciousness.

My thumbnail is about an inch long and filed to a razor's edge. I use it to cut a neat slit into my first victim's neck and sever the carotid artery. I use my thumb to apply pressure to keep the blood from spraying all over the place until I place my mouth over the wound. I look over at Lesile while I drink in the man's blood and find she has done much the same thing. It takes less than a minute for the heart to quit beating, but I continue to pull the coppery liquid from his body for several minutes.

Vampires can consume a vast quantity of blood. Not only will our stomach stretch to accommodate more than a gallon of the stuff, it quickly drains into our intestines and is shunted throughout our body and tissues. When I was running rogue in Vietnam, I had, on many occasions, consumed the greater contents of three or four people. Granted, I was all bloaty and looked like shit in a speedo, but it didn't slow me down.

Even though Lesile has certainly maintained more frequent eating habits than I have, even when taking into account her much greater age, I let her take first dibs on the last victim. I figure it's only fair since I punted her out of an airplane and probably broke almost every bone in her body. And people say I don't possess a shred of gallantry. She doesn't leave me much, but I don't really need any more than what I got from the first guy. The slight rosiness and puffiness in her cheeks give clear evidence to a recent feeding, and I resist the urge to make a fat joke. See, I'm a regular Prince Charming.

The deed is done in half an hour. We aren't in a big hurry. Meat doesn't make eye contact with us when we return. I seem to have developed a strange emotion I have heard referred to as empathy, and I actually feel a little guilty for his discomfiture. I have to assume it is linked to my relationship with Kat and the veritable wellspring of new or forgotten emotions it has produced. The price we pay for love… Our phone thingies chirp, and I'm over it. Lesile and I fish the devices out of our pockets. I wait to see that the encryption icon is displayed and hit the receive button.

"What is your status?" Agent Snow asks.

"We're on the ground and have picked up our gear. We should make it into Shuqrah in about two hours," I answer.

"I understand you made a commotion during the jump. What is Ms. Savard's condition?"

"Alive and still a cunt."

I note a stressed pause before his clipped answer. "She is in charge. Any further disruptions or disobedience will result in immediate execution of the failsafe protocol. I will not allow you to further jeopardize this mission."

"I'm sorry, could you repeat that? I kind of zoned out and was fantasizing about cutting off your head and using it for a fuck puppet."

"This is your last warning."

I shrug unconcerned and slip the phone back into my pocket.

Meat asks, "Do you really think it's smart to lip off to the guy who can push a button and turn your brain into cream of wheat?"

"Probably not, but if I always did the smart thing I'd never have any fun."

"You heard what he said," Lesile cuts in. "I am in charge, and you better behave yourself."

"You know who else was in charge? Gaddafi. You know what happened to him, right?" I make an upward stabbing motion with my thumb. "Right up the poop chute."

"Leonard, before I forget…" I find myself face down in the sand before I even register the blow. "Do not ever call me a cunt again. I find the word very offensive."

"I'll try to remember, bitch."

"That's better."

Meat crouches down next to me and grins as Lesile stalks away. "Hey, that little girl just laid you out again."

"Shut up."

CHAPTER 8

"Ugh, not only is this country hotter than Satan's nut sack, it smells twice as bad," I complain as we walk down one of Shuqrah's dirt streets.

As if one could call the space between buildings streets. A street generally runs a straight line and sections a city into easily navigable squares. The buildings and homes in this town have all the organization of scattered goat droppings.

"At least you have the option of not breathing," Meat reminds me.

"Okay, leader, what now?" I ask Lesile.

"I thought you were the expert on catching rogues?"

"Baby, we're a long way from Brooklyn."

"Lawrence darling, can you pick up their scent?"

Meat tugs at his shemagh to expose his nose and takes a whiff. "There are too many smells in the air to pick out one unless I happen to walk right into it. This place isn't that big, so I can do it if I shift, but that's probably not a good idea until it's dark."

"Yeah, if you thought an American werewolf in London was problematic, imagine one in Yemen," I quip. "They'd have to cut his head off twice."

"Leonard, shut up. You are supposed to be mute."

"No, I'm supposed to be in New York tracking down some dipshit, but Uncle Sam decided to draft me into another war started by their stupidity and tossed me into Mother Earth's stanky ass crack."

"You whine worse than a child. We will stroll around town and observe until nightfall. Perhaps we can learn something in the interim. I am serious about you two stooges. It is time to play your parts."

"Why do I always get called names when Malone acts like a prick?" Meat asks.

"Do not take it personally, Lawrence. You are a man and therefore fundamentally flawed."

"Gee, I feel much better now." He looks at me. "Was that an apology?"

"It's as close as you're going to get and far more than I have ever received."

"Yeah, but you're an asshole."

"Did I ever tell you about how she strapped me to a table, broke my bones, and gouged out my eyes?"

"Seriously?"

"Yeah, so quit bitching about a little name-calling."

Lesile spins, her incredibly beautiful eyes glaring out of the slit between her veil and head cover. "Both of you shut the fuck up!"

I tilt my head at Meat. "He started it."

Lesile steps toward me and glowers with such intensity I think she is trying to make my head explode by sheer force of will. I cast a wink, and the corner of her right eye twitches in restrained fury. I take great pleasure in getting under her normally icy façade despite knowing I could pay a heavy price for it later.

She spins and storms off, and Meat and I have to hasten after her. People crowd the streets, going about their daily business, shopping, hawking wares, or just milling around with nothing better to do. To the casual observer it might look like an ordinary day, but there's an underlying tension within the crowd. Eyes cast about nervously, and the people's movements are direct and purposeful. I see the faces of children peering out of windows instead of playing in the street. Despite the number of pedestrians, there is little in the way of talking. Not even the vendors are shouting to draw the customers' attention. These people move like a herd of spooked antelope which knows there is a lion nearby watching them, but they don't know where or when it will strike next.

We're strangers here, and everyone's eyes show they know it. People move away as we approach, creating clear paths of egress as we navigate the labyrinth of streets. They watch us guardedly as if we might be one of the lions in disguise just waiting to pick off the unwary. They aren't far from the truth.

Lesile browses numerous stands, pretending to be interested in their wares and attempts to draw the proprietors into conversation. Most are recalcitrant when the topic moves away from anything not pertaining to a sale and outright hostile when she attempts to ask about the attacks.

"I am getting nowhere with these people. Let us find a café. Perhaps I can overhear something there."

The larger, nicer coffee shops are on or near the highway cutting through the north side of the city. Most of the people, particularly the younger ones, wear more typically western style clothing, and I feel like maybe we dressed to an American stereotype of the Middle East. Fortunately, there are plenty of men and women in more traditional garb like ours, so we aren't completely out of place. Besides, it would be hard to hide our weaponry beneath a polo shirt and a pair of capris.

With smoking and the oppressing of women's rights being the national pastime, the café is a place filled with cloying tobacco smoke and testosterone, but at least people are talking. Lesile chooses an empty table and orders coffee. As the dutiful bodyguards, Meat and I sit with our chair backs toward the table so we can react without obstruction.

Lesile continues to snatch pieces of conversation out of the general din from all over the café. Many people are talking about the murders. Even in a violent territory like this, the brutality of the killings is noteworthy but it's all fearful, useless mutterings with no useful information.

An hour and three covertly discarded cups of coffee later, Lesile appears to note something of interest. She half-turns in her seat, leans toward a group of men at a nearby table, and begins asking questions. I don't speak Arabic, but I am pretty good at reading body language and I translate it as:

"Did I hear you say something about ghul attacks?"

"Mind your damn business, woman!"

"I'm interested and want to hear about the killings."

"You should only be interested in cooking, birthing boys, and pleasing your man."

"Why won't you tell me?"

"I would rather rape you and cut off your head, or perhaps cut off your head and then rape you. Then Achmed and I will go walk down the street holding hands and maybe later get in some ass play while we speak of our hatred of homosexuals and how they should all be executed."

I'm about to cap off my imaginative play with a big music and dance number when their posture turns overtly hostile. They start to stand, but Meat and I are both on our feet and have our blades parting beards before they assume the fully upright and locked position. It's two against four, but these clowns know their numbers are going to be cut in half, quite literally, before any of them can draw a weapon or make a move. Meat, being something of a freakish giant in this brown version of Munchkinland and wielding a goddam scimitar, looks like a nightmare version of something out of Arabian Nights.

A show like this back home would have people screaming, running for the exits, and jumping through the windows. These people just scoot away and duck a bit lower, some not even concerned enough to stop sipping their espressos as they hunker down to watch the show. Not for the first time I wonder what the fuck is wrong with this place.

I'm about half a second from stabbing this guy in the neck when a third party butts in and starts jabbering away. Either that or he's choking on a kebab and trying to get someone to give him the Heimlich. My vampy sense kicks in and I'm suddenly thinking this guy is a bigger threat than these four camel jockeys. Larry, Moe, and the two Curlys glare, growl out what I assume is an expletive, and spit on the floor before storming out of the coffee house.

The newcomer turns to Lesile and dips his head. "Your Arabic is very good, but you are a westerner, yes?" he asks in flawless English.

Lesile's body tenses, but she responds casually. "This is true. Would you like to join us?"

"Thank you."

I study the man as he takes a seat next to Lesile. He wears a thawb, but his fingernails are manicured and his beard and hair are neatly groomed. I get the feeling he is more accustomed to wearing a three-piece suit than a thawb and shemagh. His posture is relaxed, but it's a pretense. I'm sure he pulled a rather long stick out of his ass before crashing our little party. There's discipline and precision in his movements from years of practice that even his best acting cannot hide.

"I am Zaim Kameel Safar, and who might you be?"

"Lesile."

"Just Lesile?"

"For now."

"And your friends?" Zaim asks without taking his eyes off Lesile.

"Unimportant. They are my bodyguards. Both are mute, and the small one is a eunuch."

Meat stifles a choking sound, but the contraction in his throat is unmistakable. There is little I can do about her little jokes for now, but there will be a reckoning. There is always a reckoning.

"What brings you to this unpleasant stretch of country asking about ghuls?"

"I was once the first wife of Sheik Zafar Najid Shamoun until a ghul took him from me. I have spent the past decade learning all I could about them so I could hunt them into extinction."

"You hunt fairytales."

"Do I? I have heard of several brutal murders in the area, or are those fairytales as well?"

Zaim looks pensive. "Unfortunately, Shuqrah does not need mythical creatures to create violence and fear."

"What about the nature of some of the murders? I hear many victims were found savagely cut open, their bodies nearly drained of blood."

"So you have heard much already. Despite the military's efforts in driving the Taliban from Abyan, there are still active elements within the governorate, particularly in Shuqrah. It is likely a Taliban terror ploy to convince the uneducated that the government cannot adequately protect them. Ignorance has always been their greatest recruiting tool."

"You sound unsure."

Zaim shrugs. "Who can be sure of anything in these uncertain times?"

"You know people are being killed. What can you tell me of them?"

"You are persistent. Yet another sign you are not a born daughter of Islam." He appears to give his next words some thought before answering. "All of the attacks happen at night. They are swift and often brutal, as you said."

"No one has been able to capture or kill one?"

"Few, if any, have witnessed any of the attacks and lived to tell of it. Police and military forces have been to a murder site within minutes, but the killers have always vanished into the night before they arrive."

"What of the victims? Is there anything connecting them?"

Zaim fidgets in his chair and seems reluctant to answer. "Most of the victims have ties to the Taliban, particularly known Al-Qaeda cells operating within the city."

"That sort of pokes holes in your Taliban theory."

"It has created some contradictions," Zaim admits. "It may be an internal power struggle. With the American drone attacks killing off many of the Al-Qaeda leaders, there could be some infighting as men try to assert themselves into the hierarchy."

"You still sound unconvinced. What do you really think is happening?"

He smiles and stands up. "I wish you luck in your hunting and beg you to be very cautious. The ghuls may be nothing more than superstition, but there are real dangers in Shuqrah. Salaam."

"Wa alaykum."

We wait another ten minutes after Aladdin, or maybe Jafar, I haven't decided if he is a good guy or bad guy yet, departs before we leave as well. Sitting around irritating the locals isn't likely to get us any closer to finding our guys.

"I do not think we will accomplish much during the day," Lesile says. "We should rent a room and wait until nightfall."

"Wonderful. Let's hope the Shuqrah Ritz Carlton has a suite available. We'll probably have to pay a pet deposit."

"You should really stay in character," Meat responds.

"You mean a mute?"

"I mean a eunuch. I can't recommend extreme method acting enough."

"I think we should listen to Bob Barker and have our dogs neutered."

"I'd still mount you just to display dominance if nothing else."

"I dominated the hell out of your mother."

"Will you two boys just kiss and get it over with?" Lesile asks.

"Gross, I'd rather bang you again, and I'd rather become a real eunuch than do that."

Meat quirks an eyebrow. "You and her…?"

"Oh yeah, the sex was great. It was the whole post-coital Buffalo Bill serial killer thing that wrecked it all."

She scowls with practiced expertise. "Leonard, unless you want to play out the sequel, I suggest you stop talking."

"Will you eat my liver with some fava beans and a nice Chianti?"

"I'm warning you, Leonard," she snaps.

"Bitch, I ain't afraid of you."

Lesile reaches beneath her abaya and lunges at me. I ruin my brave façade by leaping away so fast I almost trip over the hem of my robe and fall on my ass. Lesile smirks and stalks off.

"You just got punked by a little girl."

"It was tactical retreat to give me some fighting space."

"From what I've seen, she doesn't need much space to kick your ass—twice."

"Shut up. Shouldn't you be licking your balls or chewing on your ass?"

Meat turns his eyes to Lesile. "I think I got someone for that."

I give my best Sideshow Bob shuddering groan and stop talking before he fills my mind with something even more disgusting. After a few inquiries, Lesile leads us to a three-story brick building looking as drab and decrepit as all the other structures in the town. A man sits behind the counter watching a soccer match on a TV probably half as old as I am. Lesile speaks a few words of phlegmy gibberish, hands over some money, and takes the two sets of keys the man drops onto the counter.

The room is on the top floor and, although this isn't the Ritz, it is probably the best suite in town. It's large with two bedrooms and a spacious sitting room. It's surprisingly clean, nicely furnished, and does not at all fit with the dilapidated exterior.

"Dibs on the second bedroom," Meat announces the moment we enter the room.

"Why do you get the bed?"

"Because you're smaller than me, and I won't fit on the couch. And yes, the pun was intended."

"What if I don't want the couch?"

Meat peers into the bedroom. "I suppose the bed's big enough for the both of us, but if I get an erection in my sleep you might get pushed onto the floor."

I fluff one of the sofa pillows. "The couch is looking pretty comfy."

Lesile says, "I need some rest. I expect you two boys to behave yourselves."

"Yes, mommy."

Meat and Lesile head off to their beds, and I stretch out on the couch. Stretch out is a generous term. My feet touch the end, and the arm props my head up, but several throw pillows make it comfortable. I'm not technically alive like Meat is, nor did I fall out of the back of an airplane like Lesile, so I'm not feeling the effects of fatigue. I choose to slip into a state similar to sleep since the only other option is to lie here, stare at the ceiling, and listen to Meat's hellacious snoring.

I turn my thoughts inward, particularly in regards to getting this damn bomb out of my head and shoving it up Snow's ass. He thinks he's learned from his mistakes with his super soldiers and has vampires figured out. I intend to show him how wrong he is. He might understand the basics of your generic vamp, but he doesn't know me.

My subconscious registers a change in the ambient noise

and rouses me back to the real world. The length of the easterly-pointing shadows made by the sun streaming through the window gives me a rough guess as to the passage of time. I cock my ear toward Lesile's room and know why I no longer hear Meat snoring away. I release another shuddering groan and force my mind back into peaceful oblivion.

CHAPTER 9

The sound of running water wakes me up again. Given the smell of the populace, I wasn't sure this country had showers, but I'm glad to find they do. The last thing I need is Meat and Lesile's lusty, mingling scent distracting me. I suppress the shudder resulting from the unwanted mental picture and triple-check my gear.

I'm reassembling my MP-7 when Meat walks in with a shit-eating grin plastered across his hairy face. He looks at me as if begging me to make a comment, but I refuse to give him the satisfaction. Lesile appears a few minutes later, and she and Meat make a hasty inspection of their gear as well.

Lesile slams her weapon's magazine home and slings it beneath her abaya. "We'll leave by the roof. Call me paranoid, but I would rather no one sees us depart."

"Paranoid is pretty far down the list of things I'd call you."

Lesile gives me a disdainful huff through her nose. "Lawrence, how would you like to proceed?"

"I need to get downwind. I think the wind is coming from the sea, so we should stake out the north side of town. If they show up, I should be able to sniff them out. This isn't a big city, and there isn't a lot of places to hide."

Our room has a balcony but no fire escape. Lesile balances on the wrought-iron rail and jumps the ten or twelve feet to the roof. I interlace my fingers to give Meat a boost. He sticks his oversized foot in the stirrup I make.

"Don't go looking up my dress," he says and tries to teabag me.

The thought of flinging him off the balcony crosses my mind

as I heave him upward. Lesile snatches him from the air and pulls him onto the roof. I leap up afterward and join them. One good thing about Yemen's haphazard city planning, most of the buildings are built close together. We're able to cross much of the town without dropping to street level.

Meat calls for us to stop a few blocks from the hotel. "There are a lot of cops and soldiers around here. How is that going to affect the actions of our guys?"

"It's hard to say," I answer. "It depends on how far gone they are. When I went rogue, I was far more animal than man, but I was still clever and capable of tactical decisions. They might pick a target as far from armed opposition as they can, or they might attack the cops and soldiers because it's a greater sport and a challenge."

Lesile asks, "What do you think, Lawrence. You are guiding us. You make the decision."

Meat thinks through the situation. "Frost says these guys are still somewhat following their OPORD. If they are sticking to their mission, even if out of control, they'll want to execute it as quietly and as efficiently as they can. I think they'll avoid the soldiers, so let's head east. It looks like they're concentrated mostly here in the west side of town."

We're on the move once more. It takes only minutes to cross the town, but we have to drop to the ground to cross a small wadi bisecting the city into two halves. We sprint across the two hundred yards of open ground in seconds. Meat is in partial shift and is able to keep up if we don't pour on the speed.

We take back to the rooftops once we cross the open ground. Meat sticks his elongated snout in the air and takes several deep sniffs. He doesn't detect anything, and we follow him as he lopes farther east. We're near the northeastern part of the town when he stops again to get a sensing.

"Anything?" Lesile asks.

Meat twitches his shemagh-enshrouded head. He moves his muzzle around like a wizard wielding a magic wand, picking out invisible streamers of different smells borne on the wind. He doesn't seem inclined to leave this spot for a while, so Lesile and I move to opposite sides of the building we're on and look out over the nearly lightless town. Gazing into the blackness, I'm surprised at how much we take something as simple as light for granted. It's everywhere in the States, especially in cities like mine where artificial light takes over from the sun the moment it drops below the horizon.

"I got something to the east," Meat announces.

We hop across the roofs until Meats stops, takes a sniff, and points to the north. The buildings become sparser, and we are forced onto the dark streets. I hadn't paid much attention before, but now I realize there is absolutely no one on the streets and likely hasn't been since the sun went down. This city is under siege from an enemy they simply can't fathom.

"I think they came from the north and circled around to the southern side of that compound up the road."

I use my enhanced vision to cut through the darkness and spy a long wall a couple of hundred yards away. I can see the roofs of a few buildings just peeking over its top. There's a smaller walled courtyard to our right and a stand of greenery between it and the big compound north of it. It's a good tactical approach for someone wanting to infiltrate the complex.

"How old is the scent?" I ask.

"Recent. It was made maybe half an hour ago. I can detect the trace of older scents in the area as well. They probably staked this place out before and chose tonight to hit it."

"Aren't we just the lucky bunch?"

We stick close to the wall on our right and creep toward the big compound. I don't need Meat's nose to tell me someone has recently moved through the brush near the wall. We listen for signs of activity around and within the complex for two full minutes before making the leap over the wall. In his partially shifted form, Meat is able to jump high enough to grab the top of the wall and drop over with ease, which is a good thing because I would surely have head-butted him or worse if he tried to stick his balls in my face again.

It takes us less than a minute to find the first body, its throat slit yet showing far less blood loss than such a gruesome wound should. The undischarged AK-74 lying next to him indicates he never saw his killer. This man was probably a roving guard, which means we are likely to find more corpses before long.

Sometimes being right isn't so great. We discover three more sliced and diced guards by the time we reach the first building. Assuming the rogues will strike at the main building across the way, we lope across the twenty yards of open courtyard, hunched over like a bunch of burglars. All of our stealth, or lack thereof, is a waste of effort. A sharp crack rings out and I tumble to the ground when the bullet strikes my right upper back.

"Fucking shit!" I scream like a true master of covert discipline.

Meat scoops me up and tosses me over his shoulder without missing a step. Three more shots ring out and strike the building ahead of us before we race around the corner out of sight.

Meat dumps me on the ground. "Malone, how bad is it?"

"I'm fine, but now I'm pissed."

I send an army of super platelets to stem the bleeding and clamp off some of the nerve endings to reduce the pain. I can't numb it completely without losing control of the limb. Bullets whizz by in suppressing fire.

"Where are the shots coming from?" I ask.

Meat pokes his head around the corner and nearly gets a bullet between his bushy eyebrows. "Northeast corner of the building near where we came over the wall."

"Fifty yards of open ground with direct line of sight. Super. Lesile, we'll skirt around the small building here on our right and charge him. I need you to provide suppressing fire from here. Can you do that?"

"Of course."

"Watch out for his buddies. They aren't far away."

Lights are already flaring to life as the unholy commotion outside rouses people from their beds. Meat and I sprint around the north side of the small building and wait until Lesile starts popping off controlled, single shots in the area where our sniper is hiding. Meat kicks off his boots and shifts into full wolf man form.

Bullets zing past our heads and kick up dirt as we serpentine across the fifty-yard kill zone. Meat and I shoot and move, forcing the rogue to keep his head down and to throw off his aim. We make it to the building, and the sniper tries to leap away onto the roof. Faster than I would have given him credit for, Meat surges forward, jumps up after him, and snatches him out of the air by the ankle like a cat catching a bird.

Meat gets a two-hand grip and flings him ten yards into the curtain wall. The rogue hits, bounces off, and comes up with a combat knife in one hand and a Beretta in the other. Meat spins and jumps away as the 9mm slugs spew out of the barrel. I hear him hiss in pain when one catches him in the side. I can't spare the time to be sympathetic with his plight as the soldier-made-monster slashes at me. I block the cut with my MP-7. The rogue kicks the weapon from my grip and lunges in.

I push away from him and draw my blade. Meat tries to rush him from behind, but the rogue jumps ten feet to the side and pops off three more rounds from his Beretta, forcing Meat to take cover behind the building. I rush in and swing my blade in hopes of taking his head off. The SEAL may not be the swordsman I am, but he's a skilled warrior, and it's obvious he has not been slacking off in his combatives training.

With his combat knife running down the length of his forearm, he intercepts my blade and tries to bring his pistol around to put one in my brain. I grab the weapon along its slide, give it a twist, and strip it from his hand. Before I can try to bash him with it, he kicks me in the chest and sends me sprawling to the ground. The Beretta skitters off into the darkness somewhere.

I hear Lesile shout, and gunfire erupts all around us. The other two vampires come out of hiding and alternate between shooting at Lesile and the Yemenis storming out of the buildings. Lesile is shooting back while trying to avoid being caught in a crossfire, and the locals are shooting fucking everything. Bullets are flying through the air chipping off chunks of brick from the buildings, kicking up sand in the courtyard, and sailing off into the night sky where they will probably come down and kill some poor Bedouin's goat a mile out in the desert.

The SEAL rushes in, and I block his thrusting knife out to the side. He slips inside my guard, grabs my sword arm with his right hand, and flips me over his hip. He raises his blade high and is about to plunge it into my skull when Meat's furry, clawed paws envelopes his head. Meat lifts him off me, slams and pins him to the ground with his foot, and twists. The sickening crack of bone is distinctive even over the constant rattle of gunfire. Meat heaves up and tears the rogue's head not so cleanly from his torso.

I dive, roll, fish out my MP-7 from beneath the fucking costume dress I have to wear, and start capping off rounds at the Yemenis closing in on us. A hail of bullets chases us behind the building. I see Meat has recovered his weapon as well, and we rush out from behind our cover and return fire. Ten shots drop three locals in seconds as we sprint along the wall and try to circle to where Lesile is under a lot of pressure from two opposing sides.

We're about to rush the largest concentration of resistance when Lesile appears to lose her patience. With a feral shriek audible over the automatic gunfire, she leaps onto the roof of the small building to her left and unloads her submachine gun's magazine into a group of locals. Hurling her weapon at their bodies, she vaults to the roof of the larger building, drawing her sword in mid-flight, and rushes the two rogue vampires so fast she is little more than a blur.

Multiple rounds from the former SEALs' Knight's Armament PDW tug at her flapping abaya. She plunges her rapier into the chest of one of the vampires and kicks the other one off the back side of the roof. The stuck rogue tries to punch her in the head, but she grabs his wrist, lifts him up over her head by the arm and the sword piercing his body, and slams him onto the roof.

The SEAL flings a handful of sand and gravel at her face and performs a leg sweep. Lesile falls onto her back, and the soldier pulls out a knife and throws himself atop her. Supercharged rogue or not, Lesile is an elder and terrifyingly powerful. She grabs the plunging wrist, rolls them both over into a standing position, and smashes him into the rooftop like he's a hammer driving a giant nail.

Dozens of new voices shout through the darkness. Within seconds, the whumping of several helicopters hovering overhead competes with the shouting and gunfire. Bright lights cast the entire courtyard into unnatural daylight. Dozens of men repel from helicopters, landing in the courtyard and onto the roofs, ready to gun down anyone who does not surrender immediately.

I look back to the rooftop at Lesile. At least a dozen men in uniform point Russian-made automatic weapons at her. I don't see either of the rogues and assume they fled during the few seconds of confusion. I look around for an opportunity to do likewise, but they have the entire complex surrounded and, despite my hatred for Lesile, the thought of leaving a team member behind is more repulsive to me than she is.

Realistically, I know it's a poor option at best anyway. There are so many guns on us; it's unlikely even I would make it through. I know Meat wouldn't. His body has an amazing ability to heal like mine does, but it isn't as efficient and is far more limited. We both throw down our weapons. Lesile looks ready to fight it out, but she apparently comes to the same conclusion I did and surrenders.

Not knowing what they are shouting, I follow Lesile's lead, get on my knees, and put my hands behind my head. Within seconds, someone twists my arms behind my back and zips them together with plastic disposable cuffs. If it weren't for all the guns it would be laughable. Meat and I can both tear these things apart. I lose what remains of my humor when some asshole drops a heavy cloth bag over my head. I'm beyond sick and tired of people bagging my head like groceries.

Discretion being the better part of valor, I let them shove me into the back of an armored APC. These guys aren't taking any chances and lock me up all by my little lonesome. I liked it better when I thought they were all idiots. Escaping may not be as easy as I had hoped it would be. Easy or not, it's going to happen unless they kill me right off, which I doubt.

The APC rumbles down the road, and I have to give credit to the driver as he manages to hit every pothole and piece of debris in the street while still making good time. I replay my options in my head about ten times during the minutes-long ride. The driver's compartment is sealed off, so breaking loose and stealing the vehicle is out of the question. I could snap my bonds and come out swinging the moment they open the door, but I doubt I'd get very far given how many guns I expect them to have trained on me at all times. You gotta love paranoia. My best bet is to play dead, which I can do very convincingly, and walk off from wherever they toss my corpse, but Meat can't perform that little trick, and I don't want to leave him in their clutches just yet. I can always fall back on that option later. For now, I think my best bet is to see where this goes.

The vehicle rolls to a stop, and I hear the sound of heavy doors sliding shut. Someone opens the back hatch and pulls me out. I can't see shit, but my escorts are kind enough to shove and kick me in the direction I need to go. At this point, you would think they know I don't speak a lick of their durka durka language, but they keep yelling at me as if volume will translate into meaning. Idiots, don't they know that only works when you're speaking English?

I sit when someone puts pressure on my shoulders and promptly fall on my ass. I thought this was a humorless society but, apparently, stoning and pratfall are quite the rib-ticklers. Someone yanks me to my feet and sits me back down, this time placing a chair under my ass instead of the floor. A guard tears the hood off my head, and far too much light assaults my eyes. I command my pupils to all but close, but it's still uncomfortably bright.

I'm in a solid room obviously built for containment and interrogation. There are six men armed with submachine guns, but they stand to the farthest edges of the room. I figure I can kill two, maybe three, before they fill me with more holes than even I can endure.

There's one guy in the room I mark as my torturer. Not only is he not carrying a gun, he's a little, rat-faced prick wearing a sadistic smile. Torturers are always the smallest guys. They can't fight for shit, so they make up for it by being the cruelest and are only courageous against a helpless foe. I guarantee that if I snapped the chain to my cuffs right now he'd be the first one out the door and wouldn't stop running until he reached Mecca.

"You answer questions and this goes easy. You don't answer questions and this gets fun—for me."

"Good, you speak English. I was afraid you were just going to yell incomprehensibly at me the whole time."

"Trust me; you will understand everything I want from you. I will be very clear. What is your name?"

"Goenn."

"Goenn what?"

"Goenn Fuckyurself. It's Slavic. Loosely translated, it means go and fuck yourself."

Torquemada laughs but not in the way someone laughs when they think something is funny. "You are funny guy! I like funny guys. Maybe if you are so funny you can get job on *Saturday Night Live*. You can be funny with Chris Farley."

"Buddy, you're a bit out of date with your prime-time programming lineup. You might want to check your VCR and have it record something a little newer than 1995."

"No need. I just change the channel to something more entertaining." Torquemada punches me four or five times in the face then steps back.

I spit out a bit of blood and grin. "That all you got? I dick-slapped your mother harder than that."

That one strikes a nerve. Taliban Torquemada starts going to town on my poor face. I shut down my nerve endings and barely register the blows. I laugh aloud when I hear the bones snap in his hand. He takes a few steps back and cradles his injured dick beater. Amateur. You never beat a person's face with a closed fist. It's torture 101.

Torquemada is looking pissed, so I egg him on by hawking a bloody wad of spit halfway across the room. The gory mass hits him right between the eyes. My brain pictures Apu from *The Simpsons* and I can't keep from laughing.

Angry Apu flicks out a collapsible baton and goes berserk. Okay, now it's starting to hurt a bit. I cut off my pain receptors and flop to the ground. Angry Apu keeps beating on me a minute to see if I'm faking, but even his best efforts can't break through my façade. There's little they can do to me that hasn't been done before, and I've learned to mitigate all kinds of brutality. I'm in little danger unless they set me on fire or start putting bullets in me, which is unlikely.

My torturer shouts what I must assume is a stream of curses in Arabic and storms out of the room. The guards leave me on the floor and follow him, locking the steel door behind them. I lie there unmoving and take what for my kind constitutes a nap, while my body heals the bludgeoning injuries inflicted upon it.

The seconds tick away and the hours drag by. I look up when I hear the door open and several Arab stormtroopers shamble in. Two of them grab me under the arms and drag me out. They don't bother with the hood, so I get a good look at my surroundings. The cinder block walls and barred gates give credence to this being some sort of police station or military detention facility. It's probably both, given the limited separation of duties in this country.

They march me into a slightly larger room and set me down next to Meat who is sitting next to Lesile. Meat looks a little more beat up than me, due to his slightly slower healing ability, but he still looks to have his sense of humor. Lesile's hair is mussed, but it doesn't look like she was worked over as much as me and Meat. Either that or she put discretion to the wind and cured all her ails, but I doubt she is that careless.

No one says anything as the minutes tick by. I imagine there is some kind of staring contest going on between us and whoever is watching through the two-way mirror set in the far wall. My hands are still bound, so I can't make rude gestures at them, so I content myself with mouthing unkind statements about their parentage and sexual perversions. I'm not sure if they have a lip reader or if they just got tired of their voyeurism, but the door opens to announce the show is about to begin.

"Aha!" I exclaim. "Jafar, I knew it. I can smell a fed a mile away."

Meat gives me a sidelong glance. "Explain to me how it is you came to be here again?"

"Fuck off. My sense of smell was thrown off by the stink of psycho whore."

Zaim takes a seat across from us and flips open a folder. "So, we have Goenn Fuckyurself..."

Meat grins at me. "Nice one."

"I do aim to please."

"...Paul Madique..."

"Nice twist on the classic," I say.

"I like to keep it simple yet fresh," Meat replies.

"...and Lesile Savard."

I give Lesile an annoyed look. "You told him your real name? Why would you do that when there are so many delightful options like Sofonda Cox, Amanda Doomy, Connie Lingus, Edith McCrotch, Enorma Skank, or Frieda Banger? The list is practically endless."

"Because I am not a child, and I wish to get this over with as quickly as possible."

"There's something you never hear a woman say in the bedroom."

"Right!" Meat says in agreement.

"If I might redirect this conversation back to its original course..." Zaim says.

"You mean the course where Lenny limp wrist slaps us around some more?"

"I must apologize for that. I am afraid I did not leave clear instructions before I left to attend to another matter."

"Hey, it's procedural, I understand."

"You two are American. Ms. Savard is French, if I place her accent correctly, but I am betting she too was sent by the Americans."

"Technically, I'm Canadian," Meat clarifies.

"Seriously? I knew there was something wrong aboot you," I say.

Zaim clears his throat. "You are spies sent from the American government regardless of your nationality."

"Wrong and wrong. We're independent contractors sent to deal with a problem before it creates an international incident. And why do you, or any of these third-world morons think the U.S. is spying on you? What do you possibly have that we need to find; your sand weaponization program, stealth camels?"

Lesile cuts in. "Zaim, what I told you in the café was almost entirely true. You have a problem in your region, and we're here to make it go away. That is all."

Zaim's steely façade slips, and the stress he is under rises to the surface. "I also spoke truly. I was not convinced of the existence of ghuls and attributed the killings to an American plot, but I have just returned from our medical examiner's office, and his preliminary reports and my personal observations are…unsettling. You show up and now I have two problems. I have killers running free, and I have three American spies who are going to ask to be set loose within my country as well."

"Setting us loose solves both your problems," I tell him. "We will kill these ghuls, and then we'll go back to where we came from. Let us do what we came here to do, and all your problems go away."

"How do I know you will leave?"

"Because I don't want to be here! This isn't exactly Laguna Beach. It's hot, it's filthy, it smells, and it has all the charm of an apocalyptic wasteland without the endearing, flesh-eating mutants. It's more like Daytona."

"This is my country."

"That's not my fault, and I shouldn't have to suffer being in it with you. I don't want to be here anymore than you want me here."

"You speak as though we cannot kill these creatures ourselves. We almost got them tonight."

"Only because you used us as bait, and you still lost them. You've been stepping on your own dicks since this started. Your government has been fighting Al-Qaeda for years, and you still can't throw a rock without hitting one. You've got two, thanks to us, infiltrators with more training and abilities than you can imagine. We've been here for exactly one day and cut their numbers down by a third. Maybe you can get them on your own and maybe butterflies will fly out of my ass and sing 'Yankee Doodle Dandy.'"

Zaim sinks into his chair and cradles his head. "What am I supposed to tell my superiors? How do I explain that the killers are creatures from folklore, and I let three American spies go, to hunt them down because I am incapable of doing so, despite having a battalion of soldiers and police at my disposal?"

"That sounds like a you problem."

"It is a we problem as my decision greatly affects us both,

Mr. Fuckyurself, or should I say Mr. Malone?" Zaim smiles at my surprise and his own cleverness. "Our technology and capabilities extend beyond stealth camels. It was not difficult to run a facial pattern analysis and discover your identity. You are not what one would consider low profile. Nor was it difficult to ascertain the identity of Lawrence Poole. A simple criminal background check using his fingerprints was sufficient. Ms. Savard, on the other hand, is quite the enigma."

"She's a bitch too."

"Perhaps. I'm not here to judge character, only intent. Given Mr. Poole's criminal history and your even more notorious reputation, I am inclined to believe you are not spies, but I am convinced the American government sent you. That begs the question as to why. Why does your government care about these creatures, particularly when they are in a country they dislike and killing mostly people they despise?"

I shrug. "They want the movie rights?"

"Obviously they sent them here, and having captured you gives my country some powerful bargaining chips. Sending drones to kill suspected terrorists is one thing, but inserting soldiers inside the borders of a sovereign nation to kill its citizens could have an enormous backlash for anyone seeking reelection."

"Good luck finding anyone who knows about this or us."

"Do you expect me to believe your government is ignorant of this entire debacle?"

"Do you think you have a monopoly on terrorists? Ever hear of the Boston Tea Party or the taming of the west? We practically invented terrorism. The only difference is we're actually embarrassed by it and try to stamp it out whenever it rears its ugly head instead of embracing it as part of our cultural identity."

"You westerners know nothing of our culture!"

"I know a guy spent half an hour using my face as a speed bag."

"Tell me who sent these ghuls here and who hired you to kill them, unless you would prefer our other method of extracting information."

"You can't extract your head from your own ass much less anything we know. If you want to solve this problem, let us go."

Zaim stands, his face flushed. "We shall see. You have thus far only seen the first level of interrogation we employ. There are six in total, each one exponentially more horrific than the previous. No one has ever lasted beyond level four, and he died shortly after."

I stop Zaim before he steps through the door. "I lied, Zaim. There aren't two monsters left in your country, there are five. You walk out that door and your problems become 'exponentially more horrible.'

"Malone, shut your mouth," Lesile hisses.

"No. I'm tired of playing games, and I want to go home so I can kill the sonofabitch behind this colossal fuck up!"

Zaim turns back around and pierces me with his gaze. "Who are you, Leonard Malone?"

"I'm either the best solution you have to fix your problem, or the motherfucker who is ten seconds from going nuclear all over you and everyone else topping my shit list right now."

Zaim grips the pistol holstered at his side until his knuckles turn white. I'm ready to snap my bonds and his neck before he clears leather. Lesile looks calm but I know better. I can tell by the subtle rustling of Meat's bisht that he's already shifting.

Someone knocks on the door, opens it a crack, and motions for Zaim to step out of the room. He returns a few minutes later looking pale and even more drawn than before.

"All right, I'll release you, but you will kill these things and get out of my country." He flips a business card onto the table. "You will inform me when it is done, and I expect proof."

"Why the sudden change of heart?"

Zaim appears to ignore my question but changes his mind. "The ghuls struck our headquarters building moments ago. I no longer have a superior to report to, so the decision is now mine alone." He sighs. "They have never been so brazen, and we did not expect them to attack us after they fled. I think they wanted to make a point for you killing one of their comrades. These creatures must die no matter the cost, and if that means unleashing infidels onto the street then so be it."

"This is the smartest move you've made yet. We can't leave the bodies, and you need to destroy the one you have. There are things people are better off not knowing."

Zaim nods. "I wish to Allah I did not know."

CHAPTER 10

I'm glad Zaim finally figured out that letting us go was a no lose situation. Either the two ghuls kill us or we kill them. Either way, he's better off than he was before we got here. He had already lost dozens of men trying to take the rogues down in three different towns across the country, and he was more interested in killing them than publicizing a scandal against the American government for engaging in international terrorism.

The complex they hit is owned by a businessman suspected of funding Al-Qaeda although he isn't an actual member himself. It seems that our guys are somewhat still on mission. If it were up to me, I'd leave them alone to do their work and screw the collateral damage. Of course, the problem there is that it's only a matter of time before Zaim and his unit figure out how to kill them, or worse, capture them, and then lids get blown off of all kinds of shit.

I chuckle at the fact that if any of the enclaves had known about these three spec ops vampires running amok, they would have voluntarily taken care of them and eliminated the need for Homeland Security's heavy-handed tactics. Now we have to deal with the rogue vampires and a super-covert branch of the government. The fact I'm always caught in the middle of these clusterfucks removes any doubt as to the reality of karma.

It's less than four hours before sunrise, so we decide to return to the hotel. We're all exhausted, beat to shit, and in need of some rest and time to formulate a smarter plan of attack.

I stretch out on the couch. "What's the plan, boss?"

"Zaim said they tend to lie low for a few days after an attack, especially after they engage with local forces," Lesile answers.

"Well, they blew that pattern all to hell tonight."

"Our presence obviously altered the equation. They may not know much about vampires or our society, but they surely know we are hunting them now and pose a greater threat than the local military."

Meat asks, "So, what, we wait a few days for them to regain their courage and hope to ambush them when they return?"

"Getting locked down in a firefight in the middle of the town is not an advantage for our side. We need to find out where they are hiding during the day and take them by surprise."

"Sounds like a good idea to me."

The problem with a good idea is that you're rarely the first one to think of it. Twin RPG rounds slam into the ocean side of our hotel room, obliterating the balcony and the majority of the wall. The couch back saves me from much of the stonework blasted into the room. Lesile is on her way to the shower and narrowly avoids the worst of it. Meat takes it full on in the face, and he flies back until he reaches the far wall.

Automatic weapons chatter away, and bullets stitch holes into the ceiling. I low crawl my way out from beneath the couch and across the floor. Peeking around what remains of the wall, I can barely make out the suppressed muzzle flashes on the beach. I take aim and let loose with my own barrage. My initial shots strike my target. Both vamps take off at a run with my rounds chasing after them, spitting up tiny geysers of sand the whole way.

Lesile manages to crawl to the other side of the gaping hole in our hotel room and squeezes off a few shots before the rogues disappear into the city. Meat groans and I motion to Lesile to tend to him while I keep watch.

"How is he?"

"Beat up but alive."

Meat sits up. "I have never had my ass kicked so many times in one day. Malone, this is the last fucking time I do anything with you. You're like a giant, ass-kicking magnet."

"Complain later. We need to go after them while the trail is still warm."

"Warm?" Meat asks.

"Fresh, smartass."

"Give me a minute to get my shit together."

"Hurry up before they decide to come back and push it in again."

Rearmed, we jump through the breach in the wall and hit the beach. Meat sticks his elongated snout in the air and sniffs around. "They definitely came in from the north and retreated in the same direction."

"They could be twenty miles from here by now, but I doubt it," I say. "They'll have set up a base of operation probably within half an hour to an hour away. Even if they bug out thanks to our involvement, they'll probably stop to refuel if they took some damage."

Lesile asks, "But will they return to their hideout now that they know we're after them? If it were me, I would keep running and set up in another town."

"You have to understand the mentality of a vampire gone rogue." I think about the way my mind worked back then and what I would have done. "We're invaders and a threat, threats they need to destroy. They probably know our encounter was not coincidence, and they'll want to fight us on their territory."

"These guys are bat shit crazy, right? They jumped us here, but they also attacked the army's headquarters. They're pretty much running on instinct, aren't they?" Meat asks.

I shake my head. "Think of it like your shifting. The more you shift, the more the animal in you surfaces. You're mean and savage, but you never completely lose your humanity and ability for coherent thought. It's the same for a rogue. Yeah, they're amped up like a crack addict, but they can still think. They know we're coming, and they'll be ready for us."

Meat finds some traces of blood near where I must have winged one. Because we don't have beating hearts to put our internal system under pressure, the blood trail does not lead far, but Meat doesn't need blood to follow their scent. Thankfully, the trail is fresh enough that he doesn't have to do a full shift to follow it thus requiring him to get buck naked. We sprint across town, stealth be damned. If the ghuls preying on the populace kept people in their beds, all the gunfire should have them huddling beneath them now.

A little over half a kilometer from our not so epic battle, we find a small community just past a grove of scrubby trees. Meat pauses just on the outskirts and waves his nose in the air as he inhales deeply.

"I think our friends stopped here for a midnight snack."

"Then they probably didn't stay."

We circle the small village until we reach the north end. Meat begins pacing back and forth and in expanding circles, sniffing at the air, ground, and occasional shrub.

"You trying to get the scent, or are you looking for a place to shit?"

He extends an elongated, hairy, clawed middle finger at me. "Found it. They're still heading mostly north but veering slightly west."

We've got maybe three hours of darkness left, so we kick it up to a jog and follow Meat's nose like kids in a Fruit Loops commercial. The trail takes us into a wadi running north. We skirt to the west of another small village maybe four kilometers from Shuqrah. Meat takes a minute to sniff out the cluster of homes, but he detects no sign of anyone succumbing to a violent death.

"We're probably getting close to their lair if they passed this close to these people without picking any off," I tell the group.

"Maybe they're full."

I shake my head. "Rogues don't get full. They'll kill for the thrill of killing if they can't consume any more."

"Such an exotic species you are."

"Like none of your kind ever got rabies and went on killing sprees. You're all just a bunch of fluffy, lovable lap dogs."

"You haven't been cleaning up our mess for the past year!"

"I seem to recall springing you from the pound. It's not like you got picked up by the dogcatcher for an expired tag."

"At least we're not waving our existence in front of the public like a pervert's cock at a school bus!"

"You sound as though you speak from personal experience."

"Will you two shut up?" Lesile snarls. "In case you have forgotten, our quarry has rather good hearing, and your childish bickering is carrying halfway to Egypt!"

I point an accusing finger at Meat. "He started it."

Meat gives me an unexpected shove, and I take a tumble down a small ravine and find myself tangled in a mass of thorny brush.

"Real mature."

I extricate myself from the brambles and jog to catch back up. Our trail continues to lead us north across some of the ugliest goddam land I've ever seen. With our modern modes of transportation, it confounds me as to why anyone would live here. The idea of barely eking out a living just to survive to the ripe old age of fifty is bizarre to me.

Meat stops and inhales deeply. "There's a strong scent of blood a couple hundred yards ahead."

We take a more cautious approach until I spot a bloody, wadded up garment tucked beneath a shrub. With a nod, Meat confirms this being the source of what he smelled and creeps closer. He reaches out to pick up the discarded shirt, but I grab his hand and shake my head. I kneel down and begin blowing away the sand from around the shirt.

"If you really feel the need to blow something…"

I flip him off then point triumphantly at my discovery. A strand of monofilament runs from beneath the shirt into the brush. I carefully use my sharpened fingernails and clip the thread. I follow the direction of the line deeper into the brush and find the real prize: a claymore mine set to shred anyone touching the shirt and alerting our prey to our arrival.

"Something tells me they knew we would be following them," Lesile says.

"We weren't exactly covert on our first meeting, and they didn't press their attack on the second. They may not know much about our society, but I know they marked us for what we are the moment we fought. Meat's probably the only mystery to them right now." I chuckle, "Mystery Meat."

Meat ignores my quip. "The wind is still at our backs. I suggest we circle around. If they placed this thing here, they can't be very far ahead."

We turn to the east and circle to the north side of a tiny village barely visible against the dark skyline. Meat constantly checks the air, but the only scents are goat, camel, and stale human. If his nose is right, no one has lived in the village for several weeks. Let me amend that. No living person has occupied the village in weeks. I hate it when people call vampires undead, because that's not really true, but it's not an inappropriate analogy for this situation.

We creep toward the smattering of mud-daub dwellings, sticking to the shadows and keeping the mild breeze at our faces. Meat nods, signaling that our guys are indeed here, or were recently. Two hundred yards out from the nearest building, his suspicions are confirmed.

Let me tell you what pisses me off about Hollywood depictions of military matters. First and foremost is the uniform. Respect it. You can download a copy of AR 670-1 in seconds. Read it, learn it, live it.

Second is the RPG. Every, and I mean every, single movie showing an RPG being fired fucks it all up. They are not some swishing, swooping, bottle rocket lazily streaking through the air so slowly a person can shoot it down, jump out of the way, or juke their helicopter to the side and avoid it.

They may not move as fast as a bullet, but to the human eye there isn't much difference. At two hundred yards, it takes maybe a second from the time our SEAL buddy squeezes the trigger until I feel the white-hot shrapnel tearing into my hairy, white ass.

We spot movement ahead and dive for cover. That half-second warning probably saved all our asses…mostly. Mine is on fire with searing bits of steel and copper shrapnel lodged in it.

A hail of bullets follows the blast. I fetch up against a boulder and shake off the rocket's massive concussion. Lesile and Meat are low crawling to a shallow ravine. The smell of my burning flesh assails my sensitive nostrils, but I block it and the corresponding pain out of my mind.

"I'll lay down some cover fire while you two rush them."

Meat calls out from the ditch he's lying in. "How about you two rush them and I lay down cover fire? I'm not quite as bullet tolerant as you two are!"

"I always wondered what kind of dog you were. I never took you for a pussinese. Fine, are you ready?"

"Go for it!"

I jump out from behind my rock, and Lesile sprints from the ditch while Meat lays down suppressive fire. Submachine guns are a poor weapon at this range, but our strength allows for near-recoilless firing and vastly improved accuracy. Lesile and I shoot on the run, zigzagging, diving, rolling, and sprinting across two hundred yards of rough terrain mostly bereft of cover or concealment. At least three rounds gouge new crevices or bore holes into my body. I see Lesile twitch and know she's been hit at least once during our mad dash.

We dive behind a low stone wall that may have once surrounded the tiny village but now lays in broken lengths, its bricks having crumbled to gravel over the years or been salvaged to make new dwellings. I peek over the wall and start laying down fire so Meat can bound forward. I hear the chatter of Lesile's weapon perhaps fifty yards to my right. Meat slides behind a section of broken wall a little closer to Lesile than me.

Bullets have ceased pounding into the bricks, blanketing the tiny settlement in silence. The rogues have certainly shifted their position knowing that to stay static is to invite death. Knowing the same holds true for both teams, I motion for Meat to provide overwatch while Lesile and I skirt around the flanks.

My instincts and training prove true when I spot a grenade arcing toward me the moment I dart from cover. Meat pops off several short bursts into the darkened shadows of a building from where the grenade originated. It lands damn near on the spot I had been lying and blows my little wall all to hell. I feel the concussion from the blast wash over my back like a helping hand pushing me forward to speed my charge.

I put my back to the corner of a building and listen for our targets. The only thing I hear is my own heavy breathing, which I immediately clamp off and silently curse myself for being a moron. I haven't needed to breathe for the better part of a century, but every once in a while certain situations will kick on my automatic responses and make me feel like an idiot.

Another explosion and the rattle of gunfire means Lesile

has found her target, or he has found her. I break through the door of the building I'm using for cover and burst into a room of pitch blackness. My eyes adjust quickly to the increased darkness, and I barely notice the swift movement to my left. A hand snakes out, grabs the barrel of my weapon, and strips it from my hand, snapping the nylon sling in the process.

A foot sends me flying across the room until the brick wall is kind enough to catch me and dump me onto the floor. The SEAL tosses my weapon to the floor and brings his Knight's Armament PDW to bear. I lunge for an open doorway leading to another room and draw Shalonda while bullets chase after me.

I dart around the corner, take a knee, lean back into the doorway, and fire all five rounds as fast as I can pull the trigger. My first shot blows his PDW nearly in half when the heavy round strikes it center mass of its breach. Three more bullets slam into his chest, rocking him several steps back, but he's wearing a vest, and the bullets shatter against the ceramic SAPI plates. The last and most vital misses his head and blows a fist-sized hole in the wall behind him.

He rips his Beretta 9mm from the holster, and I unsheathe my blade. Bullets chip away at the doorframe as he circles toward me for a clean shot. I sidearm a brick around the corner and clip him in the head. When he tries to duck the projectile, I lunge forward, leading with my sword. He flips the pistol in his grip so the barrel is pointing toward his elbow and uses it to block my neck-seeking blade. A combat knife appears in his other hand like magic, and I barely manage to turn and raise a shoulder to keep it from cutting into my neck.

I drop Shalonda from my grip and grab his wrist before he has time to stab me again. I look into his feral eyes as we spin around the room like a couple of ballroom dancers. He's pretty far gone, but not as bad as I was in Nam. He still has an even split between man and animal whereas my human consciousness barely registered. It's like looking into the eyes of a guy tweaked out on crack.

He launches a series of knee strikes into my gut and sides. I feel more than one rib surrender under the assault with an audible crack. I whip my head forward and head-butt him. His head snaps back but returns twice as fast. My eyes cross from the blow, and a kick to my chest sends me flying into the wall. The SEAL takes two steps back and kicks off the far wall. His leap propels him the length of the room, knife leading like a human spear.

I slam my fist down onto a floorboard. Thanks to the conservative use of nails, the eight-foot plank pivots upward on a crossbeam and catches the rogue low in the gut. His inertia shatters the wood into splinters, and he lands atop me before I can regain my feet. We roll across the floor trading punches until I manage to get a leg between us and heave him across the room.

He hits the floor, rolls to his feet, comes up with my MP-7 pointed straight at my head, and grins triumphantly. I smile back at him and hold up my hand. Only our remarkable eyesight can see the near-invisible line running between my fingers to his chest where I had stuffed the claymore behind his SAPI plate during our ground and pound.

I yank the string as if I'm starting a lawnmower and blow him all to hell. The directional charge all but cuts him in half, but the concussive force still kicks the shit out of me even being on the "safe" side of the explosive.

My head is reeling, and I struggle to get my shit together as the sound of gunfire and the occasional explosion registers. It sounds like Lesile and Meat have their hands full and could use my help. My weapon didn't fare any better than the rogue in the blast, so I retrieve and reload Shalonda before stumbling out of the building.

The firefight is happening on the other side of the village, a couple of hundred yards away. It is constantly shifting, and I assume it has been a running battle, unlike mine. The SEAL is smart and a consummate professional. He knows he's outnumbered and that Lesile is a formidable fighter. He's going to want to kill or disable her and Meat from a distance, and it sounds like he's been doing a good job of it.

I lurch drunkenly toward the battle, annoyed at my inability to shake off my injuries faster. Movement in the illumination of a muzzle flash catches my eye. A dark shape streaks across the desert to the south as bullets seek out his fleeing form. The rogue must have decided discretion was the better part of valor and is trying to break contact. I know I cannot catch him, and I think he is going to succeed in his escape until I spot another shape racing after him. Meat has gone into a full shift and is showing us all how much better four legs are than two.

I lose sight of them both in the distance, but a shot echoes out across the black desert followed by incoherent shouts and animalistic snarling. It is over in seconds, and silence falls over the area. Meat lopes back into view a minute later and disappears behind one of the brick huts. I find him and Lesile a minute later. Meat is putting his clothes back on, and Lesile is in a mild trance as she closes off numerous wounds.

"You guys all right?" I ask as I approach.

Meat nods. "I took one in the shoulder right before I brought him down, but I'll manage. I guess we're done here."

"Yeah, I guess so." My voice is heavy with bitterness.

"You do not sound pleased with our success," Lesile says.

"No, I'm pretty fucking far from pleased. These were good men turned into monsters. Even if they could have volunteered to be blood-sucking guinea pigs, they couldn't have known what they were signing up for. Snow's blood debt is starting to look like the national deficit, and it's about time for him to pay the balance."

"Kinda hard to collect with a flesh-eating bomb inside your head," Meat points out.

"Yeah, that is a problem, but I'm good at solving problems."

"Too bad you can't shoot this problem."

"True, but I got a guy who is good at the brainy ones. We need to get proof of death and burn the bodies. Let's get this over with so we can go home."

Meat and Lesile head out into the dark to recover the runner while I search through the few dwellings for things to make a pyre. I salvage a good pile of furniture and bust it up into kindling. There's also several gallons of kerosene in cans and jugs to get it burning good and hot.

We take pictures of the two men's faces to send to Snow and Jafar, or whatever his damn name is, as proof of holding up our end of the bargain. It's tough getting a recognizable image of the guy I obliterated, but it will have to do. Unfortunately, we never got a picture of the one we killed in town, so Snow will just have to take our word for it. Fuck him if it's not good enough.

Meat and I find shovels and dig a deep grave. We pile the broken furniture in the bottom and douse the bodies with kerosene. The blaze lights up most of the ghost town in an orange, wavering light that would look cheery in most any other circumstances.

Lesile stands mute, almost distracted, while Meat looks as if he might be saying a silent prayer. Like me, he's been a soldier, and he gets it. Unlike me, he had a choice, but he came anyway knowing what we had to do. I think that's why he came. These men deserved to die with more respect than those spooks likely would have shown. There won't be any congratulatory high fives or drinks shared for a successful mission, and there damn well shouldn't be. This mission ain't over until I say so, and I say it ends with Snow's head decorating my loft.

CHAPTER 11

It's a slow, somber walk back to town. No one talks much. I think we set it into our minds that this was just another rogue problem for us to deal with, but it wasn't. Not only were the SEALS unwitting, it was the government who created them then sent us to assassinate the monsters they became. That makes it a lot more personal.

I send Snow a text along with the pictures and a brief explanation for why there was no evidence for the third target. We are less than a mile from town when I get a reply in the form of an eight-digit grid coordinate.

Lesile pulls out a map, traces a delicate finger across the top then down until she finds the spot. Call me weird, but it's kind of sexy when a woman knows how to plot a location on a map to within ten meters. It still won't keep me from killing her when I get the chance.

The coordinates are ten miles offshore. I doubt Snow wants to wait for a boat to sail from Saudi Arabia's butthole back to the U.S., so I assume there's an island there with our ride waiting.

"We'll have to acquire a boat unless they have one waiting for us," I say when we reach the southeastern side of town.

A voice breaks the otherwise silent early morning. "I believe I can help you with that."

Zaim steps out of a darkened doorway. Despite his nonchalance, I can smell his anxiety. I also know he isn't alone. Obviously, he has had eyes on us from the moment we reached the town, several of which are probably peering through high-powered scopes attached to large-caliber rifles.

"Jafar, you are a sneaky little devil, aren't you?"

"I received Ms. Savard's message regarding your success. It is time for you to leave, and I wish to ensure you do so with all possible haste. These are a poor people in a poor country. I would not like to see a man's livelihood disappear just to facilitate your departure."

"That's awfully nice of you."

"Not at all. Forgive me for being a poor host, but I want you out of my country, and I hope you never return."

I'm starting to like him. "You're welcome."

Zaim takes a deep breath and looks up at the starry sky. "When you said there were still five monsters in my town…"

"I meant you need to let us go and do our job for everyone's sake."

"It appears you were true to your word, but how can I know this will not happen again? The people who sent the ghuls here also sent you."

"Our cooperation was not voluntary. The people who sent us crossed a line, came into knowledge they shouldn't have. I aim to rectify this problem. We will not allow what they did to continue. They think they learned from their first mistake, but they just replaced it with new and more dangerous ones. Sleep easy, Zaim. This place is too damn hot for ghuls. I doubt you'll see any more. You certainly won't ever see me again."

"I hope I do not see any of you again. As lovely as Ms. Savard is, I will do everything in my power to kill you, her, or anyone I think is a threat to my people."

"We are certainly of the same mind in that regard, Zaim."

Zaim takes us to a long pier jutting out a hundred yards into the Arabian Sea and shows us to a small boat tethered near the shore.

"May I presume you are going to one of the small islands a few miles out?"

"You can if you want. We won't be able to return your boat."

"I will find it."

We climb into the small fishing boat, and Meat takes the wheel. I use my phone to point him in the right direction and motor out to sea. The ocean is almost placid, and our short voyage is over in less than an hour. We find the island, which is little more than a large mound of sand rising starkly above the water. Meat runs the engine until he beaches the craft on the sandy bank. It's high tide, so Jafar has a good chance of finding his boat still here when he comes looking for it.

The sound of idling jet engines drones across the island's narrow expanse. We walk only a hundred yards up the beach's slope before we see the black CIA plane parked on a rough landing strip less than a quarter mile away.

I ask Meat, "You ever get the feeling you're being watched?"

Meat doesn't get the chance to nod before several sections of sand bulge upward to our front. Men cast off the blankets covering them just beneath the surface and train their weapons on us.

"Hands up! On the ground, now!"

"I guess this is our welcoming party."

We drop to our knees and splay ourselves out flat onto the sand. Several men rush forward and begin prodding, squeezing, and groping us all over. They stack our weapons in a pile and affix our shackles before jerking us to our feet and marching us toward the plane.

"Same thing as before," one of the spooks says. "Several of my guys have the remote on them, and they'll use it at the first sign of trouble."

It's possible he's telling the truth, but I doubt their redundancy measures are as layered as he is making out. Just like our trip over, he's the only one with his hand in his pocket instead of pointing his gun at us. I'm sure there's more than one kill switch, but not all of them are going to be given that kind of responsibility, and he's the only one with his at the ready.

Once we reach the landing strip, one of them waves a wand over our bodies. The metal detector lets out a shrill squeal over my stomach.

"What's this?"

"Probably shrapnel from a grenade, RPG, or even one of several bullets I've absorbed during this little exercise. Wave that thing over my left ass cheek and it'll probably explode." He shoves his hand inside my clothes and pats me down. "Go a little lower and you'll find my Prince Albert."

He shoves me toward the plane. "Fucking freak."

Meat and Lesile undergo a similar examination with Lesile's pat down taking a bit longer. The plane's ramp is down, and the half-dozen spooks don't waste any time hustling us on board. They seat us next to each other and attach our shackles to the seat frames like before. I was hoping they would, because it's the biggest mistake they've made in our handling.

The ramp isn't fully up before we start rocketing down the runway. The plane flies just over the surface of the ocean until we are well within international airspace. The craft makes a steep climb until leveling out a minute later at its cruising altitude. My restraints don't give me much room to stretch out, so I lean forward onto my thighs and tune out the world.

A bump and metallic clank snaps me out of my self-induced reverie. It appears we're halfway through our flight and have met our refueling plane. That's my cue to start setting up the chairs for the party. Thanks to my Ali Baba costume, it's easy for me to conceal my hands while I'm hunched over. I've been willing my fingernails to grow since my capture and now sport a set of claws almost an inch long.

Using the sharpened nail of my index finger, I make a clean incision in my stomach and fish around for the stiff wire I squirreled away. It only takes me a few unpleasant seconds to extract it and start working on my cuffs. The locks are better than your average police-style restraints, but I have nothing but time and a great deal of motivation.

Twenty minutes into my prodding, I feel more than hear the satisfying click of the lock's surrender. I nudge Meat with my elbow, but it's unnecessary. He's been casually observing my actions since I woke up. I have no doubt he knows what I'm planning and why I'm risking all our lives. Snow might keep Lesile around as long as she continues to help them in their cause, but our end results are the same: experimentation and an unpleasant death.

I covertly pass Meat my lock pick. He gives me a slight twitch of his head and slips it to Lesile. Lesile manages to unlock her cuffs in half the time I did, and I'm jealous to the point of being pissed. My shrink constantly warns me about my ego, but my pride insists I ignore him.

Now we sit and wait for our moment. Meat and Lesile don't know exactly what I plan, and they're waiting for my cue. I pretend to be disinterested and zone out, but I'm keeping very close tabs on all six members of our security detail. My guy with the button never drifts off to sleep, but his focus does waver. Two hours after our refueling, half our guards have closed their eyes and are taking catnaps. Our apparent docility has lured them into complacency.

I nudge Meat and he pokes Lesile in the thigh. I nod at the two men closest to him, and do the same for Lesile. Meat begins a subtle, partial shift. Apparently, Snow warned the button man that I was going to be the most likely source of trouble, and he keeps his eyes fixed on me the entire flight. I look over his shoulder and tilt my head in confusion. His eyes flick toward the bulkhead where I'm staring for just a second, and a second is all I need.

I cross to the other side of the fuselage before he can turn his head back toward me. My fingernails pierce the soft flesh of his exposed throat, and I tear out his windpipe. I grab his thumb with my free hand and twist it back until it touches his wrist.

Meat and Lesile move at almost the same moment. A knee to the face of the man sitting next to our executioner removes him from the equation before he can open his eyes. The other two secondary targets have just enough time to open their eyes wide and bring their weapons halfway to the ready before Meat and Lesile take them down.

Six men are dead in less than three seconds. I grab the combat knives from my two guys and sprint for the cockpit. Being a military craft, it doesn't have the reinforced door to keep out would-be hijackers. I take a single step into the cockpit and slam a blade into the pilot and copilot's heads John Woo style. I fling both bodies out of the cabin and take a seat behind the controls.

Meat sticks his shaggy head in a moment later. "Do you know how to fly this thing?"

I look at all the buttons, dials, and controls. "Not a clue. I was hoping one of you knew how to fly."

"I've only flown helicopters."

"Ask Lesile if she knows. She was probably banging one or both of the Wright brothers at Kitty Hawk."

Lesile and Meat climb into the cockpit with me. "I don't know how to fly a plane! Are you telling me you killed the only two people who can fly this thing? Why would you do something so stupid?"

"Explain it to her, Meat."

"Malone doesn't think beyond getting what he wants, like kicking the only Arabic-speaking member of our team out of a plane without a parachute."

"Idiot!"

"Relax. Go find us some chutes and we'll just bail out."

Meat darts back to the cargo hold and reappears a few minutes later. "No chutes."

"What the hell do you mean there's no chutes? How does a damn spy plane not have any chutes?"

"I don't know. Maybe they didn't want us to use them to escape in case we got free and managed to kill our guards."

"That's awfully fucking forward-looking, especially for this lot. Well, I have some good news and some bad news. The bad news is even though planes are almost as easy to fly as driving a car these days, I can't land it."

"What's the good news?"

"I have no intention of trying to land. One of you find me a phone."

"Why do you need a phone?" Meat asks.

"I need to make a call. And grab my pistol and blade while you're back there. I feel naked without them."

Meat looks like he wants to inquire further but chooses to avoid more answers that will just annoy him.

He comes back a few minutes later bearing a phone and my preciouses. "Found this on the guy with the button. I found two others with remotes as well. You're damn lucky you didn't get yours and Lesile's brains pulped."

"It was a calculated risk." I punch in the number and hope Snow isn't monitoring this phone.

"Mo' Money," says the voice on the other end.

I'm a little relieved to hear that Marvin sounds like he's given up on his thug life persona, but that probably means he's found another way to annoy me. "Marvin, It's Leo. I need your help."

"My man Leo! Sorry, man, I am booked solid. You'll have to make an appointment with my assistant. Hey, you know where I can get an assistant?"

"Marvin, my foot is going to make an appointment with your ass if you don't shut up and listen!"

"You know, I could have sworn you were calling me for help, but your words and tone make it sound the opposite. I'm really busy. So I'm going to get back to work while I ponder this conundrum."

"I have a bomb in my head!" There is a distinct pause on the other end, and for a moment I fear Marvin has hung up on me.

"You have a bomb…inside your head?"

"Yes!"

"Well, there's certainly room for one, but I gotta wonder about the exact logistics of getting it in there."

"Marvin, I need your help."

"Okay. What can you tell me about the device, what kind of explosive, trigger, etcetera?"

"It's a liquid poison in a glass vial attached to a small explosive. It has an anti-tampering mechanism. I'm assuming contact pins or something, and a satellite receiver."

"Okay, the first and most important thing to do is speak calmly and politely, because satellite receivers can easily be set off by being an asshole. I'm surprised it didn't blow up a long time ago."

"Goddammit, Marvin!"

"See, that's the attitude that's going to make the thing go boom. They can also be set off by being a cheapskate, so we need to talk about my fee."

"We can haggle over cost later, but keep in mind a dead man can't spend money."

"Threats are even worse than being rude."

"Marvin, I need you to take this seriously."

"I am serious! I'm serious you are an asshole, and I know you screwed me on our last contract."

"I gave you what you asked for!"

"You took advantage of a poor, inner-city youth!"

"You're only poor and live in the inner city because you got thrown out of MIT and NYU and you're too fucking lazy to get a real job."

"Tick, tick, tick! You best start laying plastic over the furniture, because that thing is about to blow."

Lesile strips the phone from my hand before I have a chance to shatter it against the cockpit window. "Hello, Marvin is it?"

"Oh damn, who is this? Bonjour, baby. You got what we in the hood call a boner voice."

"You're sweet, Marvin. I certainly understand letting Leo get blown up, but I too am in the same unfortunate predicament and wish to keep my lovely head a bit longer. Can you help us?"

"Oh, yeah, I can't let a sexy-voiced mademoiselle perish. I am your knight in Sean Johns."

"Merci."

"Mercy me too. Okay, let me talk to the asshole again."

Lesile hands the phone back, and I force myself to speak rationally. "What can you do for us?"

"Let me think a minute. Okay, first thing I need to do is block the incoming signal. If I can get my hands on a spectral analyzer, I should be able to determine the frequency. Then I just need to sample the signal and make a transmitter to override the original signal with my own."

"Can you make a fake receiver and transmitter that will make it look like it's still active and functioning properly? This thing has a GPS in it, and I need it to look like it's still receiving."

"Yeah, that shouldn't be too hard if I can get my hands on the tech."

"I know a guy in Queens. His name is Yuri Poplonovich."

"Yuri? I'm at his place now!"

"Why are you at Yuri's?"

"I told you I was busy. Yuri has me installing all the electronics in this building he's turned into a fortress. Man, he's got thermal imaging, IR, sonic sensors, motion activated fucking machine gun turrets, and flame throwers in the walls and shit. Oh my God, you wouldn't believe this place...wait, Yuri's making the throat cutting gesture and says he's going to kill me if I keep talking. He's so funny."

"Marvin, listen to me. Yuri is Georgian mafia, and he's not joking. Shut the fuck up right now before you end up at the bottom of the East River."

"Oh…shit."

"Let me talk to Yuri."

"I'll put us on speaker."

"Yuri, can you hear me?"

Yuri's heavy Georgian accent comes over the phone. "Yeah, I hear you. Malone?"

"Yeah. Yuri, Marvin is going to need some high-tech equipment, and he's going to need it fast to save my ass."

"Yeah, I heard spectrum analyzer and other shit. No problem, I got guy. Same guy I get Star Trek computer shit from last year for you, no problem. What trouble you get into now?"

"The feds snatched me up and pressured me into doing a job. Now that it's over, my life expectancy is ticking down rather fast."

"Focking feds. I focking hate focking feds more than I hate focking cops."

"Yeah, I kinda figured. Thanks, Yuri. Marvin."

"Yo."

"I can slow my arrival down a bit and give you…" I look at our position and airspeed and make a quick calculation, "…five and a half hours to get the stuff ready and meet me."

"Assuming Yuri can get me the stuff within an hour or two, I shouldn't have a problem."

"Good. I need you to contact Will Stepanek. Write this down." I give Marvin the latitude and longitude of where to find us. "You're going to need his boat to get to us."

"A boat? Are you in the middle of the ocean?"

"We will be, so make sure your false receiver and transmitter is waterproof to a few hundred feet."

"I can do that, but you know radio signals don't travel through water worth a damn, right?"

"No, I didn't, but let's do it anyway just in case they drop something overboard to confirm our deaths."

"Can do."

"Thanks, Marvin."

"Was that an expression of gratitude from Leo Malone? Wow, that's like a deathbed confession coming from you. You really are in trouble."

"I am, and thanks for making it weird."

"You called telling me you have a bomb in your head. It's been weird for more than a minute. Now, if you could put that sexy mademoiselle back on the phone…"

"Get to work, Marvin."

Meat looks at me when I hang up. "Your people skills suck."

"Hey, I got it done."

"No, Lesile's vagina got it done. You almost got yourself killed."

"It was my voice, my sweet, not my vagina," Lesile corrects him.

"Honey, all women's interesting features lead to their vaginas."

"Can we stop saying vagina?" I grumble.

I flinch away when Lesile strokes my cheek. "Aw, poor Leonard. It is such a troubling subject for you, isn't it? Lars, it is a dreary flight, and we do have quite a bit of time to ourselves…"

"Oh, fuck me."

"Is that a request for an invitation, Leonard? You are more than welcome to join us."

I grumble and shake my head as they make their way to the back of the plane to have near-bestial sex amongst half a dozen dead bodies.

I locate the flight control manual in a pocket on the side of the seat and spend my time learning the layout of the complex control board. Twenty minutes into my studies, I dog-ear the page I'm on and put the plane into a steep dive. My ass begins to leave the seat, and I become weightless for about five full seconds before pulling the stick back and leveling out once more. The thump of bodies hitting the deck reaches my ears.

"Malone, you fucking asshole!"

"Sorry, turbulence."

I grin like a masturbating chimp, pick up the flight manual, and start reading where I left off.

CHAPTER 12

"Attention, disgusting passengers, this is your captain speaking. Please ensure your pants are in the upright and locked position, stow away any and all genitals, and come to the cockpit to prepare for landing."

Lesile slaps me in the back of my head hard enough to knock my headset off when she enters the cabin and buckles into the copilot's seat. Meat takes the navigator's spot and straps in.

"What exactly is the plan?" Meat asks.

"We'll ditch five miles offshore. I called my people, and they're ready to meet us."

"Ditch?"

"Yeah, it's like landing except you're not on a runway and the pilot has no fucking clue how to fly a plane."

"I know what ditch means! I'm not quite as resistant to dying as you are."

I reach into a panel next to my seat and stuff a bundle into Meat's hands.

"What the fuck is this?"

"Airbag."

"It's a goddam life raft!"

"Makeshift airbag."

"God I hate you."

"That just shows you care. We're nearing our crash site, so make sure you're strapped in tight."

"Crash?"

I roll my eyes. "Fine, our ditch site if it makes you feel better. Stop being such a baby. As long as we don't burst into flames when we hit we should be fine."

"Does this we include me?"

I shrug my shoulders as if I'm not worried about it, because I'm not. Not really, well maybe a little. If I had to choose between killing Meat or Lesile, I'd definitely choose Lesile, but this is going to happen and the cards will fall where they may. What's really important is I live long enough to kill Snow.

The engines' tone drops as I reduce their power to the lowest possible speed while still maintaining flight. The ground warning alarm goes off, and it takes me a full minute to find the shut-the-fuck-up button. We're skimming over the ocean at just a few dozen feet as I deploy the flaps for maximum lift and slowly press the stick forward.

A low swell hits the plane's nose. Meat screams in panic and yanks the life raft's inflation cord. The expanding raft hits me in the side of the head and causes me to move the stick left. The port wing dips, hits the water, and sends us into a cartwheel. Sea air hits my face for a brief second when the fuselage splits open like an egg, and water rushes in.

Lesile releases her restraints and shoots for the surface as we sink to the bottom of the ocean. I unhitch the buckles tying me to my seat and set out to follow her. I glance at Meat and see that the inflated raft is pushing against his chest and has him trapped in his seat.

"You dickhead!" I shout, but the only thing that comes out is a blast of bubbles and incoherent gurgling.

I reach into the pouch in my seat and find the standard issue restraint knife tucked inside. After cutting through the tough nylon, I take a firm hold of Meat's shirt and hitch a ride as the raft shoots for the surface.

Meat gasps in a lungful of jet fuel-contaminated air when his head breaches the water. "You asshole!"

"Me? Your goddam raft nearly killed us all. I'm the one who saved your life."

"I panicked! You're the one who told me to use it as an airbag."

"Not while I was still flying the fucking plane!"

"You weren't flying, you were crashing!"

Lesile interrupts our bickering. "It is pitch-black out here. How are your friends going to find us?"

I pull out a flare gun from inside my shirt. "With this." I raise the flare gun up then point it at the water.

"You stupid sonofa…!" Meat shouts before diving below the surface.

I squeeze the trigger and the flare streaks over the water and ignites the shimmering layer of jet fuel floating on the surface. I duck below the water just before the orange corona washes over my head. It's an easy swim for me to get clear of the fire since I can hold my breath literally forever.

Lesile curses me the moment my head breaks the water. "Asshole!"

Meat emerges a second later. "Malone, what the fuck is wrong with you? Some of us have to breathe, and now my dinghy is on fire!"

"Hey, I only had one flare, and if your dinghy is burning it's probably from fucking that dirty whore in the back of the airplane!"

"I am not a dirty whore!"

"Honey, all the showers in the world can't wash out skank. Why are you all bitching at me when I'm the one facilitating our rescue?"

"Because we're in the middle of the ocean, which you managed to set on fire."

"Fire keeps the sharks away…or draws them, I really don't know."

"Wow, Malone actually admits he doesn't know something. I am truly witnessing a miracle. Praise Jesus!"

"You want to know what I do know?"

"What?"

"If you shut the fuck up and quit your whining you can hear the sound of a boat coming our way. Aaaaaaand you're welcome."

Meat puts his complaining on pause and listens. "Shit…I almost wished we drowned."

A powerful spotlight plays over the water as Will's boat draws near. "Leo!"

I wave my arms over my head while treading water. "Over here!"

Will's light washes over me, and he points the boat in my direction. When he draws close, he spins the wheel to put the stern with *Leo'$ Money* emblazoned across the back in gold letters at my face. We clamber onto the back deck, and Will and Marvin help us into the boat.

Marvin looks out across the hundreds of yards of flaming ocean. "Goddam, Leo, what the fuck did you do?"

"I crashed my airplane. Do you have the stuff with you?"

Marvin flips open a large, plastic crate and pulls out several pieces of electronics. "Yeah, hold still so I can try and get this thing's frequency."

He studies a monitor while passing his phone bearing an odd attachment on it over my head. "I got the freq, but it's encrypted."

"Is that going to be a problem?"

Marvin looks at me as if I just asked him if abolishing slavery was a good idea. He plugs a small device into his laptop, punches a few keys, and repeats the process with a second one.

"These are your fake receivers. I've copied your bomb's response to the satellite, so it shouldn't know the difference. Anyone monitoring the signal will think that's you on the bottom of the ocean along with your busted up plane."

"Can you turn off the bomb's signal?"

"That's going to be a little harder. It's encrypted, so I have to crack it before I can do anything with the signal. But I can jam it so they will only see the ones I made instead of the ones in your heads."

"Good. Let's get out of here before the coast guard shows up. I'm sure our handlers already know the plane went down and have units on the way."

Will guns the engine, and the twin inboard motors send us skimming across the water toward Manhattan Beach. Marvin continues to work on cracking the encryption despite the bumpy ride. Most of the work is done by his laptop running an algorithm, so the rough ride doesn't hinder him too much.

It takes us half an hour to reach Marine Basin Marina where Will parks his boat. "Leo, what kind of trouble are you in now?"

"Just the worst kind."

"Sounds expensive; my favorite kind."

"Sorry, this ain't the lawyer kind of trouble."

"That's a shame; I was really hoping to get a plane this year. Oh well, there's still time."

"You're all heart."

"You need a ride somewhere?"

Lesile says, "No, I have a car parked not far from here. We can take a cab."

"All right, I need to go secure my alibi if anyone asks about my late night boat ride."

"Thanks a lot, Will. Meat, are you coming with us?"

"Naw, I best gather the pack and inform them what's happening. We may not have a dog in this fight just yet, but like you said, it's only a matter of time."

"Expect us to call on you after we convene a council. Marvin, you're with us. Let's go."

Will gives me a burner phone, and I use it to call a cab. The nightlife around here is active, and the cab shows up within minutes. The driver, a man with a thick mustache and beard, likely hailing not far from where we just came from, glances in the rearview mirror as we climb into the back seat.

"What is that stuff you have there? Read the sign: no guns, no bombs in the cab."

"It's not a bomb."

"No guns. I saw a pistol sticking out of your pocket!"

"Come on, buddy, it's a short ride. Would a hundred bucks loosen your grip on the gun policy?"

His eyes flash as greed overcomes any concern he has over our weaponry. "Okay, but only because you have a beautiful woman with you. Just keep your hands where I can see them!"

"Fine."

"Avenue Plaza Hotel, you sweet man," Lesile says to the cabbie.

Yusuf grins into the mirror and hits the gas. The hotel is only a few blocks away, and we pull up to the front in just a few minutes. I fish out a twenty and pass it to the driver as we get out.

"Hey, what about the hundred?"

"I only asked if it would change your mind. I never said I would give it to you."

"You sonofabitch!"

"Yep, welcome to New York, dickhead."

"Leonard, you did not have to be so rude to the man," Lesile admonishes me as the cab peels away.

"Are you seriously going to give me lessons on polite behavior? Was it polite when you broke my bones and gouged out my eyes?"

"That's different. It was necessary."

Marvin leans in. "Wait, what about breaking bones and eye-gouging?"

"Nothing."

The Avenue Plaza is a nice place, and Lesile maintains a suite near the top floor. Our ragged, Bedouin appearance draws some looks, but no one bothers us as we take the elevator to Lesile's suite. The room, with two bedrooms and a full kitchen, is nicer and bigger than any apartment I've rented.

"I desperately need a shower and a change of clothes," she says and disappears into the master bedroom.

"Yeah, I was going to mention the smell of dog balls, but I thought it would be rude," I call after her.

Marvin sets his gear on the living room table. "So tell me about Lesile. Are you two...?"

"If you mean mortal enemies, yes."

"How can you hate something that fine?"

"Marvin, I'll warn you one time. Leave her alone, or she will eat you alive."

"That'd be a damn fine way to go."

"Shouldn't you be working on deactivating the bomb in my head?"

"Oh, right."

Marvin sits on the couch and starts plugging away at his computer. Feeling particularly grimy, I locate the guest bath and follow Lesile's example. The hot water feels great, and even though I don't sweat, rinsing off the dirt, sand, and blood that the less than pristine bay failed to wash away is invigorating. I only wish I had a change of clothes.

I return to the living room wearing a hotel bathrobe. Marvin is still plucking away at the keyboard, and Lesile seems determined to use all the hot water in the entire hotel. Marvin looks up at me when I enter.

"I think I got something."

"Can you turn it off?"

"No, but I can change the frequency. It's not quite as good as deactivating it, and they could technically set it off if they did some frequency hopping, but it's better than nothing."

"Let's just hope they don't discover we're not at the bottom of the ocean anytime soon and take extreme measures."

Lesile steps out of the bathroom scrubbing her hair with a towel as Marvin enters a few keystrokes into his laptop. "Has he made any progress?"

"He's changing the locks so their keys don't work anymore. Hopefully that will keep them out, but it's not a sure thing."

"Wonderful work, Marvin."

Marvin beams. "Ain't nothin' but a thang, baby doll."

"You are adorable. I could just eat you up."

"Maybe we should retire to the boudoir for some breakfast in bed."

"Marvin," I warn.

Marvin gets up, takes my elbow, and steers me to the side. "You have insulted me, assaulted me, and broken my phone. Do not cock-block me too."

"I'm trying to save your miserable life! She is a real life black widow—or praying mantis. Take your pick. When I say she is dangerous I mean it!"

Marvin grins at me. "Leo, you really care about me."

"I occasionally find you useful."

"Say you care about me and I'll back off."

My lip begins to twitch, and my jaw is so tight I'm about to shatter my teeth. "I care about your usefulness and don't want you to die."

"Close enough. Now say you love me. Say it!"

I shove Marvin hard enough to topple him over the couch. "Grab your shit and let's go."

"Where are we going?" Lesile asks.

"I need to go home and change. I think better in my own place."

Marvin glares at me as he picks himself up from the other side of the sofa. "This place is nice. Yours is a shit hole, and it doesn't have a mini bar."

"It also doesn't have enough guns and explosives to lay siege to Texas, so let's go."

"Fine, but I'm clearing out the mini fridge. I know you don't have shit to eat at your place."

It's a short walk to the parking structure where Lesile keeps her car. The hotel owns the garage, and security attendants on every level keep the place immaculate and safe. I feel as if I'm walking through a giant luxury car showroom instead of a parking garage. It's the lack of urine smell more than the pristine paint covering every surface that makes it truly classy.

Lesile pulls out what looks like a small, wireless mouse from her pocket and presses a button. A sleek, black sedan chirps and blinks its lights in response. I snatch the key fob from her hand, shove her in the back, and secure the driver's seat.

"I'm driving."

She glares at me. "Why should you drive? It's my car."

"I know where I'm going. Besides, I don't own a car and want to drive."

Marvin climbs into the back seat with his gear. Lesile decides not to argue and takes the passenger seat. I look at the controls and computer screens and feel like I'm back in the cockpit of our plane.

"What the fuck is this thing?"

"It's a Tesla."

"I feel like I'm on the bridge of the fucking Enterprise."

"Do you want me to drive?"

"No, I can figure it out." I cast my eyes around the various buttons and on-screen controls and speak with my best Patrick Stewart voice. "Car, engage."

Lesile sighs, leans over, and taps the large computer screen on my right. "Now just drive it like a normal car."

I grunt, slip the shifter into reverse, and press the "gas." The tires give a little bark, and the car rockets backward. I crank the wheel and we spin parallel to the parking space.

"Peppy little thing isn't it?"

"Be careful, Leonard, I like this car."

I press the accelerator a little more gently and guide the car out of the garage and onto the street. The silence, coupled with the incredibly smooth suspension, make me feel as if I'm floating down the road. Without the normal engine feedback, it's hard to maintain a proper speed. I find the experience a bit creepy and long for the rumble of a powerful V8 under the hood.

"Marvin, I need you to put your brain to work figuring out a way to get this thing out of my head."

"Our heads," Lesile clarifies.

"I'll see what I can come up with, but without knowing exactly what kind of anti-tampering mechanisms are in place I'm not sure what I can do."

"Just find out everything you can, and I'll sort through the most likely options."

"What are we going to do once we get to your place, Leonard?" Lesile asks.

"First, we rearm while Marvin figures out a way to remove these bombs. I'll have to contact the enclave and let them know what's going on. I may have an inflated opinion of myself, but I'm smart enough to know when I need help."

"I'm surprised to hear you admit it."

"This is about more than me. This is a threat to all…mother fucker!" I brake to a stop and watch the figure in a hoodie walking across a section of Prospect Park. "How do you turn the headlights off?"

Lesile taps on the control screen and the car goes dark. I turn the wheel, mash the accelerator, and speed through the grass. I spot the glow of a phone or music player and understand why he doesn't notice me until I'm right on his ass. Francis looks over his shoulder and jumps straight into the air, but he's a fraction of a second too late. He gains just enough height to make the impact truly spectacular. The bumper catches his ankle at almost eighty miles an hour, bumps his head off the top of the windshield where it meets the roof, and catapults him at least twenty feet in the air.

I slam on the brakes, spin the car sideways, and leap out of the door before it comes to a stop. I'm sprinting toward him almost before he hits the ground. Francis staggers to his feet just in time to give me a clean shot at his neck. My blade seeks home at a dead run and launches his decapitated head back into the air.

"Gotcha, bitch!"

Marvin and Lesile jump out of the car and run toward me. "Leonard, look what you did to my car!"

Marvin looks at Lesile incredulously. "Bitch, fuck your car! Look what he did to that nigga's head! Oh man, you know every brother in a five block radius just became a murder suspect." He leans down and looks at the decapitated corpse. "Aw shit, he's white too. You know the cops are gonna look for his killer. If he was black they'd put the third-string benchwarmer cops on it. Probably rule it a suicide."

"Shut up and help me put him in the trunk."

"I ain't touching a dead, headless honky!"

"You are not putting him in my trunk," Lesile insists.

"You want him in the backseat instead?"

"Hell no! This ain't Sleepy Hollow, and I ain't Niggabod Crane. No way I'm riding with him. Nope, I'll walk first, thank you very much."

Marvin does what he does best, which is exasperate the living shit out of me. "Fine, I'll call the service."

"You got a fucking service for picking up dead bodies? How often do you do this that you need a service? Damn, I have never wanted to be white more in my life than right now. That's gotta be some exclusive shit right there. You pay by the pickup or yearly like AAA?"

"Shut up, Marvin."

"Oh, I see. A black man can be president but he can't get this level of roadside assistance. I see how you are."

"Get back in the goddam car!"

"Oh, yessa, I'ze get back in the car, sah. Back seat, right? Yup, way in the back." Marvin bends down, stuffs the phone into his pocket, and gets back into the car.

The closed car does a good job of muffling Marvin's

continual complaining. I drag the body under a bush, find the head, kick it next to the body, and order in a body pickup. Since I'm technically doing a job for Vincent, the guy on the phone doesn't give me too much shit.

I pull on the car's door handle but it doesn't open. "Marvin, unlock the door."

"No, you're a psychopath!"

"You haven't seen me go psycho, but you will if you don't open this door."

"What the fuck was all that about?"

"It was business."

"How do I know you won't do me next to get rid of witnesses?"

I rap on the panoramic roof. "If I was going to kill you do you think the best place to hide is in the back seat of a car that is mostly glass?"

"I wasn't thinking clearly! I'm obviously under a great deal of stress right now. Besides, I don't know how to drive, and I've seen how fast you run. No white man should be able to run that fast. It ain't natural!"

"How do you not know how to drive?"

"I was born and raised in Manhattan. No one drives in Manhattan."

"If you don't open this door right now, I will punch through this window, drag you out through the hole, and stuff your body next to Francis'! One body or two, it costs me the same."

Marvin lifts his laptop up, and his finger hovers over the keyboard. "Bitch, I got the button! You so much as flinch and I'll turn your brain to pudding!"

I reach for my pistol and turn to Lesile. "You distract him, and I'll put one in his brainstem."

"Leonard, relax. He's just scared. Try to reason with him."

I clench and release my fists several times. "Marvin, that man has killed several people. I was hired to deal with him."

"By who?"

"By someone who doesn't want people like him causing trouble. You're working for Yuri. How many people do you think he's put down over the years? It's just business, business you have chosen to get involved in."

"Well, I don't like this business."

"Tough shit, you're in it until it's over."

"You aren't going to kill me?"

"Not unless you keep me standing out here."

"Fine, but no sudden moves. I got the button."

"Yeah, you have the button. Now unlock the goddam doors so we can get out of here."

Marvin leans between the seats and points at the car's control screen. "We're cool, right?"

I give him a tight-lipped smile and nod. "Yeah, we're cool."

The locks release with a barely audible click, and Lesile and I get in. I spot an ambulance and patrol car cutting across the grass toward us from the north, but I'm not worried. I know it's my recovery crew and not the real police.

"Marvin, do you want to tell me what the fuck was with your panic attack?"

"You ran that dude over and cut his head off! I think that warrants a little bit of panic."

"That was a lot of panic, and it's not as if you haven't seen me kill someone before."

"That guy was in your house and trying to cut *your* head off. What is with all this *Highlander* shit anyway? Why are you people running around with swords and cutting off heads? Is this going on all over the city, or is it just you?"

"It's really best if you don't know."

Lesile says, "It really is, darling."

"You're in on this too? Do you go around lopping off heads?"

Lesile smiles, stares out of the window, and stays quiet.

Marvin shakes his head and mumbles. "I have got to get me some black friends. You white people are insane, and you're going to get me killed."

CHAPTER 13

When we pull up to my loft, I'm not surprised to find Katherine's car parked in front. I should have called her as soon as I got back, but I was distracted with other things like bombs in my head and the government set to expose us and eradicate our existence.

I unlock and open the steel door leading inside and find myself looking down the gaping double barrels of a ten-gauge shotgun. Kat leans the shotgun against the wall and runs into my arms.

"Where have you been, and why are you dressed like my favorite falafel vendor?"

"It's a long story. What are you doing here?"

"I hadn't heard from you for days, and after I heard Vincent went missing, I began to think something had happened. Do you know where he is?"

"Yeah, he got wrapped up in the same mess as me. Long story short, the government found out about us and is scooping us up. That's where I was and where Vincent is now. I need to contact the enclave and call a grand council meeting."

Kat's hand flies to her mouth. "This is terrible! How did they find out?"

"Fucking Percy left an electronic trail the NSA picked up and followed. Fortunately, it sounds like the information is on an extremely need to know, and it's possible we can stamp out this fire before it burns us all."

"I'll need to tell the pack. If they know about you they could find out about us."

"Meat already knows and should be gathering them up now.

If we're going to quash this before it becomes public knowledge, it will probably take a joint strike force. We have the numbers to make a decisive attack. The biggest problem is finding them and taking them out before they can pass on any information outside their cell."

"Do you have any idea where they're at?"

"I have a few clues but nothing to give me more than a general direction. I need to talk to Marvin and get him back on track. He's a bit off his game after I caught Francis strolling through Prospect Park."

"Oh dear."

"Yeah, it wasn't pretty."

Katherine looks over at Lesile. "Speaking of pretty, who's your friend?"

"That is Lesile."

Kat glares and reaches for the shotgun. "Really?"

Lesile perks up at hearing her name and smiles. "I see Leonard has mentioned me."

"He told me how you turned and tortured him."

"Yes, that was an unusual time for me. Besides, he left me little choice. You know how he is. Had I not taken drastic measures to prepare him for the life I gave him, he would never have survived. He does not play well with others."

"But you tortured him."

"I made him strong. Had I not, someone would have killed him long ago. It is because of me he is here with you.

"You don't seem like the monster he described you as."

"Anger creates more monsters in our memories than anything else. Tell me, how did you manage to get past his awful exterior and find the tiny bit inside him that is tolerable?"

Katherine smiles and shakes her head. "It wasn't easy."

"Come sit with me. I would love to hear about it. Leonard has always been my most difficult and interesting convert."

I look over and see my nemesis and my girlfriend clucking away. "Don't get too close, Kat. I plan on killing her when it's convenient."

The two women look at me, giggle, and lean in to continue what I assume is a detailed exchange regarding my many flaws.

Knowing I could not possibly improve the conversation by participating, I decide that even talking with Marvin would be less stressful and a great deal more productive.

"Marvin, let's talk about getting this thing out of my head."

"Yeah, okay. I'm not sure how much help I'll be. You'd probably be better off talking to my father about brain surgery."

"The surgery isn't the hard part. Getting it out without it going off is."

"Aren't you the bomb expert? I thought you blew shit up all the time?"

Marvin has been strangely quiet since the park. He didn't even ask to stop for pizza on the way back, so I know he's bothered. I forget that what is a typical day at the office for me can be disturbing to others.

"Marvin, that guy murdered numerous people over the past year or more. You know the cops can't always catch the bad guy. When they can't, people call me. That's all that was. I need your help. Can I count on you?"

He takes a deep breath and nods. "Yeah, I'm good. Good enough I guess. When I shot that guy in here last year, none of it seemed real. He was going to kill us, so I didn't think about it much. It was like a video game, you know? You just never know when reality is going to hit you."

I give Marvin's shoulder an encouraging squeeze. "I know that feeling more than most."

Marvin releases a long breath and slowly wags his head. "All right, tell me how you booby trap a bomb."

"There are a lot of ways."

"Let's stick to just the ones you can cram in your skull."

"The easiest way is a depressed contact pin. Move the bomb, the pin pops up like a turkey thermometer, and it goes off. A sophisticated method would be some kind of proximity detonator. You implant two electronic objects close together. If one moves more than X distance from the other it goes off. There are a few other possibilities, of declining likelihood."

"Sounds to me like we need to x-ray your head. At least we can see if you have one object or two and narrow down the list."

I clap him on the shoulder. "There's my big-brained guy."

"Just basic troubleshooting."

I grab one of my dozens of phones and punch in the number. "Raj."

"Leo? What the hell time is it?"

"Time for you to wake up. I need your help."

"Christ, are you sending me another present?"

"No, my guys took care of him. I need you to x-ray my head. Someone stuck a bomb in it."

There's a pause on the other end. "How did you…never mind. I'll be in my office in half an hour."

"Thanks, Raj." I hang up the phone and turn to Lesile. "Hey, bitch, time to go see the doctor."

Katherine gives me the stink-eye. "Leo, you should not talk to people like that. Be polite."

"I was. I was going to use a much harsher but equally accurate descriptive word. Want a hint? It rhymes with cunt."

"Ignore him, Katherine. Despite his age, he is still a man-child."

"If he uses that word in my presence again I'm going to beat him like one."

I smile provocatively. "Promise? You know I love a good spanking when I'm naughty."

"Don't try to deflect with a show of sado-machismo." She rolls her eyes at Lesile. "I thought he was going to cry the first time we had sex."

"I did not, and shut up, Marvin!"

Marvin cuts his laughter short and hunkers back behind his computer.

"Where are we going, Leonard?"

"We need to see a friend about these bombs in our heads. Marvin, you come with us so you can monitor the signal in case we do something to piss them off."

Kat asks, "What can I do?"

"I imagine Meat is already howling from the rooftops and pissing on all the streetlights, but maybe you should make some calls too and help get everyone together."

"Okay. I can do that from here."

"Hopefully, these guys are lying low after just losing a plane full of their operatives, but you should probably stay here and be careful. They know about you and threatened to use you to hurt me."

Katherine picks up the shotgun. "Let them come. I owe them a little payback."

"Just get inside my armory if there's trouble and call me."

"Okay. Please be safe."

"I will."

"She really loves you," Lesile says as we drive across Brooklyn.

"Yeah, she does."

"I can tell you care very deeply about her too."

"Hard not to."

"I am happy you have each other. I am glad you found someone to love. I regret the circumstances of our relationship, but I knew you were special and needed…extra attention to achieve your full potential."

"Thanks." I stare out the windshield for several minutes. "I'm still going to kill you."

Lesile smiles and pats my arm. "Of course you are."

We take Lesile's spaceship to the Brooklyn medical examiner's office. One nice thing about working these hours is ample parking wherever I go. I glide in front of the building and watch for a minute out of habit before getting out of the car. Half the lights are off, and the others are dimmed in an effort to conserve electricity.

Raj appears in front of the glass door moments after I push the buzzer. He holds the door open to admit us and leads us down the hall to the exam room.

"Leo, what have you gotten yourself into now?"

"The problem is what's gotten into me."

"Yeah, how exactly did you manage to get a bomb in your head?"

"Government of course. The mechanics of it are pretty straightforward."

"Right. I'm not going to set this thing off by x-raying it, am I?"

Marvin says, "Naw, x-rays operate on a much higher

frequency than these things and by themselves don't produce any electrical current or interference that might set it off."

"Raj, this is my resident genius. Marvin, this is my corpse doctor."

"We prefer medical examiner. It sounds a little less ghoulish on our eHarmony profiles."

"Yeah, but you still poke around dead bodies, and that's gotta be a leg closer no matter what you call it."

"Sadly, yes, but not all the time. It's one reason why I stay in New York."

Marvin asks, "There's bitches who like it freaky with dead bodies?"

"You'd be surprised how many think this is a great place for a first date."

"Damn, the freakiest I ever got was with a chubby girl in the back of an Apple Genius bar."

"If you two can stop comparing your levels of deviancy, I'd like to get back to removing this bomb in my brain."

Raj lays me on the cold, metal table and maneuvers the x-ray contraption over my head. "I'm going to get three angles to give us a clear idea what's going on in there."

He steps behind the wall and pushes the button. The machine hums and clicks for a brief second.

"Everything all right, Marvin?" I call through the door.

"You ain't dead, so yeah."

Raj repositions the camera twice more. He comes back several minutes later bearing a folder. He sticks the three x-rays on the viewing light and flips it on.

"We can see the device clearly from three different angles: top, front, and side. Unless there are two devices connected to each other, we can assume there is only one."

"So that makes it likely that it has a contact trigger. If you try to pull it out it goes off and kills me."

"Pretty much. It appears to be sandwiched between the two lobes of your brain. That provides a good, stable method of depressing any kind of contact switch before arming."

"So how do we get it out without tripping the switches?"

"I really don't know. I'm not a bomb expert. I suppose we

could cut out the section of brain around it, but I don't know how much that's going to affect your memory or motor skills."

"Not to mention having no guarantee of not tripping it the moment it feels the slightest change in pressure."

Marvin chuckles from behind his laptop. "Too bad we can't freeze your head like an ice cube and chip it out."

"Raj, can you do that? The explosive is tiny and designed to shatter the vial containing the Cure, which is liquid. If it's frozen it's rendered inert…mostly."

"Whoa, Leo, you can't freeze your head," Marvin exclaims. "Freezing causes cellular rupturing and you die. It's why we haven't brought back Walt Disney."

"Marvin, you have done a lot of work for me over the last few years, and I have come to rely on you for your technical expertise."

"Genius."

"Right, genius. Since I expect us to continue our working relationship, there is something I need to tell you before you find out on your own."

"Please don't come out. I don't think I could handle that from you. If you're in the closet, you need to lock the door, push the dresser in front of it, and superglue that beard you call a girlfriend on so it never comes off."

"Goddammit, Marvin, I'm not coming out the fucking closet!"

"Thank God. I had a hard enough time adjusting to Neil Patrick Harris. I don't think I could handle it coming from you. Don't get me wrong. I got nothing against the gays, but you're not pretty enough, and you're just such an asshole."

I cast my eyes to the ceiling and search for the strength not to strangle him. "Maybe it would just be simpler to kill you."

"Golden goose, Leo, golden goose."

"What I am going to tell you, you cannot share with another living soul. You cannot blog it, tweet it, repeat it, or in any way allow anyone to find out. There are people out there who will kill you just for knowing what I am going to tell you. Do you understand?"

"Is it why you killed that guy in the park?"

"It is."

"Maybe I don't want to know."

"Tough shit, I'm going to tell you. You're too damn stupid to be trusted if you find out on your own."

"I got an IQ of 187! I'd have to get an NFL-sized concussion just to be considered smart."

"Fine, you're too damn irresponsible then!"

"Yeah, you have a point there. My mom says the same thing."

"Marvin, please focus. A lot of lives depend on your ability to keep this secret, yours paramount amongst them."

"That is my favorite one. Go ahead then, lay some serious conspiracy on me."

Marvin is hands down the smartest idiot I have ever known, and trusting him with our secret is like trusting Bill Maher to guard your pot. But he's also someone who needs to be brought in the loop before he stumbles in on his own.

"I'm a vampire. Lesile is a vampire, and the guy I killed in the park was a vampire."

Marvin leans back and looks at me skeptically. "Get the fuck outta here."

"Think about what you have seen and know about me, Marvin."

Marvin's eyes dart back and forth as he processes the vast amount of data stored inside his computer-like brain and gasps. "The refrigerator full of blood and how a white man can run so damn fast! And you never eat pizza! I knew there was something seriously wrong with anyone who doesn't eat pizza."

"It's also why Lesile and I have a bomb in our heads. The stuff you helped me with last year was to shut down one of our kind who risked exposing us in a grab for power. The government found out and used the information they discovered to make vampire soldiers and round us up. When their homemade vamps ran amok, they took us in, put bombs in our heads, and sent us to deal with them. Do you understand why it is so important that you never tell anyone or even allude to our existence?"

"Yeah, man, I get it. You're all like a super-secret hacker club, only you go around biting people's necks and cutting off their heads instead of busting into servers."

"If that helps you keep a secret, then sure."

"So you think you can freeze yourself, cut out this bomb, and still live, or whatever it is you do?"

"I don't know, but it's possible. There's one person I know who might have the answer and a method to do it. Take a cab back to my place and keep Katherine company. While you're there, see if you can figure out where the agents who took me are hiding out."

"You got anything to go on?"

"I was taken southeast on the turnpike for two, maybe two hundred and fifty miles. I guess the halfway point being near Trenton. The building was large and concrete or brick. Despite the recent renovations, I could smell the musty scent of an old building. I got the impression of an old hospital, asylum, or maybe a school of some kind."

"It's not much to go on, but I'll try."

"I'll hit up some of my contacts around the city and see if I can narrow it down any, but first I need to get this goddam thing out of my brain."

After giving Marvin fifty bucks for a cab and pizza, Lesile and I head into Manhattan. I hope Marvin can track down Snow and his group with the little information I gave him, but I'm not putting much stock in it. But Marvin has surprised me before, and I hope he does so again. You can't fight an enemy if you can't find them.

This is my second visit here, so I know right where I'm going. We take the elevator to the top floor, gain the roof, and drop three floors onto a balcony. The apartment inside is dark, as are most of them at the waning hour just before dawn. I try the sliding door, but it's locked this time. I'm about to force it open when the tenant throws back the curtain.

"Do you have some sort of aversion to using the door like a normal person?" Dr. Johnston asks when she unlocks and opens the door.

"I like to keep people guessing."

"You lose some mystique coming in the same way every time."

"Aren't you snarky in the morning? What happened to the

overwhelming fear? I like that attitude a lot better."

"The boogeyman's scarier when he stays under the bed. You also brought much nicer company, so I assume I'm not in trouble."

Lesile extends a delicate, alabaster hand. "Lesile."

"Sandra."

"Hurray, everybody knows everyone's name. Can we get down to the important stuff before we start debating our favorite Bieber haircut or delving into the exciting world of feminine hygiene products?"

"What do you want, Malone?"

"I need you to freeze my head."

"It would be my absolute pleasure."

I give her an exaggerated roll of my eyes. "I have a bomb in my head, and the only way we think it can be removed is by freezing it."

"Aw, that's tragic."

"Lesile also has one in her head."

"That really is tragic."

"Can you do it, and can I survive it?"

Sandra sits on her couch and thinks. "We have the proper cryogenic ability at the lab. I'm not nearly the expert on vampire physiology Dr. Guzman was before he took his life, but I have studied his notes extensively. I don't think we could survive a full cryo-freeze. There would be too much cellular damage with nothing available to repair it. But if we just froze your brain and kept a fresh supply of blood in your system, it might be possible to recover."

"Might?"

"No one has ever done it, so I can't guarantee the results. Even if you do survive, there could be memory loss if the brain cells and neurons suffer catastrophic damage." Her face twitches as she runs several ideas through her brain. "However, the cells responsible for memory, personality, and identity are more durable than most. With the proper cryoprotectants and our ability to spontaneously repair cellular damage, I think there is a better than even chance of pulling it off."

"Finally, some good news," Lesile says.

"Great. How soon can we get started?"

"Our laboratory is only a few blocks from here. It will take a couple of hours to set up the equipment. Give me half an hour to get ready, and I can meet you there."

Lesile smiles and cocks her head. "Maybe I can stay and walk over with you?"

Sandra returns her coy look. "Make it an hour."

My head twitches left and right between the two women. "Oh, you've got to be shitting me."

"Leonard, don't be such a prude. What good is living for so long if you are not willing to enjoy everything life has to offer? Join us if you like."

"No thanks." I make for the balcony and look over my shoulder. "But feel free to send me the link if you shoot a video."

I leave the scissor sisters to their deviant explorations and hop from balcony to balcony until I reach the street. It's apparent I have some time to burn, and I hate sitting around doing nothing.

I take Lesile's car back to Brooklyn in hopes of digging up some information on Snow's goon squad. His guys are pros and move with surprising stealth, but the shadows hide a lot of eyes, and few things go unnoticed in New York. If anyone saw any takings, I know the guy who heard about it.

Nick might be a useless, skeevy, little cocksucker, but he makes his stock and trade in information. He's also a fearful little shit, and knowing the goings-on keeps him alive. He's a cockroach by every definition. There's a good chance he's closing down his favorite club before crawling back into his dumpster to wait out the daytime hours.

The doorman has long since abandoned his post. Only the true hardcore partiers are still out, and they're already inside. I'm assaulted by a cacophony of electronic dance music sounding like R2-D2 if he were the victim of a brutal prison rape. The club is sparsely populated with only a few people still running on their favorite drug to fuel their dancing. Most lie collapsed in booths against the wall or on the floor.

I pick out a dancer whose bra size greatly exceeds her IQ. "Where's Nick?"

She looks at me with eyes more glazed than a Krispy Kreme donut and shouts over the music. "I think he had to take a shit!"

I make my way to the back of the club and find the doors leading to the bathrooms. I deduce the one guarded by the extra-large fellow in a medium T-shirt is where I'll find Nick. I make to walk past him, but he blocks me with a palm to my chest.

"Occupied, pops."

Several emotions surge through me. Firstly, yeah, I'm old, but I don't look that old. When did thirtyish become old? Okay, I'm a rough thirtyish, but still, it kind of hurts my feelings. The second thing I sense is surprise. This guy's not just an asshole seconds away from meeting Jesus, he's a goddam bloodling like Nick.

Bloodlings are victims of a non-lethal feeding who get just a tiny bit of whatever it is that turns us into vampires but who don't fully turn or die. They are so rare they make snow leopards look like an invasive species. Both those feelings are washed aside as the biggest emotion takes the fore, and that is the absolute hatred I have of people putting their hands on me.

I grab his wrist with my left hand and break both bones in his forearm. Grabbing a wad of his shirtfront, I fling him halfway across the massive room and leave a 7-10 split of dancers. Three goons jump out of a booth, and my chances of picking up the spare are looking good. Hands dive into coats and waistbands, but before they can draw, they find themselves looking into Shalonda's open mouth.

"You girls really want to dance with me?"

One of the thugs looks closely at me. "Malone?"

I hold back the flap of my coat and show the hilt of my blade. The guy splays his arms out and gestures to his cohorts to back down. Call me petty if you want, but after receiving so many ass-kickings of late, it feels damn good to get some proper, fear-induced respect.

I holster my pistol and push through the door into the bathroom. I hear some unpleasant grunting coming from the middle stall and make a beeline for it. Taking a knee, I reach under the door and grab the inseam of the jeans bunched around Nick's ankles.

"What the fuck!" Nick yelps as I pull him out from under the door.

"Oh, fuck me, Malone! I didn't do nothin'! Please! Come on!"

I drag him by his trouser-entwined legs across the dance floor and out of the back door. He scrambles to his feet and jerks up his pants when I toss his legs aside.

"Come on, Malone! What the fuck, man?"

"A little less methadone and a lot more fiber and you wouldn't have so much trouble in the bathroom."

"A lot less you and I wouldn't have any troubles at all! Why do you have to humiliate me like this every time?"

"Because you're a piece of shit, Nick, and I feel I would be neglecting my civic duty if I didn't remind you and your friends of that once in a while."

"The only shit around here is the way you treat me and the stripe now going up my back. What do you want?"

"Tell me about the vampire abductions."

"Maybe I don't know nothin'."

"Maybe I come by for a regular visit. How does once or twice a month sound to you?"

"Fine, but you gotta stop busting my balls."

"That depends on your usefulness."

"We've heard about some full bloods getting snatched up by guys in black who are carrying serious hardware. They reek of fucking feds."

"We?"

"Yeah, me and my people."

"Since when do you have people?"

Nick straightens the lapels of his jacket. "I'm a legit businessman now."

"What kind of business?"

"You know, information, drugs, a little fencing."

"How many of your people are bloodlings?"

Nick shifts nervously. "Look, I know your kind don't like us, but these are okay guys. We stick together and look out for each other. I make sure they know the rules and don't draw attention to us or you."

"When did you find these bloodlings?"

"Around the same time all the new full bloods started popping up around the city. The first one was maybe two years ago. Seven more have joined my crew over the last year."

Once again, the ghost of Percy pops into the room, cuts a fart, and leaves. It looks like his vampire formula doesn't just increase the likelihood of making vampires. This is the first I'm hearing about new bloodlings, so I assume it's not a big problem. Bloodlings don't need to feed on humans and are benign as long as they keep their heads down and don't draw attention to themselves.

"Any of your boys see me taken?"

"Yeah. When Bryce told me, I laughed so hard I almost pissed myself."

I double Nick up with a punch to the gut.

"Totally worth it," he gasps.

"What can you tell me about them?"

Nick manages to catch his breath and straightens up. "We heard some things a few months ago. People disappearing, getting snatched up by guys in black SUVs. They were mostly the new vamps I was talking about, so we didn't care much. A lot of these new guys are even bigger assholes than you, and they scare the shit out of us. I knew you were hunting some of the ones who were fucking up, so I thought I could use any information I dug up to get some favors. I started staking out some of the ones I thought might make good targets for these kidnappers. About a month ago, I got my first hit. Some loser who'd been picking off bums and whores got snatched up right in front of one of my guys."

"He have any idea of where they went?"

"He followed them on his bike, but they shook him near Philadelphia. That was our best lead."

"It helps, thanks, Nick."

Nick beams like a kid being praised by an abusive father. "I know you're chasing some of these new full bloods. I can get you a list of the ones we've identified and who's breaking the rules."

"Do that. You did good work. I tell you what; I'm going to give you a battlefield promotion. You're now a warder of whatever territory you claim as yours. This means you're the top guy amongst your bloodlings. You got a problem with someone muscling you, you let me know."

"Thanks, Leo!"

"This also means you're responsible for any misconduct. Your guys fuck up; it's your head I'm coming for, so you best keep a clean house."

"I will. I got a good crew going."

"Good, keep it that way. You keep making yourself useful, you might start getting some regular paying work from me and the council."

"I knew this was good stuff! I just didn't think I had enough to bring you. Then you got snatched up, and I didn't know what to do with it."

"Now you know. Keep your head down for a while. The shit's going to hit the fan soon, and you don't want to get caught in the blast."

"Yeah, I got enough shit on me now, thanks."

My phone chirps and buzzes as I leave Nick in the alley. "Yeah?"

"Where are you?" Lesile asks. "We're waiting for you at the lab."

"Sorry, I thought finding out where our kidnappers are hiding was a better use of my time than Indian leg wrestling with my new gal pal."

"Stop being a prick and get over here. I want this thing out as badly as you do."

"The bomb or did you lose a toy?"

She hangs up and I call Raj with the address to the lab. I take a minute to consider Nick, his bloodling gang, and his newfound usefulness. I'm not sure what the council will think about having several new bloodlings amongst the populace nor how they might deal with it if they see it as a problem. I decide it's best just not to mention it and call Marvin.

"Marvin, narrow your search to a twenty-five mile radius of Philadelphia."

"Philadelphia?"

"I got a lead, and my rough estimate of how long I was in

that truck puts their hideout within that vicinity."

"All right, but that's still a lot of territory. It's not as if Philly is short on decrepit, abandoned buildings."

"Keep outside the city limits. I would have known by smell and sound if I was near a population center."

"Okay, I'm on it."

I zip across town, narrowly avoiding the morning rush. Lesile and Dr. Johnston are waiting when I arrive, and Raj makes his appearance fifteen minutes later.

"Leo, who is this man and what is he doing here?" Sandra asks.

"He's a friend and someone I have come to rely on for quite a while now."

"If the council finds out..."

"If the council finds out, I know who to blame. I think it's in everyone's best interest that they don't."

"Does everyone who comes in contact with you face the threat of a significantly reduced lifespan?"

"Huh, yeah it seems like it. I should come with a Surgeon General's warning or something."

Dr. Johnston leads us into the lab. "Fine, but if anyone asks, I'm telling them you threatened me."

"At least you'll be telling the truth."

Raj is looking quite nervous now. "Um, Leo, I want to help and all, but I really don't want to become anyone's breakfast."

"Don't worry. Once you prove your worth, even the council will be reasonable."

"I don't know if I can remove this."

I shrug. "Best not fuck it up."

Raj is looking queasy as Dr. Johnston uses her access badge to pass through several security doors to reach the laboratory's heart.

"This is where we cryogenically freeze mostly viruses and bacteria, but I should be able to rig up something to do what we need."

"So what do we do, jump in a tub of liquid nitrogen?" I ask.

"No, that would almost certainly kill even us. We need to replace the liquids in the brain with a cryoprotectant. Then we freeze your head with dry ice, encase it in a metal container, and submerge it in the liquid nitrogen until it's frozen solid."

"This is beginning to sound unpleasant."

"Beginning?" Raj mutters.

"It is going to be very unpleasant. The freezing part shouldn't be too bad if you can close off all your sensory receptors. It's the thawing that will be truly hellish. Once frozen, your friend can then carve out the device however he sees fit."

"Hooray for me. It would be best if I open the skull and expose the brain before freezing. It would be especially helpful if I could create a path as close to the device as I can first. The less frozen brain matter I have to remove the better."

"It's not the first time someone performed brain surgery on me this week, so let's get to it. Dr. Frankenstein, I put my brain in your hands."

Raj lays me on a table and starts cutting while Sandra gathers supplies for my deepfreeze. I tune out the sound and vibration of the oscillating saw as it removes the top of my skull. Raj pokes around in my brain for several minutes until he steps back and wipes his sweat-covered brow with his sleeve.

"I managed to expose the very top of the device. I can't go any farther without risking moving the surrounding tissue and setting it off."

Dr. Johnston pushes a cart piled with equipment next to the table. "Since we only want to freeze your head, I'll have to put a tourniquet around your neck. This shouldn't be a problem and will help keep the cryoprotectant in your brain when you lose consciousness and the ability to regulate your blood flow."

"Ugh, that's just weird," Raj says when Sandra cinches the leather strap around my neck.

She then inserts a needle attached to an IV bag into my carotid and a siphon in my jugular just above the ligature. I feel a profound sense of starvation as my blood drains away. It is all I can do to keep myself from flying off the table and tearing Raj apart to get to his warm, liquid center. I feel my grip on reality slipping away as the fluid from the IV bag replaces my precious blood. Then I lose all consciousness.

I awaken to the sound of screaming and the crashing of metal. It takes me a full minute to realize I am the source of both. A metal operating table lies in a twisted wreck against the wall of a secured room. I'm writhing and shrieking on the floor. I have no idea where or even who I am. I tear at the walls with my fingernails and pound on the steel door. When it fails to yield, I do my best to tear through the wall.

A voice comes through a speaker in the ceiling. "Leo, you need to focus. Send your blood into your brain and repair it."

Blood, it's all over the room. The smell of it drives my insatiable hunger. Images of a jungle, a grass hut, crying children, and a young Vietnamese girl cursing my existence flash through my mind, but they aren't the source of the blood. An IV catheter with a length of plastic tubing hangs from the inside of my thigh. The bag containing the blood that once fed into my femoral artery lies on the floor nearby. I dive for the bag, tear it open with my teeth, and down the sweet contents as fast as I can swallow. I lie on the floor softly mewling as I force the blood to my brain.

"Leonard, are you all right? Leo?"

It takes me a minute to recover my faculties before I can form words. "Oh, fuck me. That was the most horrible thing I have ever experienced in my life. I am so glad I went first. I think I would have taken my chances with the bomb if I watched you go through this."

"It is a good thing I am more of a man than you are."

I want to issue a biting retort, but it's all I can do just to flip her off. They give me several minutes to return to my charming self before unlocking the door and letting me out.

"How'd it go?" I ask.

"Good. The freezing kept the pins from tripping and froze the liquid, so even if I did set it off, it could not have been released into your system."

"Nice work. I guess it's time to pull up a chair for the second act. I hear this is the best part of the show."

"Are you really so pathetic to take pleasure in my misery?" Lesile asks.

"Looks that way."

"You are a real shit, Leonard."

"Yep."

CHAPTER 14

I have to admit, I enjoy watching Lesile come out of her deepfreeze. Knowing what a painful, terrifying, and outright god-awful near-death experience it was, filled me with a satisfaction bordering on the sexual.

When we get back to my loft I find two cars and a van I don't recognize parked out front. Well, the cars I don't recognize, but the van is unpleasantly familiar. I mentally prepare myself as best I can before entering. Inside my loft are three enclave heads and half a dozen Sheriffs. Sven is doing his best impression of a statue of Thor and succeeding rather well. Nikolaj Henrik, Jake Hobbs, and Harriet Shaw, who is in charge with Vincent out of the picture, stand shoulder to shoulder glaring at me when I walk in.

"You guys throw a party at my house and I don't even get an invite? That's rude."

Harriet scowls even deeper and glances at Marvin who is trying to look as if he is still working. "Send your boy away. He is not one of us and cannot be privy to this conversation."

"Wow, two deeply racist comments in such a short statement. I know you're old and set in your ways, but we don't speak like that anymore."

"You know what I mean, Malone. What we have to discuss is not for outside ears."

"He's doing something useful. You go somewhere else."

"Do not tempt my patience. There are important matters to discuss and no time to waste."

"Maybe you should have called first."

"How the hell can we call when your number changes every

few days because you cannot spend a week without destroying your phone for fear of incrimination?" she shouts, finally breaking her frigid façade.

"You do have a point. You know what's really criminal, the early contract termination fees. You would think I would be smart enough to stick with pay as you go plans, but they make it look so tempting with the free phones and unlimited data."

"I do not find you amusing at the best of times, Malone, and this is one of our bleaker moments. Now send him away, or we can discuss this openly and deal with damage control afterward."

"Marvin, can you work upstairs in my office?"

"Gladly."

Marvin flips his laptop shut, bounds up the stairs two steps at a time, and disappears through the steel door at the top.

"How much does he know?"

"Enough to help us."

"He seems awfully nervous."

"He's a young black man surrounded by armed white people."

"We already have a massive security breach. We will not permit outside knowledge of our existence to continue. We have become lax in our efforts to maintain our anonymity, and it is time to take measures to correct our oversights."

"Think very carefully before you decide who gets kicked out of the club and who stays."

"Do not threaten me, Leo Malone."

"Don't threaten my...employees or business partners."

Jake Hobbs cuts in before we can draw steel and start hacking at each other. "We need to focus on the primary threat at hand. We can discuss additional security measures later and at length."

"I assume you have been talking to the wolves," I say.

"Fortunately, they have taken this problem seriously and have been more forthcoming in sharing their information than you have been. Why did you not come to us the moment you discovered the problem?"

"Well, first I was kidnapped and sent to Bumfuck, Yemen

to kill some Betty Crocker ready to bake vampires where I had to crash a jet plane into the fucking Atlantic to escape. Oh yeah, then there was the small matter of the bomb planted in my head, which necessitated turning it into a giant ice cube in order to remove it. So, sorry if I've been a little preoccupied. I was going to come to the council when I had a little more information to share than what you likely already possess, to expedite a mission plan so we didn't spend needless hours pissing up flagpoles like we are now."

Sven growls, "Watch your tone, Malone."

"Lick my sack, Jack. I can play the rhyme game too. You want to come at me? Because I'm in a really foul mood right now, and I could use the stress relief."

Sven twitches, but he doesn't show more than half a foot of steel before my blade touches his Adam's apple and I point Shalonda between Harriet's eyes. Nikolaj reacts with impressive speed, drawing his sword and slapping mine away from Bjork's neck within a second.

"Enough of this! We have a problem that threatens our existence. We do not have time for petty bickering!"

I holster my weapons. "Fine. What do you want from me?"

"Some active and cohesive participation for a start," Harriet replies.

"Active—did you not hear the part about me being kidnapped and forced to hunt rogues on the other side of the planet?"

"I mean active within the council. You have done nothing to keep us apprised of the situation. You cannot do this alone."

"I know I can't. That's why I had Meat gather his people and contact you."

"Who is Meat?"

Jake leans in. "He is the werewolf who helped Malone in Yemen and informed us of their return."

"Ah, yes."

"Do you know they abducted Vincent as well?"

"We knew within hours of his capture and have been using our full resources to locate him."

"But no one raised an eyebrow when they took me?"

"Of course we did. We raised an eyebrow as well as a glass at the party we threw. It was when Vincent failed to show up that we knew something was terribly wrong."

"There's a funny gal in there after all. What'd you do, eat Wanda Sykes before you came over? Seriously, no one knows anything about these guys?"

"We were hoping you could tell us something since you are the only one with firsthand knowledge of who they are."

"The man in charge is Agent Snow. He is leading a team out of the office of Homeland Security and running a black op."

"That explains why our people have not been successful in their intelligence gathering. We have several people in key positions throughout the government, CIA, FBI, and even the NSA, but it took years and decades to get them there. Homeland Security is a new organization and our resources have yet to advance deeply into the bureau. What else can you tell us?"

"They are highly organized and very well-armed. I saw at least two dozen people, but I suspect their numbers are much larger. They are using a large, abandoned, concrete building of some kind, I think outside Philadelphia. That is what I have Marvin looking for now. Until we find out where that building is, there isn't much we can do."

"Not true," Harriet says. "We will begin forming a strike force and coordinate with the wolves so we are ready to move the moment we find out where they are."

I shake my head. "We cannot attack this head on. Their security measures are high, and all it takes is one data blast to tell the world all about us and provide enough evidence to make it convincing. We'll need to cripple their communications before we go in guns blazing."

"Your argument has merit. Our initial entry will have to be covert so we can disable all forms of communication and get Vincent out."

"Your insistence on rescuing Vincent significantly increases the risk of failure. I have another solution. I call it *Operation Fuck Vincent*. It's a lot like your idea only, well, the op name pretty much describes the technical difference."

Harriet glowers. "We are not abandoning Vincent and will

make all effort to secure his release. Am I clear on this?"

"Am I clear when I state that we have no idea of the layout of the building or where they are holding him?"

Harriet nods to Lesile. "Does she? It is my understanding she was also on this little cleanup operation with you and has spent substantial time with these government agents."

I tell Lesile, "I think your new girlfriend ratted you out."

"I know who you are, Lesile, and know you dislike operating within the enclave. Despite your reputation and disdain for our order and laws, will you help us rescue Vincent and crush these people?"

"Of course. They abused and humiliated me, and for that, they will pay dearly."

"Excellent. When we learn more of their position, you can lead Mr. Malone in facilitating the rescue. Once Vincent is clear, we can use a heavy hand to crush them."

"Hold on, lead me? Why am I going in?" I ask.

"You have been inside, and you know how to counter the bomb implant. You do not think you will be able to walk out with him, do you? We can hope they did not inflict such barbarism upon him, but we cannot count on it."

"I hate to burst your bubble, but neither of us has the first clue how to turn it off. That's what Marvin is for."

"Then take him with you."

I laugh. "Marvin...on a tactical raid? Marvin is the poster-child for geek analysts. He's about as field-capable as a meerkat."

"It may be necessary, regardless. Since he knows all about the bomb, I presume he knows about us. If he is reluctant to do this, tell him that his knowledge of our existence comes with certain strings attached. One of them is his being at our disposal."

"This goes far beyond providing a service! You are expecting him to put himself in an extremely dangerous situation for which he has zero training."

"We will compensate him accordingly."

"You can't compensate a dead man."

"Then I suggest you keep him alive. We are done here until we discover where these vermin are hiding."

Harriet and her retinue leave without another word. All I can do is stand in the middle of the room, clench my fists, and fume. My mind races with a myriad of ways for me to enact my revenge for her callous disregard for my…assets.

"You see why I dislike the council?" Lesile asks. "They are dictators with no regard for anything or anyone except themselves. They veil their selfish natures by proclaiming the greater good, but in the end, it is about self-preservation."

"My focus right now is Marvin-preservation. He's too valuable to me to risk losing on an uptight bastard like Vincent."

"Vincent is hardly the worst of them."

"He's still about as useful to me as a third testicle."

"Why can't you admit that you want to keep Marvin safe because he is your friend?"

I spin on her and glare. "Because I don't have friends! Friends can be used against you. I have associates who exist to help me in my work, nothing more."

"But you let Katherine close to you."

"And look what happened. Snow threatened her to make me do what he wanted. Just being near me puts her at risk, and I hate it."

Kat entwines her arm through mine. "I know the risks, but I choose to take them because I think you are worth it. You cannot decide for others how they feel about you. Is knowing me not worth the risk?"

"Not if something ever happens to you. If Snow or anyone ever hurt you, I would make Timothy McVeigh look like a shoplifter."

"Talk to Marvin and let him decide."

"Fine, but I know him well enough that he is not going to be on board with this. Marvin!"

My office door opens a crack, and Marvin pokes his head through. "Are they gone? They bring a whole new level to scary white people. I felt like the guest of honor at a Klan lynching."

"Come down here. I need to talk tactics with you."

He descends the metal stairwell with his computer in hand. "What's up?"

"The head of our enclave was taken shortly after I was, and

he is still being held. That means we cannot launch a direct offensive until we free Vincent and know for sure that they can't detonate any implanted bombs."

"Oh, okay, so you need me to show you how to use the signal scrambler."

"Can you do that?"

"Sure, it's not hard. Of course, we're assuming they're using the same frequency. If it's a different one, then he's screwed."

"Could you find out the new frequency and intercept it?"

"Sure, but I'd have to be right next to him like I was with you and use the frequency analyzer to match the signal." Marvin and I exchange looks for several long, silent moments. "Oh, hell no! Look, I can wreck an entire chat room with an ego-destroying trolling, but in a face-to-face confrontation, I am as big a coward as the rest of the Internet world. I'm not proud of it, but I know the truth. If they want to come at me on Call of Duty, I'm your man, but in the meat world, count me out."

"I want to count you out, but since you know our secret, the enclave decided to count you in."

"I demand a recount!"

"Sorry, Florida, I wish I could."

"That better be an election reference and not *Good Times*. That's racist."

"Trust me, Marvin; I don't want to bring you on an op like this for a variety of reasons."

"My death being paramount I hope."

"It's in my top ten."

"Well, thank you, David Letterman, for at least putting my life on the list."

"Fine, top five. Feel better?"

"A little bit, but I should be at least in the top three."

I lay a hand on his shoulder. "Look, you saved my life, so I know you can handle yourself when it matters. You'll be going in with me and Lesile. You can't find better protection than us. I'll even let you wear one of my bulletproof coats."

"Can I have the codename Morpheus?"

"No."

"Neo?"

"No."

"Black Neo, Negro for short. Wait, that's racist. Oh, how about Blade!"

"Absolutely not."

"You take all the fun out of infiltrating a government stronghold to rescue an old ass vampire in a mission where we have a high probability of getting shot. I bet you won't even let me blog about it."

"Definitely not!"

"Tweet?"

"What part of secret are you not getting?"

Marvin sighs. "So much street cred wasted. I'm probably considered a terrorist already. I bet there's a drone circling overhead just waiting to blow my ass up the moment I step outside."

I push Marvin to the table. "Worry about drones later. Let's focus on finding these guys."

"All right, but we're still searching almost four thousand square miles."

"Can't you just do a search for abandoned hospitals?"

"Sure, but we're assuming you were in a hospital, and they might not all be listed on the web. There are a lot of large civil war era structures in the area."

"Detective work is often a process of elimination. Let's list all the ones we can find and see if we can scratch them off."

"Good idea."

"I've learned a few things in my time."

Marvin spends the next hour compiling a list of possible locations, and he was right, it is rather substantial. Since I never saw more than a few hallways and rooms, there is no way for me to assess its real size so I can narrow down the list.

"What are our options?" I ask Marvin.

"You said you thought there were some serious renovations. Other than driving to each of them and checking them out, all I can do is use Google Earth to see if anything shows up. Unless you have friends who have access to our country's spy satellites and get real-time images?"

"Not without drawing attention."

"You could search the county and state records for any kind of building permits or renovations," Kat says. "I imagine many of these kinds of buildings have been deemed historical landmarks and would require some kind of paperwork even from Homeland Security."

"I doubt they filed it under their name, but it's a possibility. Thanks, Kat."

"The DA doesn't keep me around just for my pretty face."

"I know. No one could ignore that ass."

"Pig."

Marvin says, "Building permits aren't usually on a public database, but since most of these are historical landmarks like Kat said, there's bound to be a mention of any renovations or restorations somewhere on the web. Historical societies and architect groups like to blog and post newsletters about these kinds of things, so I'll bounce some of our names around and see what comes back. Then we can use Google's eye in the sky to see if anything looks out of the ordinary."

"I think I'll step out for a bite to eat," Lesile announces. "The surgery has left me famished."

She's right. I'm far from a hundred percent myself. While the transfusion was sufficient to heal my body, there is a deeper hunger gnawing at my soul that only a full feeding will satiate. It doesn't feel right leaving Marvin with the grunt work, but there isn't anything I can contribute here.

"I'm going to go out too. Marvin, Kat, you have my number if you need me before I return."

"I should go home, I'm exhausted," Katherine says.

"I would prefer it if you stayed here until we take care of Snow. He threatened to harm you if I didn't play nice. He may not know I'm still alive, but if he suspects I might be, he would almost certainly come for you to get to me."

"I suppose you're right, but your place isn't conducive to getting a decent night's sleep. I'll hide out in one of the pack's safe houses for now."

I open the drawer of a file cabinet, take out one of the phones inside, and add its number to my current phone. "Take one of my burners. The feds are probably listening in on yours. Don't use my name, ever. Same for you, Marvin. If they can utilize the NSA's systems, they can pick my name out of any conversation going on in the country."

"Good idea," Marvin says. "We can use your codename: Hugh Janus."

It takes me a full six seconds to decipher the double entendre, which annoys me more than the joke itself. "Marvin, don't make me regret my efforts to keep you alive."

Katherine kisses me goodbye and waves to Marvin before she leaves. She's tough, and I know she can take care of herself, but I'm still worried. My life was easier without these kinds of distractions, but it wasn't nearly as complete. I had a huge hole in my existence I didn't know existed until she stepped into it, and I wouldn't trade it for anything.

Lesile took her car back, so I jump on my motorcycle and head across town. I'm particular about who I kill when I require a full feeding, and finding one who fits the bill takes some time and planning. I don't feel like driving too far, so I decide to hit Brooklyn Bridge Park. Only fools and thugs wander around New York's parks at night, and I'm hoping to find the latter, although the former will do in a pinch.

I leave my bike in front of Plymouth Church and hoof it the rest of the way. Once I reach the north side of the park, I begin hunting the more likely predators lurking in the area. It doesn't take me long to identify three primary targets and two secondary. I pick out a group of five with colors marking them as Latin Kings.

Staggering and mumbling down one of the paved pathways, I show off my best impression of a guy who had too much to drink at the nearby wine bar and doesn't have the wits to know where he's going. Three of the five gangbangers split off and shadow me just as I had hoped. Deviating from the path, I leave the minimal protection of the streetlights and stagger into the shadowy interior of the strip of trees to my right.

The thugs follow me in and make their move. There's no clichéd demand to hand over my wallet or a request of any kind. Fists and feet start raining down on me without warning or preamble. I put up a feeble resistance, just enough to make it something of a challenge so I can determine how far these guys are willing to take it. It takes five seconds to find out that it's all the way.

Switchblades snick open and plunge into my body, signaling the start of the main event. I shed my drunken disguise and come up swinging for real. My left elbow destroys one's face, and I send a second one flying twenty feet with a kick to the chest. I grab the third by the arm holding a knife, strip it from his hand, and put him in a chokehold. A quick headbutt stuns him into submission. I press a thumb against his jugular and use his knife to sever it. I clamp my mouth over the wound and release the pent-up flow from beneath my thumb.

In less than five minutes, it's all over. I don't know if the other two are dead or not, and I don't care. I could dump them in the river along with their friend, but it's not as though they're going to go running to the cops, so I leave them be. A good hunter preserves the herd after all.

I stuff the gangbanger's pockets full of rocks, poke a hole in each lung, and pitch him into the East River. It's an impromptu disposal, but I don't feel like paying for another body recovery. There's a chance the corpse will float to the surface one day, but the only wounds on him were made with his knife, and the cops don't look too hard for people who take out New York's garbage. I'm halfway back to my bike when my phone buzzes.

"Yeah?"

"Hugh, I've got a narrow list of likely vacation spots."

Marvin is enjoying his spy game a little too much. I hang up without answering. My bike is still where I left it. It's always a risk, but folks tend to steer clear of the big churches. Faith is the last flimsy barrier separating human decency from depravity. Yeah, I see the hypocrisy coming from a guy who just killed someone in a park and drank his blood, but necessity trumps depravity.

Lesile isn't back when I return, but I'm not surprised. She likes to play with her food. I'm more of a drive-through kind of guy where she prefers a dinner theater whenever possible. Marvin is practically bouncing in his seat with anticipation.

"What did you find?"

He turns the screen and shows me a list of what I assume are the buildings fitting our search parameters. "I found over a dozen places fitting your description, and most of them have undergone some sort of renovations in the last couple of years. One stands out: Pennhurst State School and Hospital. Pennhurst was closed down in 1987 after numerous lawsuits involving patient abuse. Guess who bought the property?"

"Surprise me."

"The Department of Military Affairs. Records show they were converting the upper campus into a veteran's home, and that looks legit until the project flops. In 2010, someone decided to turn it into a haunted house for tourists. That ended a year ago, and now a twelve-foot chain-link fence surrounds the central building. A composting company running operations on the property claims to have purchased the structure and closed it off for renovations as their new headquarters. It didn't take me long to follow their rather flimsy paper trail to figure out this was a shell corporation probably run by one of the federal bureaus."

"Okay, I admit it looks incriminating. Do you have anything more substantial before I call the enclave to have them send out a scouting party?"

Marvin clicks around on his screen and brings up an earth view of the area. "Look at the dates on the maps. Google Earth is a series of satellite photos stitched together like an enormous quilt. When I focus in on different areas, you can identify the individual images. Look at the dates."

"They're the same."

"Right, they're supposed to be. When the satellite passes over an area, it starts snapping pictures, so all the pictures of a given area are going to have the same date. But look at the image showing our school. Here's the one from two years ago, and here's the one taken four months ago."

"They're the same."

"Exactly. Where's the fence? Someone took the old image and changed the metadata to reflect the new date. Why would they do that unless the image showed something they didn't want people to see, and who could hack into Google's server to do it?"

"You?"

"Damn right, but I didn't, and no one I know has enough interest in an old school and composting company to bother. That leaves the feds."

"All right, that's good enough for me."

I call Harriet and tell her what Marvin discovered.

"Excellent, it appears your faith in him was worthy after all. I should be able to have eyes on the compound within the hour. Stay where you are, but be prepared to come in for a strategy meeting in a few hours. Is Lesile still with you?"

I glance at the sound of my door opening. "She just came back."

"Good, her knowledge of the inner complex is instrumental in any assault we launch. I will contact the wolves so we can bring them in on our plans. I will call you once I receive first-hand confirmation of the location."

"Sounds like a great party. Would you like me to bring anything? I make some mean deviled eggs."

"Just be ready to move."

"Yeah, this ain't my first rodeo."

"If we screw this up, it may well be your last, along with the rest of us."

Lesile asks when I hang up, "Was that the council?"

"Yeah. Marvin thinks he found out where our ops team is hiding. Harriet is sending some people out to investigate before calling us all in."

"Where do you think it is?"

"It's an abandoned boarding school and asylum northwest of Philly." I have Marvin show her what he found.

"I'm sure that's it," Lesile says. "I didn't get a good look at the outside, but I did catch a glimpse, and the distance and direction is right. What do we do now?"

"Harriet wants us to wait here until she calls."

"And we're…?"

"Going out."

"Of course we are. Leo Malone doesn't like to follow orders."

"Leo Malone doesn't like to sit on his ass when there's work to do. Leo Malone also doesn't like to speak in the third person, so stop it. Marvin, we're going to go see Yuri, so you may as well come along."

Yuri doesn't like surprise visits, so I call him once we pile back into Lesile's car. "Yuri, it's Leo. I need your help."

"What kind of help?"

"The kind that will earn you massive favors from my people. I'm on my way to see you now. You at your bunker in Queens?"

"Yeah, I'll be here waiting for you."

Yuri says a lot with just a few words. When he said he'd be waiting for me, it didn't just mean he was anticipating my arrival. It meant he was prepared to deal with any trouble I or anyone else might cause. It hurts a bit that his trust in me has dwindled since finding out I am a vampire, but I guess I can't blame him after what happened. Fucking Percy.

The changes Yuri made to not just the building but the entire block are obvious. I'm guessing he bought the surrounding buildings, if he didn't own them already, and turned each of them into a fortification. The windows in the central building are gone, leaving only a smooth, concrete surface bristling with cameras. The surrounding buildings' windows are only six inches wide like arrow slits in a medieval castle. I'm guessing these are manned by sniper crews ready to pick off anyone trying to get into Yuri's central complex. The doors to all the buildings look like bank vaults. I don't bother knocking as I stand in front of the big steel door and await recognition.

The speaker crackles to life. "You and the smart black kid can come in. The woman waits outside."

"Why you gotta label me like that?" Marvin asks.

"You want to stay in a label-free zone, wait outside with the broad."

Interesting. I wonder what kind of tech they used to determine Lesile is a vampire. If I were to guess, I'd say thermals, but we can beat those if we want to. I doubt Lesile bothered to raise her body temperature to fool it. I sure didn't think about it until now.

"I'll wait in the car," Lesile offers.

The door opens with a hiss of hydraulics, and Marvin and I step into a mantrap. The portal closes and locks us inside the small room. My ears detect a hum coming from behind the walls, likely a full body x-ray scanner like those used in some airports but much more *Total Recall*-ish. Marvin can probably tell me everything about his new security setup, but he shouldn't and I don't ask him to.

A section of the wall ejects a deep drawer. "Place your pistol and sword in the box."

I do as I'm told, and the wall swallows up my favorite toys. The far door opens into a longer hallway still bereft of a living soul. I'm starting to feel as if I'm in a sci-fi horror film where a series of short hallways ends in a room full of fiendish traps. This hallway ends in a steel door with no visible method of opening, but it swings wide at our approach.

The first signs of human life wait just beyond the portal. It doesn't make me feel any better given the intense firepower these guys are toting. Six men wear tactical vests bristling with weapons, magazines, and even a few grenades. Each of them carries a submachine gun and an assault rifle, and I'm betting the magazines are loaded with incendiary rounds.

They surround Marvin and me and march us down the hallway toward the heart of the building. These guys aren't the usual Russian and Georgian thugs Yuri typically employs. Their movements indicate a high level of military training. I'm guessing Yuri has contracted some outside help.

We stop at a secure elevator, and one of the mercs punches in a five-digit code on a keypad. The doors open, and they gesture for us to enter alone. People seem to be as willing to share an elevator with me as they are with the entire Klump family.

Yuri's regular goons are waiting for us when we arrive, but their weaponry is similar to those of the frontline mercs. I notice the ceilings are lower, and I can only guess what kind of nasty surprises lurk within them. The entire building is designed to be one big killing ground.

We finally arrive at Yuri's office, which is now inside his panic room. They enlarged the chamber and installed what I'm guessing is an elevator in the back. He's sitting behind his usual desk doing whatever kingpins do.

"I love what you've done with the place."

"Is upgrade. Yuri fortress 2.0."

"I see you got some new help as well."

"Russian spetsnaz. Best value for the dollar. You said I can earn favors from your people. I like doing favors."

"You like cashing in favors."

"There is another reason for doing favors? What can Molotov do for you?"

I take a seat across from him. "I told you the feds found out about us." Yuri's face twists with a look of revulsion. "We think we know where their base of operations is, but I'm guessing their security is a lot like yours."

Yuri glares at Marvin. "What do you know about my security?"

"Nothing other than what I've seen walking in here and what my imagination conjures up. Marvin hasn't told me anything, and I'll never ask. A chain-link fence surrounds the complex, and I'm sure it has active sensors to warn of any tampering. If I were securing an area against my kind, I would have thermal cameras and ground vibration sensors throughout. No one would be able to get within a quarter mile without me knowing."

The mob boss nods. "It is sound theory."

"They have the head of our enclave, and I'm betting they put a bomb in his head like they did me and another of my people."

"The woman outside?"

"Yeah, that's her."

"Very pretty, but I'm guessing even more dangerous."

"You guess right. The biggest problem is that her, Marvin, and I need to get inside quietly, disable the bomb in Vincent's head, and get out, preferably undetected. The only way I can think of is dropping in by parachute, but Marvin doesn't skydive, and the risk of being seen is too high."

"So you need to be invited in." Yuri glances at the ceiling and scratches at the corner of his left eye. "Someone goes in and out. You must take their place."

"The only ones I know who leave are their hit teams. I don't see a way to infiltrate them that way."

"They must bring in some kind of supplies—food, toilet paper."

"Probably, but they could have months' worth of supplies stored up. Who knows when they will receive another delivery. Agent Snow, the guy in charge, said they were completely self-sufficient and off the grid. Not even their own department is aware of their operation."

"No such thing as self-sufficient. How do they get their power?"

"I heard some low-decibel industrial generators when they took me to the basement to install the bomb."

Yuri smiles. "That is our way in. A friend of mine was serving life sentence in a Kiev prison. Every two weeks, big fuel truck makes delivery. I make secret chamber in tanker. My guys go in, take my friend from the kitchen, and drive him out the front gates. No problem."

"We could do the same thing with the fuel deliveries for their generators. But even if we get an identical trailer, how are we going to swap it out with ours?"

"We take the truck. Is easy. My men take trucks all the time."

"The guards aren't going to let just anyone drive a truck into their compound, Yuri."

"Is no problem. I got guy who does incredible makeup with latex. Works for big movies. I once had to fly back to Georgia for business with the focking feds watching me. He make me look like Eastern Bloc Mrs. Doubtfire."

I nod. "I guess it's the best we've got. Let's just hope they don't get drawn into any conversations. We'll need your guys to drive the truck. I'm sure they have equipment to tell who's human and who's not."

Yuri grimaces. "This will cost more than favors. Big risk for my guys."

"How much?"

Yuri scribbles a number down on a piece of paper and slides it across the table. I take the paper and read the ridiculously long number printed on it.

"Big risk equals big money," Yuri explains.

"If they pay this, and they probably will, I'll need to raise my rates, because I've been lowballing them for years."

"That's why I hire you. You're good but cheap as shit. You

are like spetsnaz of vampire bodyguards."

"Thanks. So what do we do now?"

"I make phone calls. We need to find truck and get pictures of drivers to make masks. There are only a few diesel distributors around Philly. Black market fuel is good money. I know some guys."

"Thanks, Yuri. I'll take the plan and your bill to the enclave. I'm assuming the annoying buzzing in my pocket for the last fifteen minutes is them trying to call me. If we come out of this intact, they'll owe you big time."

"And one day I will collect big time."

Yuri's goons show us out the same way we came in. He's definitely put a lot of thought and work into protecting himself from a very specific threat, and he's done a hell of a job. Short of dropping a bomb and leveling the entire block, even the might of the entire enclave would find this a costly nut to crack. There's no way they could do it quietly, and our compulsive requirement for anonymity is as great a protection for Yuri as his concrete walls and massive weaponry.

"The enclave has been calling you," Lesile says the moment I drop into the passenger seat.

"I know. All the vibration was giving me a boner and making it difficult to have my meeting."

"Is your friend going to help us?"

"Yeah, he's got an idea to get us inside, but it's going to take a little time to get everything coordinated."

"I don't think the council is going to like waiting on anyone."

"Guess how many shits I give about what the council wants? I'll give you a hint, it's a number between zero and kiss my ass. Speaking of the council, there goes my phone and my erection again. I guess I shouldn't keep it in my front pocket."

Lesile slides a hand over my thigh. "I know how we can take care of that little problem."

"And it's gone. Thanks, slut." I return my attention to the phone call. "Malone."

"Where the hell have you been?" Harriet squawks.

"I've been pooling my resources and contracting help to get us into the feds' compound."

"You don't even know for certain where it is!"

"It's Pennhurst, right?"

"Yes, but you didn't know that, and now you have wasted precious time by going off on your own and ignoring my calls."

"I have been saving precious time by not sitting on my ass."

"This is an enclave operation, and you will do what I say when I say it! Is that clear?"

"Is this clear?" I press the end call button. "Three, two, one… Yello."

"You better not have hung up on me!"

"It's possible. Did it sound like this?"

End call.

"Hola."

"Do you think this is a game?"

"I'm having fun."

"Vincent has afforded you far more tolerance than I will ever allow. Now you listen to me…"

"No, you listen to me. Not having someone nag me is why I've never been married."

"You've never been married because you're an insufferable little shi-!"

End Call

Lesile asks, "Leonard, are you trying to get yourself killed?"

"I'm trying to get her to understand I'm no one's puppet, and if they want my help and cooperation they need to not dictate and order me about."

"You walk a dangerous line."

"I walk it, hop over it, and piss on the other side of it. I don't care. I'll live my life my way, or I won't live it at all. Aloha."

I hear Harriet take a deep breath before speaking. "Listen very carefully, Malone. We need you to come in so we can exchange information. We are looking forward to hearing what you have found out and your plans for extracting Vincent."

"You see how much more productive our conversations are when we use a little restraint and courtesy?"

She takes a long pause before answering. "Please come in. The entire council, along with representatives from the wolf pack, is waiting."

"I'm on my way."

"Thank you."

"No, thank you." The connection drops. "She hung up without saying goodbye. How rude. Oh well, to the bat cave!"

Lesile smiles, shakes her head, and puts the car into drive or whatever makes this thing go.

"If it's all the same to you, you can just drop me off at Leo's place, or anywhere close by is fine," Marvin pipes up from the back seat. "I'd rather not dangle my tasty flesh in front of a room full of...you people."

"What do you mean 'you people'?" I ask using my best Marvin impression.

"Don't even try, Leo. That's my thing, and you can't have it."

Lesile says, "You seem in a good mood considering everything that's happening."

"I always get giddy when I know I'm close to kicking teeth in and blowing some shit up."

Lesile shakes her head. "Boys..."

CHAPTER 15

Security around the tower is tighter than I have ever seen it. Sheriffs stand in force around the entrances and guide us into the private parking garage located beneath the building. A pair of vamps flanks the elevator and has to receive confirmation before allowing us to pass.

The guard punches the basement level button. It's been a long time since I visited the enclave chamber. Stepping out of the elevator and into the cathedral-like subterranean room makes me reminisce about my trial for killing the German enclave's ambassador. Just as it was then, the council sits upon a high dais like the Supreme Court justices posing for a photo op, only one seat is conspicuously vacant.

The room is needlessly large. The bulk of the east coast enclave is present yet they barely fill a hundred seats. Even the dozen representatives from the werewolf pack fail to make an appreciable dent in the chamber's maximum capacity. Of course, the room isn't designed to seat a huge audience, its purpose is to intimidate those within it. It does a good job.

"Lesile, Mr. Malone, thank you for heeding our summons," Harriet intones from on high.

Her voice echoes hollowly from the darkened seats upon the dais. I cover my derisive snort with a cough. Lesile's sidelong glance reminds me how stupid a gesture it was. Harriet's pause shows the failed attempt was not lost on her either.

The de facto enclave head continues. "Our people have confirmed that the federal task force is indeed holed up in the old Pennhurst complex, and we assume Vincent is still there."

"Yeah, I thought as much and have been working on a plan to infiltrate the place."

"It is my understanding you have been in contact with Yuri Poplonovich and enlisted his aid in our operation. Why have you shared our problem with a warm blood?"

"Because he has resources and experience we do not possess."

"Why would he help us?"

"Profit, of course, and future considerations he will call in later."

"Profit...What is his price?"

"Ten million dollars."

"That is ridiculous."

"That is a pittance."

"I refuse to be extorted by a weakling."

"So operation Fuck Vincent is back on?"

"Of course not!"

"Because it makes my job a lot easier and has a lot less risk."

"I am not suggesting that."

"Of course, there is the increased chance of them sending a data blast telling the entire American government about a subspecies of people who feed on the populace, unless you have multiple satellite jamming systems stored in a closet somewhere. Do you have satellite signal jamming devices stuffed away somewhere? Maybe in your ass? Go ahead and take a quick look around since that's where your collective heads are at most of the time anyway."

"Enough, Malone! You will conduct yourself in accordance with the rules of the forum!"

"This is a forum now? Because I thought it was a dictatorial tribunal the way you perch yourselves way up there above the rest of us common folk."

Harriet looks ready to explode, but she composes herself. "Everyone within the enclave has a voice. Convince us that Mr. Poplonovich is acting in good faith and not taking advantage of our desperate situation."

"The price has more to do with cementing a trusting business relationship between his people and ours than being about profit. He fears us."

"He damn well should."

"And that attitude is why you are going to pay him. He didn't ask to be let in on our little secret. It was one of yours who put it in a paper bag, dropped it on his doorstep, and lit it on fire. He has the knowledge and the technology to give us the best chance of pulling this off. I think that and the trust we will build through cooperation is well worth the cost. Most people in his situation would let us try on our own. If we succeed, he's no worse off than he was before. If we fail, what he views as his biggest threat takes a potentially fatal blow."

"Again I ask, why help us then?"

"Yuri is a businessman before all else. He is forward-thinking and sees potential in harvesting a cooperative relationship between his house and ours. He is risking the wrath of the federal government to help us, and we owe it to him to show some good faith. Ten million dollars' worth of it."

Heads begin bobbing and words of agreement echo through the chamber. The vampire community, especially the old ones like those on the council, hates having to work with humans. Knowing Yuri has capabilities they do not possess is akin to blasphemy.

Harriet confers with her fellow council leaders. "Very well, we will pay Mr. Poplonovich. Recovering Vincent and preventing this information from spreading beyond the current government operation is of paramount importance. If this helps reassure Mr. Poplonovich and creates a mutual understanding it is worth the expense."

"Yuri knows how to keep secrets. He is no more a fan of the government than we are when it comes to inner knowledge of our operations."

"Where do we stand now with our preparations, particularly in regards to Mr. Poplonovich?"

"Our best hope for sneaking into the compound is by hijacking the truck used to refuel their generators. Yuri proposes that we take the driver and crew, disguise his people as the crew, and use a trailer with a hidden compartment to sneak our team inside. Once inside, Lesile, Marvin, and I will make our way to the top level where they lock up the captured vampires. When we find Vincent, Marvin will change the frequency so no one can remotely detonate it. Once we secure Vincent, your team waiting outside the compound will turn on the signal jammers so no traffic can get out, then storm the place. After that, it's just a cleanup operation."

"Do you think a simple disguise will get his people past their security? I do not like relying on frail humans."

"Yuri says he has a guy who can create dead ringers. Because of the countermeasures I suspect Snow and his people to employ, we'll need Yuri's people to pose as the fuel truck crew. Snow knows how to identify vampires, and I'm sure some of these measures are passive types and in constant use, likely thermal imaging being primary amongst them. Since we cannot know what other measures are in place, it is best we not use our people."

"We are putting a lot of faith in Mr. Poplonovich and his people."

"No more than he is putting in us. Yuri is placing himself in a very dangerous position for no reason other than cementing a mutual tolerance of each other's existence."

"And ten million dollars and some favors," Harriet reminds me.

"That too."

Mason, the werewolves' pack leader asks me, "What would you have of my people?"

I have been thinking about the wolves' involvement from the get-go. No doubt they will provide some valuable shock troops, but if this operation goes south, I don't want to expose them to discovery as well. It was bad enough I had to involve Meat, but I needed him.

"I think it is best for you and your pack to stay behind the lines and pick off anyone trying to escape. Just in case Snow has another way of getting information out, I don't want to compromise your people as well."

Mason nods. "I understand, and we appreciate your consideration. It is a bit unexpected coming from you."

"What can I say? I have a vested interest now."

Mason's face twitches as if he just bit into a turd-filled éclair.

Obviously, Kat's and my relationship does not sit well with the pack. As if I give two shits.

"Lesile Savard," Harriet cuts in, "your conduct has been the topic of numerous discussions within the council. You toe a very fine line, but if you acquit yourself well during this operation, we will pardon your past indiscretions. Be warned, this does not give you license to continue acting recklessly."

Lesile's condescending smile indicates she cares about the opinions and goodwill of the council about as much as I do. It's an odd feeling realizing we are more similar than different. Maybe that's why I hate her so damn much.

"If there is no further business, this council is adjourned. We will reconvene once we hear back from Mr. Poplonovich regarding the acquisition of the truck and crew."

I shake my head at her continued formality. Even when everything is a clusterfuck, she and the rest of the old blood still can't pry the sticks out of their asses. It's doubtful, but I hope her and the other council leaders put themselves on the front line. When bullets start flying and explosions are rocking your bones, rules and protocols get thrown out the window. You learn to be flexible real fast or become real dead.

Lesile and I take that as our cue to leave. I stare out of the car window as we cross over the Brooklyn Bridge. Looking out at the lights of the city, I can't help but think about what a fiasco this all is. I don't think I realized how close to Armageddon we really are. If we fail to prevent the information of our existence from spreading beyond Snow's organization, it's Judgment Day for us. Snow might be willing and able to keep our secret for a year or two, but it will become common knowledge soon enough, especially if they succeed in creating their super soldiers.

This has to go down perfectly, or we're screwed. The entire world will create task forces to eradicate our kind. For a minute, I start to wonder if I care. I've spent so long hating my existence I can't help but think that maybe it wouldn't be so bad if that happened. Then I think of Kat and even Meat and his people. The humans wouldn't stop with us. Someone would find out about the werewolves, in their hunt for vampires. Kat deserves better than that. She is a good person and not a parasite.

But we're not parasites either, not all of us. We made some of the greatest achievements in human history. Our long lives allow us to learn far more and develop insights well beyond those of most mortals. Sure, there are assholes like Francis and greedy dipshits like Percy who come along and fuck it up for the rest of us on occasion, but are we any worse than the warm bloods? We don't exactly corner the market on killing people, and our motivation is a damn sight better than most murderers.

Maybe I've been too hard on myself and my kind. Hell, I like me, and I like what I do despite my bitching about it all the time. I'm not sure I would have admitted that before meeting Katherine. Whatever the reason, I'm not going out without a fight.

CHAPTER 16

Castillo smiled as she pushed the button that released the chemicals into Malone's body until a voice woke her from her dream. Her hand covered her right eye as it cradled her head and acted as a kickstand to keep it from dropping onto the desk. The detective's left eye focused on the open military record belonging to someone who looked an awful lot like Malone, only it was from 1972, so it couldn't possibly be him unless he was the youngest-looking senior citizen on the planet.

"Castillo, some kid wants to talk to you. You got a minute?" a detective asked.

She lifted her head up and blinked away the fog. "Sure, send him back. Thanks, Callahan."

"It's late even for you. Why don't you kick off and call it a night?"

"Yeah, I will, right after this."

Callahan gave her a concerned look before stepping out. He returned escorting a Latino kid, who looked to be around seventeen, to her desk. Both of his eyes were blackened, and the entire left side of his face was a massive bruise. Castillo was no doctor, but she suspected there were some fractures as well. The kid occupied the chair next to her desk. He looked around nervously, desperate to be anywhere else than here. The tattoo of a crown on his neck was new and marked him as a member of the Latin Kings. Something must be pretty bad for him to walk willingly into the police station.

"What's your name?"

The kid flinched at the sound of Castillo's voice. "R-Rafael."

"What brings you here?" Rafael looked around the room

again and struggled with what to say. "Look, I can't help if you don't tell me what's wrong."

He swallowed and nodded. "Me and some of my homies were hanging out at Brooklyn Bridge Park. We got into it with this guy. He hit me in the face and I blacked out. I've never been hit so hard in my life. It felt like he used a baseball bat, but it was just his fist."

"What caused the fight?"

The kid looked down at his shoes but did not talk.

"What did the guy look like?"

"He was just a gringo in a black coat. He acted like he was drunk, but I think he was faking." He looked at Castillo intently. "I swear he wanted us to do something! He baited us into the park so he could kill Miguel!"

"He killed Miguel?"

Rafael shook his head. "I don't know. He knocked me out, and when I came to, Miguel was gone. I can't find him. No one can find him."

"Rafael, I need you to be a hundred percent honest with me. I need you to tell me exactly what happened."

He shook his head again. "I can't. I shouldn't even be here, but I'm afraid he's going to come back for me too. He wasn't human."

"What was he?"

Rafael began to tremble and he whispered, "*El Diablo.* I've sinned, and he's coming for my soul. He's coming for all of us!"

Castillo pulled out a picture of Malone from her desk. "Is this the man?"

Rafael nearly fell out of his chair, hugged his arms around his chest, and nodded. "That's The Devil, and he's in New York."

"Rafael, I want you to tell me exactly what happened. Whatever you say is just between us, I promise."

"You believe me?"

"I do. Tell me what happened. Why do you think he is The Devil?"

"Me and some of the gang were just chilling at the park. This guy, we thought it was just a guy, staggers past us. Me, Miguel, and Julio follow him. We're going to roll him for his wallet. It's supposed to be my final initiation. We follow him off the path and jump him. We start beating him, and he goes down like he's supposed to. Julio and Miguel, they start stabbing him. I'm freaked out. We were just supposed to roll him. Suddenly, the guy jumps up like it's nothing. Julio and Miguel must have stabbed him like ten times and he doesn't care. He hits me, and I go down. When I wake up, Julio is lying in the grass with me, but Miguel is gone. Everyone looked for him, but he's gone. *El Diablo* took him to hell."

"Why did you come to me?"

"I didn't know where else to go. A couple of the guys, they know you. They said you were cool if you played straight with you. I don't know what else to do."

"If you really think it's The Devil, I suggest you get out of your gang and start going to church."

Rafael's head bobbed up and down. "I will!"

"Go home. Get out of the gang, get a job, get that thing removed from your neck, and go to church if you want to save yourself."

"I will, I swear. Can you do anything for Miguel?"

"I'm going to try."

Castillo was going to have to make a stop before she went home. She refused to believe Malone was The Devil or any other kind of immortal monster, but there were things she had seen that made it hard for her to maintain her belief. She did know he was a threat to the city, and she was going to stop him whatever the cost.

CHAPTER 17

"Do you have an outlet outside?" Lesile asks as she parks the car.

"What for?"

"I need to plug in my car."

"Are you serious, like a toaster?"

"It can't go forever without refueling, just like a regular car."

I point past the side of the building. "Around the corner in the back near the stairs. Just put a condom on it. I don't want your gay car to give my house AIDS. God only knows how many strange sockets it's plugged into."

Lesile rolls her eyes and moves the car around as I enter my loft. Marvin is in the corner, lit up by his computer screen. The shotgun is leaning against the table, and he flinches toward it when I come in.

"Good news, Leo. Yuri's people have been studying the security tapes of the fuel suppliers in the area, and he thinks they have their guys. A truck comes every two weeks and takes on a load of diesel. It's always the same two people. Yuri looked into their paperwork and says it's bullshit. He's got his Hollywood guy using the images to make the masks."

"I better call him." I punch in Yuri's number. "Yuri, Marvin tells me you're already working on the truck thing. Thanks. The council agreed to your terms by the way."

"I knew they would, so I got my people on it right away. You need to get to Philadelphia. These guys are smart, and they vary schedule by a couple of days. Could come maybe three days or could come tomorrow. Very small window to take truck, switch trailer, and put you inside."

"I'll pass it on to the council and get down there." Yuri gives me the address, and I call Harriet. "Yuri's found our truck, and we need to get on station ASAP. Get your strike team in place, and have whoever is coordinating the attack meet us at the fuel distributor. Me, Marvin and Lesile will set up camp there so we're ready to deploy in an instant."

"Excellent work. You are quite capable when you put your mind to it. I'm starting to understand why Vincent allows you so much leeway."

"My taut Italian buns?"

Harriet sighs and hangs up. No one appreciates my baser attributes. Someone starts banging on my door with what I assume is a brick. Kat's knocking is more delicate, so that narrows down the list of likely visitors to a determined Jehovah's Witness or someone even less welcome.

I swing the heavy door open. "Speak of the devil and his girlfriend shows up."

"Shut it, Malone," Castillo snaps.

"I've been out of town for a while, so unless you're here with a welcome home gift, I'm a little busy."

"Out of town where?"

"A quaint little beach resort on the coast of none of your fucking business. I'm sure you've heard of it."

"How long were you gone?"

"Just long enough to miss your sirenesque voice."

"How long have you been back?"

"Long enough to remember it was an ear-piercing police siren."

"Real cute, Malone."

"Thank you, I was just remarking on how no one appreciates my roguish good looks." I turn and flex my butt cheeks at her. "What do you want? I really am in a hurry."

"There were two suspected murders in the last two nights."

"I'm sure there was more than that. I think Chicago alone likes to rack up at least a dozen a day."

"Where were you last night?"

"Right here."

"Can anyone corroborate your alibi?"

"Why do I need an alibi?"

"I'm just checking up on some reports."

"I can," Marvin says and hastens across the room.

"Who are you?"

"I'm Leo's technical guy. We've been here the past couple days working on his alarm system and a website for his company." He hands Castillo a business card. "I do all kinds of freelance computer and network service. If your department ever needs a computer guy, I'm your man."

Castillo gives Marvin a dubious look and takes the card as if it might be infected with Ebola. "Thanks, I'll keep it in mind. Can anyone else place you here?"

"I was also here," Lesile says.

Castillo flinches at the voice behind her but does an admirable job of not screaming and pulling her piece. "Who the fuck are you?"

Lesile edges past the detective and squeezes through the door. "She's a client."

"What kind of client?"

"My husband is a cheating sonofabitch, and I hired Mr. Malone to catch him in the act."

"Cheating spouses? That seems a bit pedestrian for you, Malone."

I shrug. "I got bills to pay."

"You keep weird hours, Malone."

"Yeah, and you're cutting into them. Now, do you have anything specific you want to ask, or are you just here to check up on my itinerary?"

"Someone called in a disturbance at Prospect Park two nights ago. We found tire tracks, a discarded shoe, and blood but no body."

"I don't own a car, so why are you bugging me about it?"

"The people we questioned claim they saw what they thought was a police unit come in and clean up the scene."

"It sounds like you should be calling your department instead of sniffing around here."

"I did, but no one covered a hit and run in the area, and

the cleanup was completed before any units could respond. Sound familiar?"

"Should it?"

Her eyes lock onto my face in search of the subtlest clue that I'm fucking with her. I don't give her one, but we both know what she's referring to.

"Tonight, a kid came in beat to shit. He says one guy took out all three of them."

"It sounds like they picked the wrong guy to fuck with."

"His buddy is gone, and he thinks this guy, who did a good job of matching your description, killed him."

"You think I could take out three thugs all by myself?"

Castillo leans in. "I remember what you did in that cell. I don't know what you're capable of, but I know what I saw."

"Let's suppose I did get jumped by three hooligans and stomped their heads in. Why do you care? Three guys try to mug someone in the park. Sounds like they got what they deserved."

"I didn't say anything about a mugging, and I sure as hell didn't mention it was in a park."

"I'm a detective, I deduced. One man isn't going to take on three criminals, so obviously they initiated the attack. Most nighttime muggings take place in a park, so I naturally assumed that's where it happened. Besides, you seem to have a fixation on park-related violence. Maybe I got confused."

"Bullshit."

"Regardless, I have an alibi. I also have a dirty, cheating husband to find, so unless you have a warrant, or better, probable cause to take me in, you're trespassing."

Castillo's posture says she wants nothing more than to slam me to the ground, slap cuffs on me, and bring me in, but she takes a step back out of the doorway.

"I'm watching you, Malone. I will bring you in and, when I do, I'll have enough evidence to put you away for life, and you won't weasel your way out of it."

"You know, when you took your oath to protect and defend, they meant the citizens of New York not bad clothes and a shitty haircut." I slam the door in her face before she can reply. "Where's your car?"

"I hid it inside one of the buildings around back. It is nice having a silent vehicle sometimes."

"I don't think Francis would agree with you. Marvin, let's get you suited up. Lesile, how long will it take to charge up your Barbie dream car enough to get us to Philly?"

"It wasn't drained, but at least four hours."

"Shit, I was hoping to leave sooner than that."

"I can take it back to my hotel. They have a rapid charger in the parking garage. We can leave for Philadelphia in an hour."

"All right, Marvin and I will meet you there. Look around before you leave. I wouldn't put it past Castillo to stake me out."

Marvin makes a stabbing motion at my heart. "Ha, stake. Get it? Because you're a vampire."

"Shut up, Marvin."

"Someone got up on the wrong side of the coffin."

I restrain my urge to strangle Marvin and open my armory. This is going to be close-quarter combat within a confined area, so I pick out a pair of Brügger & Thomet TP9 and an MP5, all suppressed to the max. I slip the weapons, half a dozen spare magazines for each one, and a few concussion grenades into a duffle bag and return to my loft.

"Marvin, what kind of equipment are you going to need once we're inside?"

"I gave Yuri a list. He said he'll have it waiting for us in Philly." He nods toward the bag in my hand. "Is that our gear?"

"Yeah."

Marvin abandons his nerd corner and strides across the room. "Let me check this out."

I slap his grasping hands away. "They're not toys. I'll issue you your weapon when we're ready to deploy, not before."

"Yes sir. Captain Killjoy."

"Come here, I do have something you can wear now."

I cross to the large antique wardrobe where I keep my jackets and pretty much my entire mono-stylistic apparel. I hand Marvin a ballistic vest and pull out one of my Miguel Caballero trench coats. Marvin slips the vest over his head, cinches down the Velcro straps, and shrugs on the coat.

"Damn, this stuff is heavy."

"I have some black cotton tees if you prefer to go in light."

"No and hell no. Not only am I partial to not getting shot, I am totally rocking the coat look. Tell me I don't look like a thinner, younger, smarter, better-looking Morpheus."

"You need to take this seriously, Marvin. This is not a game or a movie. This is real."

"What is real? How do you define 'real'? If you're talking about what you can feel, what you can smell, what you can taste and see, then 'real' is simply electrical signals interpreted by your brain," Marvin quotes.

I slap him on the side of the head. "Was that real?"

Marvin rubs his stinging cranium. "Yeah, a real dick move. Hey, what if someone shoots me in my head?"

"I suggest you keep your head down and out of the path of bullets."

"Oh, that's great advice. I might be a genius, but that is truly brilliant and insightful. I never would have considered that as part of my overall strategy."

"Your strategy is to do exactly what I say. You got it?"

I grab Marvin's wrist before he can bring his hand up to salute. "Yeah, I got it," he says and pulls his arm from my grip.

The cab takes almost half an hour to reach my place after I make the call. The only reason I can get one here at all is due to my frequent customer status, otherwise no cabby with an ounce of sense would come down my dark streets for a fare. This isn't exactly the West Village.

I continually check our six, but I don't spot a tail. Castillo seemed to be a bit more reserved than usual, and Angel wasn't with her. I think maybe Will convinced her superiors to get her off my back before he sued them into Third World poverty.

We draw some looks from the few people populating Lesile's opulent hotel lobby. Dressed in black trench coats and carrying a bag full of automatic weapons and explosives, I can't help but think about the firefight in *The Matrix* thanks to Marvin's constant movie references.

"Don't say a damn word."

Marvin looks at me and grins. "You were thinking it, weren't you? Yeah, you know you were. Epic!"

I struggle to endure the elevator ride to Lesile's suite while Marvin chatters away as if he's reading the movie's screenplay to me. Only the thought of soon getting to shoot people I currently find more deserving to die keeps me from strangling him. That and the fact I need him to get the job done.

Lesile answers the door in a black, form-fitting jumpsuit.

I shove the vest into her arms. "I wasn't sure if you had your own vest, so I brought you one."

"How thoughtful of you. Bulletproof vests are not part of my regular wardrobe."

"Huh, they are mine."

"Okay," Marvin interjects, "I know I'm not the only one who notices we look exactly like Morpheus, Neo, and Trinity."

"Jesus Christ, Marvin, would you get off that goddam movie?"

"It's not my fault we got a white guy and a black guy in black coats, a hot chick in a tight outfit looking all catwomanish, a bag full of machine guns, and we're on our way to storm a government building full of secret agents! I mean come on! Tell me the guy's name isn't Agent Smith."

"It's not. It's Snow."

"Still starts with an S. Does he call you 'Mr. Malone'?" Marvin asks in a monotone voice.

"No...he uses a little more inflection."

"How much more?"

"Not much."

"See."

"Shut up, Marvin."

"You know what, I'm going to start translating 'shut up, Marvin' as: You're right, Marvin. You are as insightful as you are smart and good-looking, and I am only mad because your genius reminds me how mean and dumb I am."

"Shut up, Marvin!"

"Thank you."

I shove Marvin toward the door. "Get in the goddam car."

Lesile is grinning at me and chuckling under her breath as we speed out of the parking garage.

"What?" I demand.

"I see why you like him so much."

"What the hell are you talking about?"

"I understand why you are friends with Marvin."

"We're not friends, we're occasional work associates, and there's only one reason for that: lack of options."

"Leonard, it is okay to like someone and for someone to like you."

Marvin leans forward and sticks his head between the seat backs. "Yeah, you don't fool me with all your growling and name-calling. You know you like me. Marvin and Leo sitting in a tree...you know what, I'm going to go ahead and stop, because this is taking an unhealthy turn."

"You're entire life has been a series of unhealthy turns."

"It only gets unhealthy when I'm around you! I never had to shoot anyone in the face with a shotgun because he was about to cut my employer's head off when I worked at the Apple Genius Bar. I've been installing computers, surveillance equipment, and security systems in the Russian mafia's headquarters for the past nine months, and I ain't so much as gotten a paper cut. I've been working with you for like three days, and I've pulled you out of the ocean after a plane crash, disarmed a bomb in a vampire's head, and been a witness to you running over some dude just before decapitating him. As if that weren't enough, now I'm on my way to infiltrate the government's anti-terrorist organization, and I cannot figure out for the life of me how the hell I came to be doing all this!"

"Shut up, Marvin."

"Don't try to flatter me. I'm not in the mood!"

"Marvin, take a deep breath. Take a few deep breaths."

Marvin presses himself back against his seat and breathes deeply. "I should have listened to my grandmother."

"She told you to stay in college?"

"No, she told me 'don't ever trust whitey.' I'm sorry, mama Beatie, I didn't listen, and now your baby's gonna die!"

"Calm down, Marvin! If all goes according to plan, we'll get in, you'll kill the security systems and the bomb in Vincent's head, and we'll be out without a shot fired."

"And if it don't go according to plan?"

"Then *The Matrix* just got real," I reply.

"Don't try using my fantasies to make me feel better about this!"

"Doesn't it?"

Marvin crosses his arms and sulks. "Yeah, a little."

"Listen, I've done this sort of thing before, and I'm pretty damn good at it. My primary focus, other than stopping the knowledge of our existence getting out, is keeping you alive. I will literally be between you and the bullets."

Marvin leans forward again, sticks his head between the seats, and grins at me. "You really do like me."

"I have a vested interest in keeping you alive. Don't read into it."

"But you would take a bullet for me."

"Only because bullets are rarely lethal for my kind."

"Yeah! Tell me about this whole vampire thing. Show me your fangs!"

"I don't have fangs."

"What about all that other shit? Can you turn into a bat or climb walls like a spider? What about mirrors, can you see yourself in them?"

"No, I can't climb walls, and why the hell would I want to turn into a bat even if I could? You're supposed to be something of a scientist, so how could a mirror not reflect my image?"

"Oh, yeah, that is kind of dumb."

"Most of what you see in movies is dumb."

"So no stake through the heart either, huh?"

"Not unless you really want to piss me off."

"So you're just strong, fast, and mean. Kinda like a steroid user."

"Pretty much."

I'm hoping Marvin is out of inane questions, but I should have known better. He continues prattling on for most of the drive, the majority of his pestering inquiries I answer with a grunt or halfhearted backhand. He takes refuge behind my seat but still rambles on until we reach the fuel depot.

We drive through the open chain-link gates and creep into the yard. A massive warehouse and office building abuts the naval yard to our left. We follow the roadway past it, a large parking lot, and a few smaller buildings until we navigate to the far corner of the depot. Trucks of various sizes are parked in an area to our right. To the left and just ahead are massive tanks holding what I presume are various forms of petroleum products.

A man in a yellow hard hat waves us over. We pull up next to a trailer like those often found on construction sites. He leans against my open window ledge and sticks his head in the car.

"You Malone?"

"Yeah."

"Yuri told us to expect you and the kid." He juts his chin at Lesile. "Who's she?"

"She's part of my team."

"You can park behind that building there then meet us in the trailer."

Lesile parks the car behind a nearby structure. I grab the weapons bag, and we make our way to the trailer. With the three of us adding to the four people already inside, it is a bit cramped. The man who told us where to park stands just inside the doorway. Two more men are playing cards at a small table, and a fourth is lounging on a couch at the far end.

"I'm Lenny, that's Rick and Dimitri," he says as soon as we enter.

I look to the skinny man on the couch. "And that is…?"

"Fucking annoying."

The guy slinks off the couch with the supple grace of a ferret, sashays across the room, and tilts a wrist in front of my face. "I'm Blaine, Yuri's transformation genius, and I wouldn't be so fucking annoying if you people would have brought me the right fucking water," he says in a lisping, lilting voice.

"What's wrong with the water?" I ask, deliberately ignoring his hand.

"I told them I only drink Veen straight from Finland when I'm on set, and they brought me fucking Aquafina from like Costco or some shit. I may as well drink out of the fucking toilet."

"It can be arranged," Lenny growls. Blaine sucks his teeth

and returns to his couch. "Anyway, these guys are due to show up in the next few days. They don't keep a regular schedule, but it never varies more than about forty-eight hours. Tactically, it's a good idea, but it made them stand out. It's one of the things that drew our attention."

"And you're sure these are our feds? I would really hate to get it wrong."

"No doubt these are our guys. They're less convincing as truck drivers than Twinkle Toes over there."

Blaine flips Lenny a lazy, swooping finger from the couch.

"Leo, Yuri's supposed to have my gear here. I'd like to check it out and get it prepped," Marvin says.

Lenny points to the other end of the room. "Yeah, it's over there behind the desk. Have at it."

Marvin starts popping open military-style plastic cases and setting the contents on the table. I don't know what a lot of the stuff is, but I recognize the signal analyzer he used before. He flips open the lid of a laptop that looks like it could take a bullet and live, sticks a thumb drive into a port, and begins tapping on the keys.

I tell Lenny, "We're going to need to block all forms of cellular, satellite, and radio communications once this kicks off."

"That broad who seems to be running the show talked to Yuri last night. He furnished her group with some signal scramblers. We got guys ready to take out all the cell towers as soon as you give us the word."

"It sounds like you have all the bases covered."

"Yuri likes to be thorough."

"Who's going to be driving the truck?"

"Rick and Dimitri. They look the closest like the feds. They've been studying the tapes and have been practicing their voices. They won't fool someone who knows them well, but they're getting pretty good."

"Let's hope it's good enough."

Marvin has plenty to occupy his time. I on the other hand have little recourse but to sit and listen to Blaine's incessant complaining. It takes me less than half an hour before I begin to fantasize about killing him, which I discuss with Lenny and company and learn that I now hold the record for tolerance, as their best only managed twenty-two minutes. Only the knowledge that we need him, and Yuri seems to want him around, keeps us from snapping his scrawny neck.

Marvin never seems to run out of things to do on his computer. I wish I were so fortunate. I manage to sneak out of the trailer once and take a stroll around the depot. There's a navy ship moored at the dock, which is interesting for about five minutes. My escape goes unnoticed for close to fifteen minutes before Lenny politely tells me to get my ass back inside before I blow our cover. There's little fear of that. He says they never come before nightfall, but I guess I should be more careful.

I slip into one of my trances and manage to block out Blaine and his marathon viewing of the most idiotic reality shows ever aired. Even if I wanted to talk to Lesile, which I most assuredly do not, she mentally checked out shortly after we got here and hasn't moved since.

Lenny wakes us both up by poking us with a broom handle. I guess he doesn't want to be too close if we are the sort of people who wake up swinging. Smart man. It's dark out, but a pair of headlights shines through the trailer window between the slats of the venetian blinds.

Lenny nods to Dimitri. "Ready?"

"Let's do it."

The two mobsters exit the trailer and approach the truck. I peer between the blinds and watch the scene unfold. The driver and passenger are standing in front of the truck. They are attentive but not on alert.

Lenny raises a hand. "Hey there, is it time to top off again?"

"Yeah," the driver responds, "late like usual. I don't know why the day shift can't do it and always leaves it for the night crew to do."

"Ain't that always the way."

"Do you need me to pull closer to the tanks?"

"Naw, you're fine where you're at."

Rick steps out from behind the trailer, closes to within fifteen feet of the passenger, and puts a bullet in the back of his head. The report from the silenced .22 automatic is a barely audible pop from where I'm standing. The driver reacts instantly, spinning and drawing his weapon before his partner hits the ground. He doesn't get a chance to fire. Lenny pulls his own silenced pistol from inside his coat and puts one behind the driver's right ear.

Lenny grabs the driver beneath his arms and drags him to the trailer while Dimitri and Rick scoop up the passenger. They bring the two dead men into the trailer, lay them out on the floor, and begin stripping them. While Dimitri and Rick swap clothes with the feds, Blaine opens a suitcase containing liquid latex, glue, and a veritable Ralph Lauren mobile warehouse of makeup supplies. Lenny darts back out the door, and I hear the truck fire up.

"Okay, so did you want me to recreate the huge, gaping hole in this one's forehead or no?" Blaine asks. "Seriously, could you be more disgusting?"

"Just do your job," Dimitri snaps.

Blaine affixes the latex masks he created from the videos to the two mobsters and uses putty and bits of plastic to change the shape of their faces. He paints over them with a liquid that dries with a texture similar to skin. He then uses his vast assortment of powders and creams to match the dead men's coloring and paints in additional contours and creases. I don't give compliments easy, but Blaine is without a doubt a true artist. When he finishes, I bet their own mothers wouldn't know it's not them, at least in the dark.

Lenny reappears just as Blaine is putting on the final touches. "I got the trailer hooked up. Is everyone ready?"

"Ready as we're gonna be," I answer.

Marvin's complexion goes from Wesley Snipes to Tiger Woods, and he looks near to throwing up. His hands shake and his breathing is near hyperventilating as he closes up the cases containing his various electronics.

"Marvin, are you going to be okay?" I ask.

"Why shouldn't I be? There's two half-naked dead guys just lying on the floor, and I'm about to embark on a job where there's bound to be a whole lot more dead guys, and these ones have guns and want to kill me. Naw, I'm fucking great. I'm a little confused at how all this came about, but I'm doing super."

"You're doing the right thing. You are on the right side, and I will make sure nothing happens to you."

"These guys got you once before. How you gonna keep me safe when you can't protect your damn self?"

"They got the jump on me. This time, we have the jump on them."

Marvin lugs his case toward the door. "You just better be ready to jump your ass in front of any bullets coming my way, because I will come back and haunt you."

I look to Lesile, but she is unwilling to come to my aid. Thankfully, Marvin lets it drop. Lenny is standing next to the truck and waves us to the trailer.

"Lenny, this isn't the same trailer. It doesn't look anything like the other one."

"Like Yuri says, 'is no problem,'" Lenny says using his best Yuri impression. "We'll tell them the other trailer had some mechanical problems. They'll check it out and wave you through."

"I hope you're right."

"We all do. If this goes tits up, the feds are going to come down hard on all of us. Yuri is betting it all on black, so we want this to go smooth."

"How do we get in this thing?"

Lenny hunkers down and waddles under the trailer near the front. He pushes against the bottom and a hatch opens up to the inside.

"The seam is almost invisible, and the hatch locks from inside. It's a tight fit, but you won't be in there long. The rest of the trailer is filled with fuel, so even if the feds inspect it, they'll find what they're looking for. Like most fuel tanks, it's double-walled, but the space between is packed with a couple hundred pounds of explosives. Dimitri has a remote, but it also has a secondary timer in case something goes wrong. You don't have a huge window, so don't take too long getting your guy out. You don't want to be inside when this thing goes off."

"I don't want to be inside at all," Marvin mumbles.

"Got it."

"Rick or Dimitri will rap on the side like this," Lenny knocks on the metal tank, "when it's clear to come out. They'll stay by the truck as long as they can, but if the shit hits the fan, it's everyone for himself. Get out however you can."

"Understood. We best get going. We don't want to make the feds any more suspicious than we already have."

Marvin and Lesile climb into the belly of the aluminum beast before me. Lenny wasn't kidding about the tight confines, but it's not intolerable as long as Marvin doesn't start talking. I'm hit with my first real feelings of anxiety when the truck begins to rumble down the road. This isn't the first time I've thrown myself in the middle of a hornet's nest, but it's the first time failure will result in a catastrophe that reaches beyond me. One of the reasons I prefer to stick to myself is I don't like being responsible for someone else if I fuck up. Man, when responsibility comes calling, it brings the whole damn family with it.

CHAPTER 18

The truck ride lasts less than an hour, but I can tell everyone is counting the seconds. Marvin's fear is evident on his face, in his posture, and seeping from every pore in his body. Lesile is harder to read. She remains impassive and silent. She is stiff but not indifferent or aloof. The truck slows to a stop with the hiss of air brakes. I put a finger to my lips and press an ear to the tanker wall.

"Easy, guys," I hear Rick say from the driver's seat.

"Frank, Mark, you're running late."

I hear several footsteps approach the trailer from both sides. I'm assuming a small tactical squad, hidden off the road, broke cover when we pulled up and is now surrounding us.

"Why are you in a different truck?" the man at the gate asks.

"It's the same truck, just a different trailer. The brakes took a shit on the other one, so the guys at the depot set us up with this one. It was either that or leave it there and come back in a couple of days once they get it fixed, and you know Snow doesn't like us making extra trips or stretching our fuel supply thin."

"Yeah, are you feeling all right? You sound a bit hoarse."

"I think I'm coming down with the crud, and I'm not the only one. Too many people in a place with shitty ventilation, I guess. It won't be long before we're all seeing the doc, assuming she's capable of more than Dr. Frankenstein-type experiments."

The man at the gate chuckles. "Yeah, she'd probably cure your cold by injecting you with polio or something. Stand fast a minute. We need to check out the truck."

"Knock yourselves out."

I hear movement all around the vehicle. A scraping sound

just beneath us is likely an under vehicle search mirror. Someone climbs up the back ladder and is opening the manholes on the top of the tanker. It's a good thing these guys aren't petroleum experts or they would know the difference between diesel and jet fuel. The hatches clang shut, and the guard climbs down to the ground.

"It's clear."

The truck rolls on at a sedate pace until stopping and backing up. The trailer tilts downward as we descend the ramp leading beneath the building. The droning of an industrial generator thrums through the double walls of the trailer. The truck stops and I hear Rick and Dimitri get out. A full minute passes before one of them raps out the code against the tank.

"Go straight out to the other side of me," Rick says as I drop through the hatch.

Lesile comes out next followed by Marvin. We take up a position hunkered next to the side of the cab where Dimitri is standing.

"There are two cameras I can see. If you follow the wall and go behind the generator, you can get to the one covering the stairs leading up," Dimitri says.

I ask, "Marvin, can you take care of the camera?"

"Probably. If it's connected to their computer network, I can probably take care of all of them from here."

"That would be extremely useful."

"That's me, extremely useful."

"Don't screw up, or you'll be extremely dead."

"What did we say about creating a hostile work environment? It is not conducive to utilizing my full genius."

"Marvin, just do your best," Lesile says. "Leonard, shut up."

"Yeah, Leonard."

I grab Marvin by a strap on his tactical vest and pull him close. "Call me Leonard again and I will burn us all here and now."

"I'm sorry; I didn't know that was one of your buttons. You have so damn many," he mutters.

"Just keep your mouth shut and focus, if it is at all possible for you."

"Sorry, I get shitty when I'm scared, and I'm scared as hell right now."

"I get it. Just focus."

"I'm focused…and a little hungry. Can we stop for pizza on the way home?"

"Marvin, that is not being focused."

"It's easier to focus on a full stomach."

"And impossible when you're dead, which you are going to be if you don't shut up and move."

Dimitri cuts in, "You two want to finish your little lovers' quarrel some other time?"

I feel chagrined enough to keep my mouth shut and move against the wall. Lesile pushes Marvin ahead of her and keeps him sandwiched between us. I spot the camera in the far corner of the room catty-corner from the stairwell doorway. Dimitri was right, we can avoid its field of view if we stick to the wall and sneak behind the generator.

We sidle along the wall, watchful for both cameras' panning, and time our movements accordingly. The second camera pans away from our hiding spot behind the generator, and we move beneath the stairwell camera. Marvin pulls a camera out of his pack and peels the paper off the sticker backing it.

"Leo, I need you to lift me up on your shoulders."

I hunker down, and Marvin throws his legs over my shoulders. He sticks his camera to the underside of the one in place.

"Lesile, hand me my laptop."

Lesile hands him his computer, and he props it on my head.

"My head is not a table, Marvin."

"This should only take a minute. I just need to spoof their MAC address and record a full pan so I can play back the loop." Marvin waits for the camera to complete its rotation. "Got it." He disconnects the cable from the feds' camera and plugs it into his. "Okay, you can put me down."

"Didn't they see the camera lose signal when you unplugged it?"

"Yeah, but only for a few seconds while I pull an IP address from their DHCP server."

"Huh?"

"Nothing, I got it. Sweet, they have their cameras running on the internal network instead of a closed circuit."

"What does that mean?"

"It means I can gain access to their computers and all the cameras attached to the network. I should be able to record a snippet from all the cameras and play it back instead of having a live feed."

"Can you tell if they have outside internet access?"

"It will take me a minute to get access to everything, but since I'm inside the firewall, it shouldn't take long."

Marvin starts plucking away at the keys, and all Lesile and I can do is stand and wait.

"I'm in. The WAN port on their router is shut off, but that doesn't mean there's nothing on the other side of it. It's possible they could turn it on and gain access to the outside world."

"Can you make it so they can't turn it on?"

Marvin gives me an annoyed look. "Leo...come on."

"Sorry I asked."

"You should be. I left a nice little package that will crash the entire system the instant someone activates the port. I also set a trigger event to the alarm system, so if the alarms go off it will activate my data nuke."

"Good work. Now we just have to find Vincent and get him out before we kick the anthill."

Lesile says, "Vincent should be on the top floor in one of the secure rooms. We can take the stairwell all the way up, but the top floor is locked behind a security door."

"Great. Don't these people understand the importance of following building codes and fire safety?"

It's a good thing Marvin was able to take command of the cameras from the sublevel, because we would never have made it past the first floor landing without the stairwell cam picking us up. It never panned away, and we could not have disabled it without them seeing us.

The sound of our footsteps and Marvin's breathing echoes off the stairwell walls. The noise and our inability to see beyond half a flight of stairs make this the most dangerous section of our infiltration. If we come upon anyone in the stairwell, we may not be able to neutralize them before they sound the alarm. Marvin's access to the security monitors would have come in handy, but he lost the wireless signal to his camera the moment we entered the stairwell.

Keeping our backs against the wall and our weapons trained on the stairs above us, we move our way to the top floor. Luck is with us, and we don't encounter any sentries or someone sneaking into the stairwell for a quick smoke.

I try the door at the top of the stairs and find it locked just as Lesile says, "Marvin, you have any tools in your kit?"

He rifles through his pack and hands me a toolkit. I use the screwdriver to pop the cover plate off and gain access to the inner workings. Once I remove a few hex screws, I have the entire assembly in my hands within seconds. After extracting the bolt, I crack the door open just far enough to peer through with one eye.

"There are two men in the hallway. One is just beyond this door, and the other is maybe fifty feet farther down. I think he's guarding Vincent. I should be able to put them both down before they sound the alarm."

"Let me. They know my face and will be slower to react," Lesile says.

I nod and Lesile strips out of most of her tactical gear. She slips a silenced Walther PPK into the back of her waistband and steps into the hall. I keep the door open a crack and peek through. Both men jump and bring up their guns. Lesile stops and raises her hands chest-high.

"Easy, boys, it's just me."

They lower their guns to their waists. "We thought you were killed in the plane crash," the one nearest Lesile says.

"Almost. I was trapped in the wreckage for days. It's a good thing too since Snow told me he had pushed the button to my implant to make sure."

"What about Malone, did he make it?"

"Sure, he's right behind me on the stairs."

Both men's eyes dart to the door where I'm hiding. Lesile whips out the Walther, smashes it against the nearest one's head, and puts two rounds in the other's chest before he can bring his firearm to bear.

She glances back at me. "Clear."

I dart into the hallway with Marvin close on my heels. I motion to the man Lesile clobbered. "Grab him. I'll search the other one for keys."

I don't bother with the search when I reach the door and see the keypad set in the wall. "It's digital." I raise my gun to put a bullet in the control panel.

"Stop, what are you doing?" Marvin exclaims.

"I'm going to shoot the keypad so the door will open."

"When has breaking something ever made anything work? Man, you say I watch too many movies. If you break the thing that opens the door, we'll never get it unlocked."

"Fine, you do it then. We wouldn't have this problem if Lesile hadn't killed the guy with the code and brained the other."

"That's called deflecting, Leo, and it ain't cool. Sack up and let me work."

"Sack up…I'll sack you up," I mumble and step aside.

Marvin uses an electric screwdriver to remove the panel, strips a pair of wires inside the control box, and attaches a set of clips attached to a USB cable plugged into his laptop. He executes one of his custom programs, and the door opens a few seconds later.

We drag the dead guard and the unconscious one inside the room and find Vincent chained to the wall. It's obvious he has been a source of the doctor's abusive experimentations, but he does a fantastic job of looking bored and unsurprised by our rescue.

"Ah, when Agent Snow informed me of your assumed demise, I guessed it was only a matter of time before you came for me."

"Your faith in me is quite touching. Marvin, the bomb?"

Marvin pulls out his scanner and jammer from the bag. "Already on it."

Lesile drops the unconscious man at Vincent's feet. "I thought you might need dinner."

"Indeed I do. Bless you, child." Vincent makes a slit across the man's carotid and clamps his mouth over the spraying wound.

"Oh, now that's just nasty," Marvin says and keeps his eyes focused on his equipment.

Vincent looks up from his meal. "Mr. Malone, who is this young man?"

"This is Marvin, and he's the only reason we haven't had our brains turned to mush."

"I presume he is not going to be a problem?"

"Marvin is always a problem, but he's not a threat."

"That's me, Marvin the nonthreatening black man. Get your cameras, white people, because like a comet, you may not recognize another one for years."

"The implant?" I ask.

"Done. It was on the same frequency and used the same countermeasures. Like yours, I can't disable it, but I have changed the frequency so they can't detonate it."

"Good work, now let's get the hell out of here."

CHAPTER 19

"Sir, gatekeeper reports that Gasman has returned."

Agent Snow keyed his encrypted radio. "Gatekeeper, this is Frosty. Was there a situation with Gasman?"

"Roger, Frosty. Gasman had a brake failure and needed to switch out tanks. We checked the cargo and everything's fine."

He stared at his radio for a few seconds. "Have Gasman report to me once he finishes topping off the generators."

"Wilco, Frosty."

"Sir," Agent Henning said, "seismic sensors are picking up movement to our south and east."

Snow faced the analyst. "Can we get eyes on it?"

"No sir, they're outside camera range. It's probably just deer again."

"Probably. Have Jacobs and Eisner do an unscheduled walk of the fence."

"Yes sir."

Snow had been feeling paranoid since he lost the plane, six tactical agents, and two pilots. The electronics package he had sent down near the crash site confirmed Malone and Lesile were amongst the wreckage. He had used the remote transmitter-receiver to detonate their implants just to be safe, but he still could not shake an uneasy feeling. Snow tried to pass Malone off as a smartass with a big mouth and even bigger ego, but there was justification to take his threats seriously. He was sure what he had been able to dig up on him showed only a small part of a bigger picture he represented, and he had no doubt the man was adept at killing. It wouldn't surprise him if he had caused the crash.

The entire operation was starting to turn into a clusterfuck. It was one thing to manage a black op, it was another thing to keep the death of ten members of his task force quiet for long.

It took a lot of maneuvering and outright lying to make everyone think this was a counter terrorism operation, but Snow had had no choice. If anyone found out the truth before Dr. Birch perfected the Cure, it would put the country in a state of chaos. Half would want to scour the streets; the other half would deny they existed. Even with all the evidence he'd collected, the deniers would be too timid to take the necessary action.

Dr. Birch was close to a breakthrough. They thought they had it with the SEALs. Snow's team was on the verge of being able to cure every disease known to man. They would be able to create soldiers who could drop deep into enemy territory and surgically remove threatening targets without the need to employ thousands of troops and spend billions of dollars like they had done in Iraq and Afghanistan. He just had to keep this quiet a little longer so he could provide the congressional hearing he was bound to face with a working serum and real world results. It was the only way he was going to be able to justify the expense and avoid going to prison.

"Sir, team five is three minutes late checking in. Do you want me to radio them?"

A chill ran down Snow's spine. "No. Send a team to the containment floor—quietly."

His people did not miss radio checks. Could Malone have survived the crash and infiltrated their base? What about the implants and the signals they detected? Snow didn't see how it was possible, but he had underestimated his kind once. He could not afford to do it again.

The radio squawked to life, and the sound of gunfire nearly drowned out the panicked voice. "Contact! We have hostiles in the containment room!"

"Malone," Snow whispered. "Code red, people!"

"Sir, we have multiple contacts inbound!"

"How many?"

"Ten, no, twenty...Christ, there might be thirty or more

coming in from all directions, and they're moving fast!"

"Lock it all down! I want heavy machine guns guarding every exit. Get us online and send the data package to all federal agencies. We have a breach, people. Let's plug it." Snow took out a cell phone and tried to call headquarters, but there was no signal.

He tossed it aside and made for the safe where he locked up the secure sat phone. The lights went out, and the alarm klaxons fell silent for a couple of seconds until the batteries turned on the emergency backups.

"What the hell was that?" Snow demanded.

Agent Henning shook his head. "I don't know, but we don't have any outside comms. The whole damn network is dead."

Snow fished the key from his pocket, opened the safe, and retrieved the satellite phone. He tried to make the call, but the phone was unable connect to anything. It took some serious hardware to jam the sat phones. These creatures were far more organized and had greater resources than he could have imagined.

"If Malone or his friends are springing our prisoner, they'll have to use the stairwell to get out. I want a team on every door. These creatures are responsible for the deaths of our friends and God only knows how many of our citizens. Let's make them pay."

CHAPTER 20

I glance through the door, dart to the other side of the hallway, and wave the rest of my team forward. Marvin has just cleared the door when gunfire erupts from down the hall. Bullets whizz past, and a few thump against my jacket. Marvin screams and unloads his entire magazine on the walls, floor, and ceiling. Vincent and Lesile dart back into the room. I sprint across the hall, pick Marvin up with my free hand while laying down suppressive fire, and hurl us both back through the doorway.

"Blackhawk down! Blackhawk down! Oh, I'm coming, mama Beatie!" Marvin screams as he lies on the floor.

"Marvin, get ahold of yourself!"

Marvin opens his eyes. "Damn, mama Beatie, you got ugly."

"You're fine. The bullet went through the jacket, but the vest stopped it."

"I thought this piece of shit was bulletproof?"

"It is, but it's not a perfect system."

"No, Obama Care ain't a perfect system! This is fucked up. I hope they don't make condoms too."

"Quit bitching, you're not the only one who was shot."

"Yeah, but bullets don't kill you."

"Both of you stop whining!" Lesile shouts between bursts from her weapon. "Keep the hell out of the bullets' path and neither of you has to worry about it!"

I give her a push into the hallway and grin when she screams from multiple impacts. She lunges back into the room and looks as though she wants to shoot me.

"Not so easy, is it?" I remark.

"You are such an asshole!"

Vincent grabs the open door, braces a foot against the wall, and tears it from its hinges. "If you two are quite through fucking around, I would like to leave now. If I am not mistaken, I believe those are grenades hanging from your bandolier?"

"They are."

"Then how about putting them to use?"

"Oh, right..."

I fling a pair of flashbangs down the hallway. The moment they detonate, Vincent springs out of the room and sprints down the corridor using the metal door like an oversized Roman centurion's shield. Bullets ping off its surface until he reaches the knot of agents pinning us down at the end of the hall. The elder vampire flings the door at the group on the left and wades into the one on his right with his bare hands. I hear strangled cries and spot a blur of movement as I run to provide support. In the two seconds it takes me to reach the end, Vincent is already standing amongst five corpses. I try to make a mental note of never pushing him too far.

I pull out my phone and start shouting before Harriet gets the chance to say hello. "We have Vincent, but the mission is FUBAR. Blow the towers and fire up the scramblers!"

My phone goes dead and shows zero bars, so I assume the cell towers are out of commission and just pray the satellite scramblers work.

Vincent says, "I think our best egress is by way of the roof."

I shake my head. "Marvin can't make the jump."

Vincent looks as if he is ready to abandon Marvin, but he picks up two of the fallen agents' MP5s. "The stairwell it is then. Lead the way, Mr. Malone."

Alarm klaxons unleash a banshee's wail throughout the building with strobe lights matching their cadence. The power goes out, likely Rick and Dimitri's doing, and emergency lights flare to life, throwing us into a red, flickering hellscape.

We run for the stairwell while keeping close to the wall with Marvin tucked in the middle. The door opens just wide enough to stick an arm through, and a grenade bounces and skitters across the floor in our direction. I take two long strides and bend it like Beckham back the way it came. The grenade explodes and shakes the hell out of the stairwell door. I hope the concussion rattled anyone standing just on the other side. If so, I'm not going to give them the chance to recover.

Sprinting to the door, I jerk it partway open, blindly fire a few bursts inside, and drop in a concussion grenade for good measure. Even through the door, the blast gives my body a solid kick. I tear the door back open and step through, firing. Two feds lie crumpled on the top landing, but I put a couple of rounds into them to make sure they don't get back up.

I stick my arm through the door and wave the rest of my team forward. "Clear!"

The four of us pack into the corridor and start to make our way down when a barrage of bullets erupts from below and chews up the ceiling.

"Kinda clear," I amend.

Lesile and Vincent point their weapons over the rail and fire at the lower levels. I glance over the side and mark the location of greatest resistance. They're approximately thirty feet down, and my grenades have a five second fuse. I pull the pin, count to three and a half, and drop it. My timing is dead on, and the grenade goes off a few feet shy of hitting the ground floor. I'm not accustomed to fighting as a team and my game was off a bit, but I'm catching my stride now.

"Hug the wall and follow me," I order my group.

I wedge a piece of the door handle under the door to secure our rear. Keeping our backs against the wall, we descend the stairs. A few rounds zip through the open shaft, but they can't get the angle on us. I spin around and shove everyone back up the stairs.

"Back!"

The claymore shreds the stairs where I was just standing. Pieces of the casing and ricocheting steel balls pelt my jacket like a bunch of tiny but powerful fists.

"Give it up, Malone!" Agent Snow shouts. "I've got heavy machine guns covering the hallways above and below you. There's no way you're getting out of this stairwell alive."

"Just like there was no way I could defeat your brain bomb,

hijack your airplane, crash it into the ocean, and come back here to kick your ass?"

"I'll admit I underestimated you and your kind."

"It seems to be a habit with you."

"It's one I'm intent on breaking. I see you brought friends, but I've locked the building down. It will be a costly endeavor taking us out. How about we make a deal?"

"All right, you and all your men shoot yourselves in the head and I won't kill you."

"You're a funny man, Malone, but we both know you're trapped in here with me."

I tighten the sling on my weapon, and pull the pin on a grenade. "Wrong, you're trapped in here with me."

I jump into the stairwell shaft, hit the railing below, hook my legs over the steel bar, and hang down over the ceiling of the first floor hallway. I arch backward, fling my grenade at the machine gun nest, and spray the hell out of the place. The machine gun rattles to life, spewing dozens of rounds per second just below my hanging head. I swing up and out of view. Several bullets shred the dangling back of my jacket. Half a second slower and it would have been my beautiful face. Vincent and the grenade go off almost at the same time. I see him flash past me as he drops from the landing above, stalks down the hallway with both weapons extended at arm's length, and fires at anything with a pulse. There's a pause in the shooting. The sound of Vincent's expended magazines striking the floor breaks the eerie silence.

"Clear," the elder vampire calls out from just down the hall.

I drop to the floor and go to survey the damage. I glance back and find Lesile towing Marvin behind her. I stride past Vincent and find Snow amongst the bodies. He grabs feebly for an Uzi lying next to him. I step on his wrist and bear down until I hear the bones crack. He tries to shout but only sprays a frothy spattering of blood onto the floor.

"You lose."

The agent spits out another wad of blood. "I found you. Someone else...will put the pieces together...like I did. I just hope...they eradicate your species...like I should have done."

"That's the first thing you've gotten right since you started this little war."

I point my weapon at his head and end his existence. No one in this building is going to get out alive, and I wonder for a brief moment who's the good guys and who's the bad guys. The agents are just doing their job, but so am I. It reminds me once again that the world is never black and white. It is a multitude of greys. How dark a grey just depends on your angle.

Vincent turns to me. "If we exit the building on this floor, I believe we will have to shoot our way out."

"And likely get shot at by our own people as well. Let's continue to the basement. If Yuri's men are stuck down there, we need to take them with us."

"Let us proceed then."

We traverse the last flight of stairs and reach the sublevel. I ease the door open, and a single shot narrowly misses my head.

"Shit, Malone, is that you?" Rick calls out.

"Yeah, you want to not shoot me in the face?"

"Sorry. Come on out, it's clear."

Despite his reassuring words, I cautiously open the door and peer through before exposing my more vital parts. Dimitri and Rick are crouched next to the front of the truck. Three agents lie dead not far from the stairwell door.

"Looks like you had some trouble," I say as I step over one of the bodies.

"Yeah, just a bit. I don't think they're aware of how many are down here and decided to just let us sit since they know we aren't going anywhere." Dimitri points to the roll-down barrier now sealing the sublevel exit. "There's another door near the stairwell, but it's locked tight, and nothing short of a demolition charge is going to crack it open."

"That is the door leading to the laboratory," Lesile tells us.

"If she's in there, then let it be her tomb," I declare. "We'll set the timer on the explosives and crash the gate with the truck."

Rick nods. "That was our plan as well, so we unhitched

the trailer. But it sounded like a war zone out there, and we weren't going to jump into the middle of it until we had to."

"You two take Marvin and Lesile in the cab. Vincent and I will cling to the back. Hopefully, our people will recognize us before they shoot us to shit."

Lesile and the three breathers clamor into the truck while Vincent and I crouch behind the cab and get a tight grip. Rick fires up the engine and guns it. The barrier doesn't stand a chance. The gate gives way with a crash and shrieking of metal. Rick blasts the horn and flashes his lights in hopes of signaling our people not to shoot. Vincent and I lean out, hang off the sides, and wave our arms.

Several rounds zip past and ping off the trailer coupling, but they are coming from behind us. Our people holding the gate redirect their aim back to the building and wave us through. Several flares streak skyward in a prearranged signal to get clear of the building. The suppressive fire increases to cover our people's withdrawal. Rick guns the engine once we're through the gate until we reach Harriet and her command group.

The senior council and a squad of Sheriffs are blocking the road five hundred yards from the front line. News and police helicopters circle overhead, and the blare of sirens draws near.

"Vincent, I am pleased we were able to retrieve you," Harriet says as we hop off the back of the truck.

"As am I. I do wish we could have accomplished it without drawing quite so much attention."

"We have it all in hand. Do not concern yourself."

More than a dozen police cars and a SWAT truck skid to a stop just short of our roadblock. Cops pile out of the cars and van, but appear unsure how to respond. All are gripping weapons and taking cover behind their vehicles, but they aren't pointing them at us. Harriet and another of her senior council approach the nearest squad car.

"Who is in charge here?"

A man wearing a bulletproof vest over a cheap suit stands up from behind the lead car. "I am."

"Wrong!" Harriet and her posse whip out badges and ID.

"I am Special Agent Harriet Winslow. You are interfering in a joint FBI and Homeland Security operation. Your department was told to stand back before this started. Was there something ambiguous in that order?"

"No, but..."

"Then what the hell are you doing here blocking my road?"

"It sounds like goddam downtown Fallujah over here!" The trailer we left in the sublevel explodes, and the powerful concussive force shakes the vehicles and slams into everyone like a gust of strong wind. "Holy fucking Christ!"

"We are why the entire city is not Fallujah. That explosion marks the end of a very large terrorist cell operating right under your nose. The explosives you just witnessed were three days from being parked in front of the Capitol Building. If you feel the need to be part of this, then set up an outer perimeter one mile out from my operation, or I will charge you with obstruction. If I'm in a particularly bad mood, I might even levy charges of aiding terrorism. And get those goddam helicopters out of my airspace before I call in a pair of strike fighters and shoot them down. Now move!"

The police captain looks furious, but he turns to his people and shouts, "Everyone, move back five thousand feet and form a perimeter. I want every road, creek, and deer path leading from this area covered."

Harriet turns back to Vincent once the local police disperse. "Dr. Johnston is expecting you at your facility if they implanted you with one of their fiendish devices."

"They did indeed," Vincent extends an arm toward Marvin, "but thanks to this young man, I am told it is inert for the moment."

"All the same, I think it is best if we do not delay in removing it. I must warn you, Dr. Johnston claims it is a very unpleasant procedure."

"Unpleasantness seems to be the meal of the day of late. Best to finish quickly so I may go on to better things."

"We have a helicopter waiting in the clearing just through the woods over there."

Vincent glances in the direction Harriet points and drapes

an arm over Marvin's shoulder. "Excellent, the flight should give me and my young friend time to chat."

Marvin looks to me with pleading eyes and appears torn between fainting and throwing up.

"It's okay, Marvin. Vincent knows if anything happens to you I'll finish what Snow started."

"You surprise me, Mr. Malone. I did not think you were capable of compassion."

"I don't like people breaking my toys, especially when I'm not done playing with them."

Vincent smiles. "Indeed."

Marvin gives me one last fearful glance as Vincent leads him away. He'll be fine. Vincent's just a cautious sort and wants to gauge Marvin's character and impress upon him the need for secrecy.

"Hey, Rick, you guys want to give me and Lesile a ride back to the fuel depot so we can pick up her car? I think we're done here." I look at Harriet. "Right?"

"We'll handle the cleanup. Thank you, Mr. Malone. I'm starting to see why Vincent places some value on you."

"You checking out my ass now too?"

"And yet dislikes you so much."

I give her a military-style salute, which I then snap down to give her the finger. It's a snug fit for the four of us in the cab, but not overmuch. Once we get back to the fuel depot, Rick and Dimitri disappear into the trailer to update Yuri on the situation now that we are within range of a functioning cell tower. I follow Lesile to her car.

"Can I give you a ride home?" Lesile asks me.

"I'll catch a lift with Rick and Dimitri. I need to square away some things with Yuri before I leave."

"Leonard, I hope this time together has made you understand why I did what I did to you. I am sorry for how traumatic it was for you, but I do not apologize for the results. You were special to me, and I wanted you to succeed in your new life. I hope maybe you understand now, even just a little."

I look up at the sky, sigh, and nod. "Yeah, I guess maybe I can find a little forgiveness."

Lesile smiles, kisses me on the cheek, and gets in her car. I watch her drive away, pull out my phone, and hit the speed dial. The explosion lights up the block, shatters nearby windows, and sets off a barrage of car alarms.

"Now that you're dead."

EPILOGUE

The sharp reports of weapons' fire echoed through the woods, and the occasional blast of hurled grenades sent subtle tremors through the ground. A massive blast rolled a concussive wave through the trees and shook the leaves from their branches. It also carried the scent of a human to Henrik's sensitive nose.

He crept through the woods, careful not to step on any branches that might betray his presence. He spotted a form crouched in a stand of bushes ahead. He stalked closer and seated his M4 tighter against his shoulder.

"Let me see your hands!"

The woman let out a fearful shriek and nearly fell over. She raised her hands and held out a small video camera. "Please don't shoot!"

"Who are you?"

"Jennifer Conway, Action News 5," she answered nervously.

"How'd you get this close?"

"There's a large culvert not far from here. I crawled through it to try to get some video of what's going on. I know, not very dignified, but anything for a story, right?" She let out a nervous laugh.

Henrik leaned forward, snatched the camera from her hand, and smashed it with the butt of his weapon. "Crawl back the way you came, and don't come back here, or your camera won't be the only thing left in pieces in these woods."

"Hey, you can't do that! You ever hear of freedom of the press?"

"You ever hear of reporters accidentally getting shot because they were someplace they weren't supposed to be?"

"Fine, but you'll be hearing from my station's lawyers!"

Dr. Margaret Birch controlled her deep sigh of relief and made a beeline for the culvert with the aggressive man shadowing her every move. She was certain he wasn't a vampire, but he was obviously in league with them.

Agent Snow had thought he understood these creatures, but he didn't, not like she did. He considered them little more than animals, like wild tigers or other creatures that occasionally preyed on humans, but she knew they were much more. She had seen this eventuality and had prepared for her escape should they ever lose control.

A maintenance tunnel ran from her laboratory to one of the outermost buildings of the complex. From there, it was only a short ways to the tunnel-like culvert on the other side of the woods. She lamented the disruption to her research. These so-called vampires were fascinating creatures, but she would set up her lab again and resume her work. It would be an expensive endeavor, and she no longer had the government's deep pockets to fund her research. It was still only a minor setback. She had the potential to make people immortal, and there were wealthy men and women who would pay anything for it. The Cure had some bugs to work out, but none of them was insurmountable given enough time and money.

She looked back at the man still training his gun on her before squatting down and climbing into the galvanized steel pipe. It was a long duckwalk to the other end, but the discomfort was well worth her life.

Lesile shook her head while she watched the orange flames devour what was left of her car. "Leonard, you are such an asshole, but at least you are a predictable asshole."

The council had gotten too close. Harriet may have said they forgave her prior transgressions, but old grudges died hard. Thanks to Leo, she could now disappear once again and return to the shadowy, enigmatic life she preferred.

She hoped that with her apparent death, Leo would find some closure to ease his troubled soul, but she doubted it. Lesile knew he found comfort in blaming her for his tormented spirit, but it was obvious his pain went far deeper than the trauma she had inflicted. Thinking he had killed her might make him feel better today, but tomorrow those ghosts that were the true cause of his anguish would return. Lesile hoped his relationship with Katherine would bring him some happiness, but she knew it was a salve at best. Leo would have to seek out his demons and face them, or they would surely come for him.

"Castillo, did you hear about the shitstorm last night outside Philly?" Angel asked.

Castillo shoved the folder she'd been reading into her desk drawer. "No, I was up late looking into the park murders and went straight to bed. What happened?"

"My buddy down there says the shit really hit the fan. Something about the feds taking out a terrorist cell." Angel fished a thumb drive from his shirt pocket. "He sent me a copy of his cop cam. You gotta see this."

Angel plugged the drive into her computer and hit play when the menu appeared. The video showed a plain-clothes detective having a heated discussion with a short but stern woman who appeared to be in her mid-fifties. Two men of equally severe disposition flanked her. The woman was verbally emasculating the detective when a massive explosion rocked the scene.

"Look at that!" Angel exclaimed. "That blast broke windows half a mile away."

Castillo nodded, but it wasn't the explosion that caught her eye. She paused the video and rewound it to the moment of the blast. Her stomach churned with a wild mix of emotions.

She jabbed her finger against the screen. "Who does that look like to you?"

Angel leaned in and looked at the figure partially illuminated by the flash of the explosion. "I know who it looks like, but that don't mean it's him."

"Goddammit, Angel, we both know that's Malone!"

"I don't know shit, and you don't either. The captain is going to have your ass if you go busting down his door and haul him in here without concrete evidence. Why would Leo even be there? You think he's a terrorist now?"

"I don't know what the hell he is, but I'm damn well going to find out."

Angel sat on the corner of Castillo's desk. "If that is Malone, and he's obviously not under arrest here, then maybe he's a fed."

"Leo Malone is not a fucking fed!"

"You're right; maybe he's something worse. Maybe he's a spook. You ever think of that?"

"Like CIA or some bullshit?"

Angel shrugged. "How many times have you had him in here? How many times did you have enough evidence on him that would have put any other perp in jail, only for it to fall apart long before it reaches trial?"

"That's because of his slimy, sewer rat of a lawyer."

"No lawyer is that good. I'm telling you, stop chasing the dragon before it turns around and eats you."

Castillo stared at the mostly silhouetted figure on the screen for a solid minute. She didn't know who or what Malone was, but she was not going to rest until she found out. No one was above the law. Castillo didn't care if Malone was CIA or a goddam alien from outer space. She was going to bury him.

I'm about to make a call when someone knocks on my door. Katherine is the only person who stops by for visits, and she's at trial today. My sign directs customers to use the stairs to my office. That pretty much leaves Castillo here to bust my balls some more.

Imagine my surprise when I find Vincent standing outside. Any meeting he ever wanted to have with me was always done by his order and within his Tower office. He doesn't wait for an invitation before pushing past and walking into my loft.

He looks around the room in obvious disdain. "How old are you now, eighty-one, eighty-two?"

"Eighty-one."

"By the time I was your age, I was a reasonably wealthy man. It is not as though what I, or even most of your clients, pay you is a pittance. I fail to understand why you cannot afford something a little less…third-worldly."

I shrug. "I guess I'm just not money savvy."

"No, this goes beyond business acumen. It borders on economic retardation, or ambivalence at the very least."

"Did you come here just to insult me?"

"No, I came here to express my appreciation for what you did."

"I'm sorry; I must have misunderstood the context of you calling me retarded."

"It is no secret that I do not particularly like you. Other than Katherine, I don't know anyone who does. Your friend Marvin has some affection for you, but his fear makes it a complicated friendship. We had a long talk about fear and the responsibilities inherent to his newfound knowledge."

"Marvin's all right when he isn't driving you into a homicidal rage. Was there something else you wanted other than to tell me I have no friends and nobody likes me, because recess is almost over and I don't want to be late for class. One more time and I'll get detention."

Vincent indulges me with a chuckle. "I am often asked why I tolerate and even seek you out for help. Do you know why?"

"We most desire that which we can never have," I answer philosophically.

"It is because despite your abrasive personality, I can count on you doing what you know in your heart to be the right thing. You are not persuaded by allegiance and politics. You have a freedom to act as you see fit that, due to my position and responsibility, I do not. And while publicly I must condemn some of your actions and behavior, I admire your unwavering sense of duty."

"It's nice to know I'm appreciated even if you have to keep it a secret. I had a girlfriend in high school like that. I think they call them moped chicks these days."

Vincent chuckles again, bringing the grand total of the number of times I've seen a hint of humor from him to two. It is truly a historic day. I guess having a bomb planted in your head brings about a profound sense of appreciation.

"Speaking of keeping secrets, do we know if we plugged the leak?"

"Our senior assets within the FBI and CIA have buried or

destroyed the few reports that put Snow onto us. He was telling the truth about the level of covertness of his operation. There was a single hard copy file on record with Homeland Security. A file clerk belonging to us managed to get her hands on it. Agent Snow and his people died heroes, killed in the line of duty thwarting the biggest terrorist act on American soil since 9-11."

"It sounds like we really dodged a bullet."

"We certainly did. You have taken the liberty of bringing your young friend and doctor into our circle. While their services have proven to be a great benefit to us all, we cannot condone any further outside knowledge of our existence. We are watching those two men, as well as Mr. Poplonovich, very closely. It would be good to remind them of that on occasion."

He turns to leave but pauses at the door. "Oh, there is one other thing, Mr. Malone. There have been seven calls to have you expelled from the enclave over the years. I was the deciding vote in four of them. You may want to keep that in mind the next time you want to coordinate an offensive like *Operation Fuck Vincent*."

I watch him climb into the backseat of his chauffeured town car and resume making my phone call as he drives away.

"Orphans of War Foundation, this is Cynthia. How may I help you?"

"Hello, Cynthia, this is Leon Mallory."

"Hello, Mr. Mallory! It's always wonderful to hear from you. How can I be of service?"

"The usual."

"Wonderful! Will this donation be coming from your Cayman account?"

"Yes."

"And how much would you like to donate today?"

"A hundred and fifty thousand American. Anonymous."

"Of course, Mr. Mallory."

"Thank you, Cynthia."

"We all thank you very much for your continued, generous support, Mr. Mallory. Have a wonderful day."

I lay my recliner back and stare at the ceiling. Dr. Morrison thinks my PTSD and my social disorder is due to all the dead

I've left in my wake throughout the decades, but he's wrong. It's the living who haunt me. I've been in three major wars and several freelance mercenary conflicts. It was a life I chose. I killed without thought until I lost it in Nam.

When I finally snapped out of my insanity, it made me think about all the people I had killed. I was able to reconcile myself to most of them. What I could not contend with were those I left alive. I killed hundreds, maybe as many as a thousand or more, but the real toll was much higher than that. How many families did I destroy? How many children did I leave without fathers or mothers? What kind of suffering did I impart that stayed with them as they grew to adulthood? How many more inherited the suffering I laid upon their parents?

People think I'm an asshole and a loner because I don't care. Apathy would be a blessing. Do I think throwing money at it absolves me of my crimes? No, but I don't have anything else to give.

Two very different young women performed two very different activities within a loft looking out over Lake Michigan. Carol, her hair cropped short and died black with subtle streaks of blue, tapped at a computer keyboard. Her nails were enameled to match her hair as well as the gratuitous eye shadow outlining her large, blue eyes.

Trinh looked several years older than Carol's twenty-two years but was in fact much older. Her black braid whipped about as she spun around the large, open floor like a dervish, her sword slashing almost too fast for the eye to see. The brown orbs set behind narrowed, tan eyelids matched the fury of her blade routine.

"Holy shit, Trinh," Carol said from behind her computer screen, her voice a valley girl drawl, "you gotta come see this."

Trinh sank to the floor, her right leg spinning low in a leg sweep as her sword followed a second behind to cut at her invisible foe as he fell. She held her pose a moment, leg extended with her sword held perfectly parallel to it, before springing up as if the laws of gravity did not apply to her.

"What is it?" she asked in a slightly clipped Southeast Asian accent.

Carol turned her laptop in the direction of Trinh's approach. "Some shit just kicked off in Philadelphia. The news claims it was a terrorist cell destroyed by homeland security, but the Blood Boards are saying it was a nest of vampires."

Trinh curled her lip in disdain. While most of her information on vampire activity came from the dark web chat room, only one or two percent of it was actionable intelligence, with the rest being fantasies dreamed up by conspiracy theorists or vampire fan boys and girls.

Carol raised a hand. "I know, most of it's bullshit, but the last report brought us here, and you've killed three of the blood-sucker fuckers this month."

"No, the last one said Barack Obama was a vampire and that he was using his vampire hypnosis to control the country through the TV."

"Well, this one has a video, a video that was removed from YouTube minutes after it was posted."

Trinh watched the video Carol played back, her eyes narrowing as her hatred spiked. "Stop! Back it up to the explosion and play it back frame by frame."

Carol rewound the video and tapped the arrow key on her laptop with the cadence of the second hand on a clock. She stopped when Trinh's face paled at the sight of a man in a black trench coat backlit by a fiery explosion.

"Pack your things," Trinh ordered. "It's time to go."

Trinh, rooted in place by shock, continued to stare at the blurry, pixilated image on the screen. The man's face clarified in her mind and turned to look at her. His lips parted, and his maniacal laughter filled her ears.

Trinh touched the brand made by her own hand by heating an army dog tag and searing it onto her chest when she was just a girl. "After all these years, I will make you pay for what you have done, Leonard Malone."

The rain pattering down upon the pawnshop's canvas awning made Delia feel like she was inside a drum, but at least she was dry. There were better spots to turn tricks, places with a little more traffic, but that would have required standing in the drizzling rain and competing with other prostitutes in the better areas. It was the price she paid for a little comfort and minimal competition. Even here, she should still make enough to pay her rent and get high.

Delia's prospects started to look up as a man carrying a black umbrella strolled up the sidewalk whistling a tune she didn't recognize. Not many people walked this area at night, and none in the rain. Her clients usually pulled up in their cars for some drive-through servicing.

"Hey there, sweetie, looking for a good time?" Delia asked the man when he drew near.

He smiled beneath his umbrella. "I am indeed."

"Oh, you sound like James Bond. Are you from England?"

"I am, but I haven't visited my home in more than a century."

She giggled at the man's joke. It was an unwritten rule of whoring. You always complimented him on the size of his manhood and sexual prowess, and you had to laugh at his jokes.

"So what'll it be?"

"I think a quickie just around the corner will suffice."

"In the rain? I know a cheap motel with hourly rates half a block up the street."

"My brolly should suffice to keep us both from the elements."

Delia glanced at the big umbrella and understood what he wanted. "Sure. Oral is fifty bucks."

She led him to the side of the building, and he handed over three twenties. Delia folded them in half, stuffed them in her shirt, and set a piece of cardboard down at her client's feet to protect her stockings.

"So what's your name, or should I just call you James?"

"My friends call me Jack," he answered, "Jack the Ripper."

LOOK FOR BOOK 3 IN THE BROOKLYN SHADOWS SERIES

PRIMACY OF DARKNESS

ABOUT THE AUTHOR

Brock Deskins was born in a small town located in rural Oregon. At age twenty, he joined the army and served as an M1A1 tank crewman, dental specialist, and computer analyst. While in the military, he became an accomplished traveler, husband, and father of three wonderful children. His military career completed, attended college to brush up on his skills as a computer analyst and gain new skills as a writer. Brock received his degree in computer networking and is now devoting his full time and limited attention span to writing.

BIBLIOGRAPHY

THE SORCERER'S PATH

The Sorcerer's Ascension
The Sorcerer's Torment
The Sorcerer's Legacy
The Sorcerer's Vengeance
The Sorcerer's Scourge
The Sorcerer's Abyss
The Sorcerer's Return
The Sorcerer's Destiny
The Sorcerer's Rebirth

BROOKLYN SHADOWS

Shrouds of Darkness
Blood Conspiracy
Primacy of Darkness

THE TRANSCENDED CHRONICLES

The Miscreant
The Agent

EMPIRE OF MASKS

Highlords of Phaer
Nightbird
Mourningbird

STANDALONE NOVELS

The Portal
Amelia: Battle for Ardentia

CROSSROAD
PRESS

www.ingramcontent.com/pod-product-compliance
Lightning Source LLC
LaVergne TN
LVHW091053080826
845145LV00002B/733

9781951510572